EX-Girlfriends

KYLIE ADAMS

KENSINGTON BOOKS
http://www.kensingtonbooks.com

KENSINGTON BOOKS are published by

Kensington Publishing Corp.
850 Third Avenue
New York, NY 10022

ISBN: 0-7582-0499-X

First Kensington trade paperback printing: April 2004
10 9 8 7 6 5 4 3 2 1

Printed in the United States of America

Outstanding praise for Kylie Adams and
EX-GIRLFRIENDS

"Ex-Girlfriends is wonderful—I tore through it like a sales rack at Bloomingdale's. Kylie Adams writes with the sass of Candace Bushnell and the brass of Jackie Collins. *Ex-Girlfriends* is cutting, cunning and real. I couldn't turn the pages fast enough, couldn't forget the characters when it ended. *Ex-Girlfriends* is *ex*-actly what a girl needs to get over—or under—an old flame."
Stephanie Bond, author of *Cover Me*

"Ex-Girlfriends is as smart as it is sexy, combining thrilling insider views of the fast-paced, high-power worlds of celebrity photography, entertainment television, party planning and the music industry, with a truly moving story of three women recovering from the devastating effects of one very gorgeous man. Any woman who's ever loved, lost and lingered over that ultra-special guy will totally relate to this story of three fabulous women who finally ditch the heartbreak and choose real happiness—in friendship, career and romance."
Holly Chamberlin, author of *The Summer of Us*

"Ex-Girlfriends is my favorite flavor . . . spicy! Kylie Adams's wit and intelligence make this book impossible to put down. Kylie has graduated from Diva Princess to Diva Diva with *Ex-Girlfriends*. Standing-O for this exceptional work!"
Carmen Green, author of *Atlanta Live!*

"Achingly hip, furiously funny and thoroughly unputdownable. I loved it!"
Emma Gold, author of *Easy* and *Hard*

"Here's a story that will twitch many a Botox lip. *Ex-Girlfriends* is a smile that never falters—tabloid hilarity with a heart."
Roz Bailey, author of *Party Girls* and *Girls' Night Out*

"Only the slyly savvy Kylie Adams could come up with a plot this fresh and funny. Reality television meets *Page Six* meets chick-lit in a laugh-out-loud romp—and dead-on parody—with more dramatic twists than a rose ceremony on *The Bachelor.*"
Wendy Markham, author of *Slightly Settled*

"A razor sharp novel about the power of female friendships. Smart and funny! Don't miss it!"
Patrick Sanchez, author of *Girlfriends* and *The Way It Is*

ACKNOWLEDGMENTS

With this—my fifth Kylie novel—it's high time that I paid tribute to teachers. Not the poorly dressed ones who made me spit out my gum and screamed at me for talking in class, but the truly great women who inspired, encouraged, and sometimes gave me a kick in the ass to do more and get better.

Nancy Rogers—My fourth-grade teacher. She adored my little stories about the Super Friends and insisted that I read them to the class, even when I rewrote history and had Wonder Woman exploring side by side with Hernando de Soto.

Janice Winokur—My tenth-grade English teacher. She loved my first adult-themed short story, "Tempt Me," but maintained that it was *too* adult to represent Central High in a districtwide contest. Banned at fifteen! I felt like a teenage Jackie Collins.

Phyllis Ward—My eleventh- and twelfth-grade English teacher. She went banana cake for my essay on the American character and pushed me to develop my talent. Then we bonded like thieves when I let her borrow treasures from my trashy-novel shelf— Sidney Sheldon, Judith Krantz, Shirley Conran. Forget Steinbeck. I wanted to discuss *Lace!* "Which one of you bitches is my mother?" It's one of the most fascinating questions in all of literature.

Lynn Adrian—My graduate school advisor. She was the first to read my earliest attempt at a full-length novel—a true kitchen-sink production of every genre but historical fiction. I skim it now and wonder how on earth I assembled such a disaster. But she took my effort seriously and encouraged my scholarship to find out everything that made Jacqueline Susann tick. Then she pushed me out into the world to make use of it.

When you look back on your life, you hardly recognize the person you once were. Like a snake shedding skins.
—Jackie Kennedy

THE IT PARADE
BY JINX WIATT

Fill in the Blanks

Heavier things than rice might be thrown at this weekend's Hamptons wedding. Everyone knows that America's celebrated golden son is saying "I do" to that reality television semistarlet. But more than one of the infamous heartbreaker's ex-girlfriends are on the guest list. All together now. *Meow.*

1

Lara

"Is there anything worse than being a guest at the wedding of the only man you've ever wanted to marry?" Lara Ward asked.

"Yes," Finn Robards answered matter-of-factly. "Being a bridesmaid at the same wedding. I think the only upside to the puffy sleeves on those awful dresses is that the girls will probably float if someone pushes them into the pool."

Lara covered her mouth to mask her laughter.

"So rejoice," Finn went on. "You're the beautiful, exquisitely stylish ex-girlfriend, which means our blushing bride is more insecure than smug. Excellent work."

"You're the perfect escort for situations like these," Lara said, grabbing her second glass of champagne from a passing server.

"Why? Because I cried with you when he kissed the whore in white? Believe me, I had my own reasons. I've always harbored the tiny hope that Dean Paul might be gay."

Lara admonished Finn with a look. "You think everyone is gay. It's ridiculous."

"Not true. Some men are unworthy of speculation. Bob Dylan, for instance. His orientation has never crossed my mind. Now, son Jakob is another story."

Lara tipped back the Cristal and clutched Finn's arm affectionately, her gaze locked on the groom. A little sigh escaped her painted lips. "Have you ever seen a more impossibly handsome man?"

It was almost painful to look at him—tall, blond, bronzed, and confident in his Ralph Lauren Purple Label tuxedo. Oh, God, he was beautiful, as much today as when she'd seen him for the first time . . .

Freshman year. Brown University. Lara had been sitting on the Blue Room steps. Dean Paul Lockhart had been playing Frisbee on the main green—barefoot, shirtless, low-slung khaki cutoffs revealing the elastic band of his Calvin Klein underwear.

Instantly, she had known who he was. Everybody did. His father, Robert Lockhart, was a New York senator. And his mother, Sophia Mills, had walked away from a successful acting career for marriage and children. They were the Kennedys without the scandal and the tragedy. Postcard-perfect American royalty.

Lara watched Dean Paul go through the social motions. Every guest deserved a special moment in his rarefied orbit. He knew this, and had been raised not to deny. That smile began to kill her a little bit. The movie star teeth, the adorable dimples, the little crinkle around those piercing blue eyes. The same eyes that had seared her soul when she stared into them the night she gave up her virginity. It had happened just before midnight on a Thursday in the bedroom of his off-campus apartment in the Center Place complex. She wondered if he remembered.

Suddenly, the bride stepped into Lara's line of sight and flipped her off.

Lara gasped, glancing around to see if anyone else had witnessed this.

Finn had missed everything, his eyes glued to an attractive cater-waiter.

Head down, heart picking up speed, Lara looked again. Bridezilla's offending extended middle finger was still in formation.

How mortifying. The incongruity of it all astounded her. A custom-made Vera Wang gown. A four-carat rock from Fred

Leighton. A perfect manicure. And the universal symbol of vulgarity.

Lara spun quickly, finishing the rest of her champagne and attempting to compose herself. "I can't believe it," she whispered to Finn.

"What?" he asked, still distracted. "I don't think that waiter's wearing any underwear."

"She shot me the bird."

"Who?"

"*Aspen*," Lara hissed.

"I would, too," Finn said easily. "Look at you."

Lara started to protest, then thought better of it. What was the point? Finn was no fool. He knew that her look for this event was the result of more strategic planning than George W. Bush had employed to invade Iraq.

The Celine by Michael Kors icicle minidress. The forty-five-carat three-strand diamond necklace. The Giorgio Armani stiletto heels with pavé Swarovski crystal toe straps. The long, naturally blond hair that fell to the small of her back, straightened to perfection by Yoshi of the Oscar Blandi Salon just minutes before the car service arrived.

So she looked fabulous. Big deal. The intent had never been to upstage the bride. Okay. The truth was, that had been the point all along. Oh, God. Did this make her a terrible person?

"Your love is lifting me higher . . ." The gorgeous voice of Rita Coolidge wafted from the state-of-the-art sound system at the Bridgehampton Yacht Club. The thumping bass line kicked in, and the singer swayed back and forth on the raised dais.

Lara tried to lose herself in the music, to forget the ugly incident.

Aspen Bauer-Lockhart. According to "Page Six," the new bride was insisting on the hyphenated name because she already enjoyed a "high-profile public persona of her own." Lara sniffed at the thought. A stint on MTV's *The Real World* was the only thing of note on this girl's resume.

Guests were beginning to migrate toward the dance floor.

Finn put out a hand for Lara to accept. "Shall we?"

She shrugged. At least it would give her something to do. Better to boogie than to wake up with a hangover. One more champagne, and that's exactly where she was headed. Lara couldn't hold her liquor to begin with, and the bubbly in particular could be especially unforgiving the next morning.

Finn had the moves. He didn't try to be sexy on the dance floor. He just *was*.

Lara adored her deliciously bratty friend. His grandfather had built an incredible real estate fortune, his father had improved upon it, and Finn had merely congratulated them on a job well done. Instead of working, he dabbled. Sailing in America's Cup. Walking the runway in a Diane von Furstenberg show. Writing (but never finishing) a screenplay.

Like Dean Paul, Finn had been a college discovery. Despite her good breeding (the daughter of two highly respected Providence, Rhode Island surgeons), Lara had known little of Brown University's complicated social structure. Finn had fixed that in a snap, rescuing her from an odd clique at the campus dining hall, which everyone called "the Ratty," and leading her to the dark smoking section known simply as "the cave." There, she had fallen in with a mix of Europeans and New York private school types, friendships that later helped put her boutique event-planning firm, Regrets Only, on the social map.

Lara's hip jutted out in snap-perfect synchronization with the drop of a heavy drum beat. A move shamelessly stolen from Beyoncé's dance card, but Lara didn't care. In this dress, a girl was entitled to vamp. Just a little.

Finn guided her into a half spin, and Lara nearly stopped cold.

The eyes of Joaquin Cruz were locked on to her. He was biting his lower lip and punching his neck to the beat. It was a look of total appreciation. It was a look of pure sex.

Lara knew exactly who he was but had never seen him in person. The Argentine ten-goaler. The reference was to the highest handicap in polo's zero-to-ten rating system. His lightning-fast play style made him a high-scoring threat in any match. But he was better known for his ability to score elsewhere. Women threw themselves at his feet. Lara could name half a dozen famous names who'd been linked to him in the past year alone.

It took a nanosecond to agree with the masses. His photographs were stunning, but in person, Joaquin Cruz affected the central nervous system. He got away with things that would be tragic on other men. Black hair slicked into a ponytail. White shirt unbuttoned to his torso, revealing a mat of thick, dark chest hair and a gleaming gold medallion. Tight pants. Black leather boots with slightly elevated heels. He should look ridiculous. But he made everything work. Lara had to admit it. Some men were hot. This one was on fire.

She smiled her appreciation and spun back to face Finn.

Her ambitiously unambitious friend leaned forward to whisper in her ear. "I'm trying not to look. Otherwise, I might have a wet dream, even though I'm fully awake."

Lara laughed, shaking her head. Finn could be so crude.

"Do you think it's true about him doing the Kometani twins in the dressing room at Tennis East?" Finn asked.

Lara covered her ears. "Don't tell me that! I'm meeting with them tomorrow about their birthday party."

"Good. That's a great opportunity to find out."

Lara groaned. "Believe me when I say that I have no use for that information." Deep down, she surmised that it must be true, though. Those Japanese teen socialites were building a notorious reputation for shopping and sexual excess.

"I hear it's as thick as a man's wrist," Finn said. He raised an eyebrow. "I'm talking about his d—"

"Finn!" Lara exclaimed, effectively cutting him off. Still, she swung her hair and stole another glance, marveling at Joaquin's cafe au lait skin tone, secretly wondering if the second rumor was true. *As thick as a man's wrist?* All of a sudden, she grabbed Finn's hand and began leading him off the dance floor, fanning herself.

"I'm so hot. One more drink, I'll wish the groom a happy life, and then—"

Someone took possession of her free hand. It was Joaquin. "I'm cutting in." He glanced at Finn. "Do you mind?"

Finn released Lara with a snarl. "You lucky bitch." And then he was off.

Joaquin's moves were effortless, equal parts graceful bullfighter and sensual flamenco dancer. "So . . . who are you here for? The bride or the groom?"

"Groom."

"Don't tell me you're an ex-girlfriend."

She confirmed this with a coy, affirmative nod.

"He should be committed. You're the most beautiful woman at this wedding."

Lara attempted to dance away the compliment. "It was back in college. Practically a lifetime ago." Who was she kidding? It'd been eleven years, and she still thought about him every day.

Joaquin moved in closer, cradling her waist with both hands. "His loss."

Lara could feel the heat of his fingertips burning through the icicle dress. She smiled. "That's the way I prefer to look at it, too. Who are you here for?"

"The groom. We've played in charity matches together." He gave her a long, silent, flirtatious stare. "So why won't you invite me to any of your parties?"

Lara grinned. "Technically, they're not *my* parties. I put them on for other people. If anyone's not inviting you, it's *them*."

Joaquin winked. "You could add me to the guest list. No one would know."

"Actually," Lara began, unable to resist the opening, "I might be doing a birthday party for the Kometani twins. Maybe I could snag you an invitation to that." She leveled a ray-gun gaze. "Do you know them?"

A mischievous smile curled on to his lips. "I do. In fact, I've already had the pleasure of giving them a very special gift."

Lara pursed her lips. An image of Joaquin with Mio and Mako Kometani flashed into her mind. It was disgusting . . . it was titillating. She banished the thought. Without warning, she stopped dancing. "I should get back to my date."

"Who? The fag?"

She glared at him. "That's a hateful word."

"Excuse me. The gay guy?" Joaquin shot a glance over her shoulder. "He's busy hitting on one of the waiters."

Lara didn't bother turning around. She knew he was telling the truth.

Joaquin moved in to continue the dance.

Lara took a step backward.

He gestured to Dean Paul, who was dancing with one of his nieces, a precious young girl no older than six and utterly entranced by her charismatic uncle. "I've been watching you watching him all night," Joaquin said.

Lara opened her mouth to protest.

Joaquin pressed a finger to her lips, hushing her. "I could make you forget him. I could fuck the melancholy out of you so good that it would never come back."

Lara didn't know which was worse—the things he said or the fact that she was still attracted to him. In fact, his crude offer triggered a surge of desire that filled her with a moment of self-loathing. But in the end, she maintained her dignity. "This dance is over, Mr. Cruz. I don't care for the way you lead."

She spun around, leaving him there like a fool as the band went from funky to funkier on an extended instrumental break.

Finn intercepted her right away. "What did he say to you?"

Lara hesitated. No way could she repeat it. "He's a vile man. Let's just leave it at that." She regarded her friend with implicit disapproval. "What happened to your flavor of the night?"

Finn groaned. "He wanted me to buy him drugs. Which I'm not above, mind you. But he seemed to need them a little too much. You have to be careful. I have a friend who was held at knifepoint by a pickup until he surrendered his ATM code."

"I wish you would meet a nice man and settle into a normal relationship."

Finn rolled his eyes. "Please. There's no such thing."

Lara watched Dean Paul kiss his niece on both cheeks and usher her back to one of the kids' tables.

Suddenly, his gaze met hers. The smile that followed almost ripped her apart. He made a beeline for her, stopping to pump Finn's hand before kissing her lightly on the lips. "You look gorgeous. I can't believe you're here. I wasn't sure that you'd come."

"Don't be silly, I would never miss this," Lara lied. In the last month, she'd made at least a hundred silent vows not to show up. "I'm so happy for you. Aspen seems like a . . . lovely girl."

"She is," Dean Paul agreed. "People think they know her from watching *The Real World*, but they don't. That show is so contrived." He glanced down at the elegant white gold band around his ring finger, then held up his hand for show-and-tell. "Can you believe I did this?"

Lara laughed a little. "It's official."

Dean Paul really looked at her. "Did you ever think that this would be us?"

All the time. "Maybe . . . a million years ago." *Before you dumped me for one of my best friends. And even after that.*

"This is wild, isn't it?" He shook his head. "I always thought I would show up at your wedding before mine. Are you seeing anyone special?"

Lara wondered if Dean Paul realized how cruel it was to ask that question in this setting—he, just married; she, on the arm of an openly gay society boy. "No, not even someone special-*ish*," she answered bravely, unwilling to compound the misery of the moment by lying. Besides, her personal psychic, Karen Keener, had recently counseled her about the importance of truth, about how one lie can do so much to undo what you're ultimately working toward. Granted, she had lied moments ago regarding her feelings about this wedding, her feelings for him. But that was simply self-preservation. If she could walk out of here with just a modicum of humiliation, she would be mollified.

Dean Paul smiled. "Not for long. Not in a dress like that."

Lara felt a blushing heat rush to her cheeks. She could barely stand to look at him. His bow tie was history, the first three buttons of his shirt undone, offering just a peek of his tanned, smooth, defined chest. He had always maintained the athletic build of an Olympic swimmer. Standing there, she fought the battle of trying to act naturally and trying to drink him in at the same time. Dean Paul was a time-capsule moment. Robert Redford in *The Way We Were*. Ryan O'Neal in *Love Story*. Shiny. Golden. Romantic. Heart stopping.

"Do you ever run into Babe or Gabby?" He asked this with wide-eyed, sincere, innocent interest.

Lara stood firm as the memory slammed into her. Back in college, Dean Paul's self-absorption had been epic in its magnitude. Apparently, nothing had changed. Babe had been the friend he dumped Lara for. Gabrielle had been the friend he dumped Babe for. But he probably remembered it all quite differently.

"I occasionally see Babe at an event," Lara began, "but she's so busy we never really talk. As for Gabrielle . . . Well, I rarely find myself immersed in the hip-hop scene."

Dean Paul nodded, barely listening as he tracked the room with a circular gaze. "I invited both of them."

Suddenly, Aspen crashed the scene. She iced down Lara with a go-to-hell glare and looped a possessive arm through Dean Paul's. "Do you mind if I steal my husband back? There's someone I want him to meet."

Lara splayed open her arms. "There's nothing to steal. He's yours legally. Congratulations."

"I think there's a single groomsman around here somewhere," Aspen said. "Maybe you can latch on to him." And then she pulled Dean Paul toward a gaggle of what looked to be older relatives from Florida.

Rita Coolidge began crooning the opening verse of "We're All Alone."

It was too much. Lara embarked upon a seek-and-destroy champagne mission. She needed another glass. And maybe another one after that. Payback might be brutal, but even the worst hangover had to feel better than this. She stopped a passing waiter and helped herself to two flutes, downing the first glass immediately.

Lara cased the surroundings. That's when she saw Babe Mancini.

Men were ogling. Women were scowling.

She was a rock-chick fantasy, her long legs sheathed in a skintight, handcrafted pair of art-deco leather pants. Lara knew the trousers were by Elise Overland. The Norwegian designer's clients included Lenny Kravitz and Shakira. Her low-end price tag was easily two thousand dollars. Babe's look was polished off with a midriff-baring sleeveless top, a studded Chanel cuff bracelet, and black leather pointed-toe pumps with kitten heels. Her hair was cropped dangerously short, the kind of style that only truly beautiful women can get away with.

From across the room, Babe made eye contact with Lara.

Right after that, Lara sent the second champagne down the hatch. She was going to need it.

THE IT PARADE
BY JINX WIATT

Fill in the Blanks

That sexy cable news hothead was recently seen and heard in the Church Lounge of the Tribeca Grand Hotel, claiming he had the chance to be a "plus one" at the Hamptons wedding that has everyone's tongue wagging. You see, the dreamy motormouth is currently locking lips with one of the groom's exes. But he would rather "have a colonoscopy than show up at that circus for Ken doll and *Girls Gone Wild* Barbie." Ouch. Tell us how you really feel.

2

Babe

She was a woman with a great ass. As good—if not better—than Kylie Minogue's. And she knew it.

Babe Mancini caught the evil glare of a fat lady spooning up the lobster bisque. And on this week's episode of *The Overweight and the Hostile* . . . Whatever. She was sick of the dirty looks. Get a treadmill. Get over it.

Nobody knew how hard she worked to look like this. First, there were the Mesotherapy sessions, homeopathic treatments where a cellulite-fighting formula is injected (very painfully) four millimeters deep into the skin to break down fat cells.

And then there were the punishing sessions with David Kirsch at the Madison Square Club on Fifth Avenue. Platypus walks, plié toe squats, reverse-prone scissor kicks, rumo lunges, and frog jumps.

At the end of the day, a great ass will kick your ass.

Babe grimaced. And, of course, women like Lara Ward were around to remind her how unfair the world could be. Did Lara exercise to the point of nausea? Did she make it a daily practice to force down an ounce of water for every pound of body weight? Did she withstand 105-degree temperatures in a Hot Yoga class three days a week?

Hell no. Lara's perfect figure was the result of nothing more than an enviable gene pool. She was the kind of tall and slender girl that designers went mad over. In fact, she was their precise sample size, which gave her the benefit of seasonal giveaways and discreet loaners. Case in point—that drop-dead-gorgeous icicle dress. Babe had salivated over the Michael Kors number, eventually coming to her senses when she saw the fifteen-thousand-dollar price tag. But Lara in all her glorious Twiggyness could just borrow the fucking frock like a cup of sugar. What a bitch.

Babe approached Lara and her walker-cum-date with thinly veiled disdain. "Nice dress." The compliment came spitting out of her mouth like the sour grapes it was.

Lara's smile was thin. For a Rhode Island girl, she played the cool Upper East Side act like a veteran. "Thank you. I love your pants."

"Really? They killed the entire credit line on a Visa. Did you sink fifteen grand into that dress?"

Lara managed a guilty little smile. "Not exactly. Michael Kors is a friend. I did a birthday party for his assistant. He was an angel to let me borrow it."

"There you are!"

Those three words greeted Babe wherever she went. She turned to face the source—a facelift-fresh actress who was currently stinking up the Broadway stage in a clunky turn as Roxie Hart in the long-running *Chicago*.

"Will you take our picture? *Please.*" She draped herself over her young, virile, blandly handsome, nightclub-promoting husband, both of them mugging for the camera Babe didn't have.

"I'm not working tonight," Babe explained. "*212* got scooped. *InStyle* has the exclusive."

"But we always look so good in your pictures," the actress whined.

Babe shrugged helplessly. "Sorry." Most of the time she hated her job. Being a social-scene photographer for *212*, a glossy weekly dedicated to high-profile Manhattanites, meant being nice to her subjects. In fact, actually liking them went a long way toward success.

The actress and the sleazy husband (her fourth) left in a funk, presumably in search of the official photographer. After all, if it wasn't documented and published that they were at the biggest wedding of the year, then why had they spent the day dressing up and coughed up a small fortune for the helicopter charter? The husband's jeweled hand (thumb, index, and pinky rings) planted itself on the actress's lipo-sculpted rear end.

At that moment, Babe surreptitiously brushed back a tendril of hair, pretended to adjust her Chanel cuff bracelet, and snapped the image.

Click.

The sound was ever so faint. She could barely make it out over Rita Coolidge and the band. But the first shot was in the tiny bowel of the itty-bitty camera. Granted, the resolution would be mediocre. What else could she expect from an over-the-counter spy gadget? At the end of the day, though, it would serve its purpose.

The Lockharts' decision to grant *InStyle* an exclusive had infuriated the celebrity magazine brigade. *People, Us, In Touch, Star*— each and every editor was so ravenous for guerilla shots of the goings-on that good or bad didn't apply. Any photo would do.

Her covert act sent a little tingle up Babe's spine. It was thrilling. She felt just like Jennifer Garner in *Alias*. The reception shots would net her a nice sum. And the images from the ceremony would be worth a bundle. Poor Dean Paul and Aspen. So controlling in how their nuptials would be presented to the fawning public, only to be foiled by a rogue guest. Ah, the taste of subterfuge. How sweet. While the *InStyle* editors waxed lyrical over their *official* photographs, the highest-bidding weekly rag would be rushing to press with Babe's secret-cam chronicles. Even the fear of a potential lawsuit wouldn't be enough to hold back. This was too big. Sorry, Michael Douglas and Catherine Zeta-Jones. Your little legal tantrum taught nobody a life lesson.

"I almost didn't recognize you without your camera. There's actually a real person behind the lens. Imagine that."

Finn was talking. Babe was ignoring. She scanned the area in search of another money shot.

Kaching!

Blushing bride at two o'clock, eating a salmon wrap with her eyes rolled back. Unflattering as hell. Translation: Worth a fortune. The weeklies loved pictures of celebrities looking ugly, clumsy, and idiotic. Spreads like that made readers feel better about themselves.

Babe took in a quick breath. Another brush of the hair. A turn of the wrist. A slight bracelet adjustment.

Click.

She turned her attention back to Finn, giving him an annoyed look. The gay social buck drove her crazy. All she remembered him doing in college was buzzing around campus on his Vespa, hosting parties at his expensive apartment, and piling friends into his BMW for the hour-long ride to Club Nicole in Boston. These days, he seemed to do even less. "Have you ever thought about getting a job?"

For a fleeting moment, Finn had the look of a man under attack. "I work," he insisted with a defensive sniff. "I'm a writer."

Babe snorted. "Let me guess . . . screenplays."

Finn's eyes went wide. "How did you know?"

"Because books require too much attention. Even models and kids can dabble in screenplays that go nowhere."

Finn stiffened. "Just because you never made it as an art photographer and got stuck doing candids on the party beat doesn't give you the right to judge me."

Babe kept up a bulletproof face, but inside she was wounded. "It was just an observation, Finn, not a judgment."

"You know, that chip on your shoulder has been weighing you down for at least eleven years. I'm surprised you don't walk with a limp." He turned to Lara. "I'm in the mood for a real drink. Can I get you anything?"

Lara shook her head. "I'm fine. Thanks." She stood her ground, as if waiting for Finn to leave. Once he did, she regarded Babe knowingly. "You always pick fights when you're nervous. What's going on?"

Babe revealed nothing.

"My guess is that you haven't talked to him yet," Lara said.

"*Him*," Babe repeated bitterly. "Isn't it just a little sick that whenever we talk about that son of a bitch, we never have to mention his name? It's just *him*. Like he's the only man in the whole fucking world."

Lara shifted slightly, a move of cool indifference. "Well, he is the only man we have in common. There's really no point to name identification."

Babe laughed a little. "Do you realize that this is the longest conversation we've had since college? Usually it's just a quick hello and you asking me not to photograph Britney with a cigarette in her mouth."

Lara looked at her, a gleam of superiority in her eyes. "I guess there hasn't been much to say. As a general rule, I tend to lose interest in girl talk when you sleep with my boyfriend."

"Lara, please!" Babe exclaimed with more bite than apology. "It's been a decade or more. It's time for a new grudge. Would you like to get even and fuck my boyfriend? What's your address? I'll send Jake over."

"Thanks for the offer, but I think I'll pass," Lara said. There was a beat of silence, and then a shadow of discovery swept across her face. "You don't mean Jake *James*."

Babe grinned. "Somebody alert the media. Above-it-all Lara Ward reads the trashy 'It Parade' column just like the rest of us."

Lara shook her head disapprovingly. "Do you really like him, or are you just trying to make Dean Paul crazy?"

Now it was Babe's turn to look superior. "Unlike you, Lara, everything I do isn't predicated on my feelings for Dean Paul."

"What explains your attraction to Jake then? Personal taste? That's even worse."

"At least Jake's an adult. Dean Paul still can't decide what he wants to be when he grows up. And speaking of taste, don't you hold anything against him for walking down the aisle with that reality TV slut?"

"I don't know anything about her. *The Real World* is a waste of time. I've never watched it."

"She took off her top in the first episode. And that was Aspen at her most conservative."

"Dean Paul is free to make his own choices," Lara said tightly.

Babe laughed again. "Jesus Christ, Lara, you've *still* got it bad. You're not even at the anger stage yet. You'll never get over a guy if you can't think of him as an asshole."

Lara shot back a fiery glare. "I'd rather carry a torch than crawl into bed with a creep like Jake James. Take a look at yourself, Babe. You've got it worse than I do." And then she left to join Finn at the bar.

Babe stopped a passing waiter to grab a glass of champagne. Her inner revolution started up again. All the negative self-talk that cranked in her mind whenever she was surrounded by people with better jobs, bigger money, and higher social standing. Deep down, she possessed little faith that she had equal value in the greater cosmic scheme. And being in this setting—without her equipment—only fueled the insecurity. Her Contax G2 with the Zeiss lens was her weapon against the world. Drinking deep of the Cristal, Babe remembered how it had evolved to this . . .

It was easy to be smart enough for the Ivy Leagues. But being rich enough—that was another story. Her parents weren't surgeons or senators or movie stars. They were divorced, at each other's throats, and stuck in middle management. Two miserable neurotics making enough income to take her out of the running for financial aid but not enough to put her through school. So much for the lovely graduation gift. All she got was the baggage of a fucked-up childhood.

By the time Babe left college, she was buried eighty thousand dollars deep in student loans. But Brown University had been her first choice. She'd wanted a free educational environment, and the school's New Curriculum concept appealed to her. There were no tedious core courses to sludge through. You created your own interdisciplinary concentration. Babe majored in art history, punching up her studies with photography classes at the Rhode Island School of Design.

The same freedoms that attracted Babe to Brown pulled her perceived foes there like magnets, too. Snots from old money, brats from new money, dubiously talented children of celebrities, six degrees of European royalty—they all flocked to the school, longing for unchained fun after years of lockup in rigid boarding schools.

From day one, Babe had struggled to find her place. She could never hang with the money crowd. Their gluttony sickened her. While she watched every penny and fretted about her mounting debt, they were booking houses in Newport or Block Island to host weekend-long parties.

She fared no better with the rest of the students. Too uptight to lope around with the Doc Martens stoner types. Not brainy enough for the cerebral semioticians who debated ancient philosophers on the College Green. As for seeking out the theater crowd or preppy/jock scene, Babe would have rather thrown herself in front of a moving bus.

In the beginning, it was high school all over again. Starring Babe Mancini in the edgy role of the cynical loner. But this time it didn't stay that way. Her budding photography skills were constantly pushing her into the mix, mainly because she harbored no interest in taking pictures of landscapes, still lifes, or architecture. To her developing eye, people were the most fascinating subjects. So in no time, she was a fixture on the busy Brown party scene.

Babe did Underground, the campus bar. Every Thursday was Funk Night. She never missed it. Ditto for the caravans to Viva, the nightclub in Providence that was a favorite of the Euro students. And then there were the wild theme events like the annual Naked Party and Campus Dance.

Her visual documentation style caused a stir. The images got people talking. She crafted mixed-media collages of her lens targets

for art classes, earning raves from professors and cautious approval
from her peers. Babe didn't do smile-and-say-cheese good-time
candids. Her images were disoriented, drunk in appearance, always
operating on the edge—just like her subjects. A daring cleavage
shot. Porn star–worthy scarlet lips on a beer bottle. A guy's manicured hand riding up a girl's naked thigh. Her flair for beheaded
bodies and unorthodox angles quickly became campus legend.
Soon it was a mark of social status to be a violently cropped party-
goer in a Babe Mancini original.

But she didn't limit herself to the avant-garde. To enhance her
portfolio, Babe decided to produce a series of more traditional
fashion shots. That's how she met Lara. The tall, dazzling blonde
with the elegant shoulders was polished, slick, and exuded amazing
style. Though aloof at first, she had eventually warmed to Babe and
agreed to be photographed on the steps of the John Carter Brown
Library. By the end of the shoot, they had become instant friends,
a rare feat for Babe, who had always struggled to form bonds with
other girls.

With one girlfriend in Lara, Babe actually got a second in the
form of Gabrielle, a stunning black girl, one of Lara's fellow dwellers
in "the cave" and an on-air talent for WBRU, the school's 50,000-
watt commercial radio station operated by students. For a too brief
stretch of time, they had been an impressive triumvirate. It was, in
fact, one of the happier times in Babe's life. From grade school on,
she had steered herself away from female cliques, hating the social
policing, the pressure to dress, think, and sound alike. But for Babe,
Lara, and Gabrielle, none of that came into play . . . until *him*.

Like all the other women on campus, Babe found herself mes-
merized by Dean Paul Lockhart. Maybe it was the crazy contradic-
tions, the way he could be so utterly vain yet unconcerned about
his own beauty. An eager exhibitionist, he was always quick to take
off his shirt, proud of his rippling back and that long, tan torso
quilted with muscle. Yet at the same time, he could be so careless
about his hair and clothes, showing up to classes and social gather-
ings uncombed, unironed, even unclean, as yesterday's stains on his

shirt and pants would reveal. But the real magic was simply the awesome power of his charisma, the way he could transform a room when he entered or left it.

That he was Lara's boyfriend did little to discourage Babe's crush. Her new friendship only brought her closer to Dean Paul more often. She was intuitive enough to realize the fierce loyalty expected from a close girls' club, but she lacked the experience to see it through. Babe had been a virgin to all of it—the sisterhood, the heady rush of a man with TNT for DNA. So it had been easy to fall in love, fall into bed, and fall out of favor.

She remembered the scene like it was yesterday. Brown was wilder than most colleges. The weekends started on Wednesday, not Thursday. Finn had rented an abandoned warehouse in downtown Providence, turning it into an instant disco with a DJ and a full bar. He had invited at least four hundred people. Lara had felt sick and Gabrielle had to cover for someone at the radio station, which left Babe and Dean Paul to party together. And party they did. Until almost four o'clock in the morning. Too trashed to drive back up the hill, they had crashed at the Biltmore Hotel . . . and then stayed in the room for two days.

By the time they checked out, news of the scandal had rocked the campus. Social lines were drawn, and surprise, surprise, Babe was odd woman out. The troika of Babe, Lara, and Gabrielle was no more; she was alone again. Even girls she didn't know hissed at her on the college green. She wondered why. Because she had betrayed a friend, or because she had landed the man they all wanted?

For all the destruction left in its wake, Babe's romance with Dean Paul didn't last long. It turned out to be a hot affair that burned as fast as a pink meteorite speeding across the dark night sky. He moved on. She wanted more. Typical Dean Paul math when it came to his relationships with women. And thanks to the wrecking ball that was his fling with Babe, all bets were off now. He took up with Gabrielle next. And after her, some other girl waiting for her chance.

Leaving Brown had been a relief. Babe couldn't wait to start over again, to get on with the rest of her life. She had moved to New York with dreams of making a living as an art photographer. It turned out to be frustrating as hell. Gallery after gallery snubbed her. She watched in disgust as other upstarts with less technical skill and a less interesting eye got ahead in the game. They were landing solo shows, selling images for top dollar, garnering attention from art critics. Meanwhile, she was going nowhere. A stint as an assistant for a legendary photographer proved short-lived. The genius had been a manic-depressive, drug-snorting lesbian. For six months, all Babe did was play victim to her pendulum mood swings and score coke from her dealer.

A stringer job on the *New York Times* improved Babe's life—but not by much. She tried hard news. Too many elbows jockeying to snap the perfect shot. Her heart just wasn't in it. A run at sports fouled out, too. Action photography? Not her strength. Getting on as a party photographer had been a fluke. One night a double-booked freelancer called Babe to help him out of a jam. Two hours later she was recording the scene at a Christmas party being hosted by Brae Group, a hot venture-capital firm. An editor from *212* had been there, drunk on spiked eggnog and offering everything from a full-time position to a three-way with her stock analyst boyfriend. By the end of the holiday bash, they had exchanged business cards. By the first of the year, Babe had a new job—*212*'s official nightlife photographer.

There were worse gigs. Hell, she'd worked all of them. People from her graduating class were earning megabucks practicing law. They were being paged to surgery in major hospitals. And here Babe was, thankful to finally have a good salary with benefits. Her phone usually started ringing at noon with details about the night ahead. On a typical beat she would hit four events over the course of an evening.

Somewhere between the first flash and the millionth, resentment had kicked in. There was so much wealth. Every gig reminded Babe of what she didn't have, and, at the rate she was going, what she would never be able to afford. But then the culture began to shift. And the opportunities began to present themselves. So many celebrity magazines. So many paparazzi shots needed to keep them in business.

The world was operating on a whole new shutter speed. Reese Witherspoon glowing on the red carpet in Emanuel Ungaro was good. But Reese exiting a supermarket rest room with toilet paper stuck to the bottom of her Adidas was better.

Babe had been aware of the new order, but hardly paid attention—until a colleague earned ten thousand dollars for a one-off sale of Jennifer Lopez getting out of her Rolls Royce. That's when the trend captured Babe's full interest.

There were things that she wanted for herself. Nicer clothes. A great apartment with a rooftop garden. Exotic vacations. Maybe even a weekend place in the country. She knew that true dedication to the task and a few lucky breaks could get her all of that and more.

The trick was to avoid biting the hand that feeds you. If *212* ever found out that she was moonlighting as a paparazzo, then she would be over. So over. Banished from the A-list scene. Blacklisted from the masthead of credible magazines. She could just see herself after that, waiting at the airport with the other semi-psychotic pic hunters, drinking 200 ounces of Coke a day, boasting about her inside sources—doormen at the best hotels, Brad Pitt's body double, the jealous loser brother of a sitcom star. Such a scenario was imminently possible. That's why Babe executed her every move with paranoid caution.

For the stealth missions, she shot in digital format only. The Nikon D1 was her baby. This eliminated film processing. Plus, sources with cash to burn wanted to see pictures right away, either the same night or early the next morning. Babe set up a dummy corporation to facilitate payment, negotiated prices by e-mail, and launched an on-line file-transfer program that was accessible to buyers by password only.

Tonight's Jane Bond routine was unusual. She only did the secret agent act on those rare occasions where the risk was worth the potential payout. Wedding photos of Dean Paul and Aspen could easily command a price in the low six figures. On a typical project, Babe kept a safe distance, turning out surveillance-quality pictures of the famous in captivating situations—Calista Flockhart calming her irate son in Central Park, Sarah Jessica Parker arguing with Matthew Broderick outside their apartment building, Renee Zellweger on Bleecker Street stuffing a Magnolia Bakery cupcake with pink icing into her mouth.

"Hey, baby, can I see your backstage pass?"

She jolted as Dean Paul's mellifluous voice shattered her reverie. His warm breath bathed her neck. The bastard was closer than skin. Babe smiled in spite of herself, turning to face him. "I don't need one. I'm with the band."

He moved in to kiss her hello.

Babe turned her head so that his lips met her cheek. It was bad enough that she already wanted to rip off his clothes. Why pile on the misery?

"Those pants are in strict violation of the dress code," he teased, checking her out in an obviously approving way.

She challenged him with her eyes. "So throw me out."

"Nah . . . I don't want to cause a scene." He winked.

She almost sighed. *Damn him.*

"It's good to see you, Babe. It means a lot to me that you're here."

"I'd be a fool to miss it," she said silkily. How would he feel if he ever found out that his wedding had earned her the down payment on a fabulous apartment?

Dean Paul leaned in to whisper conspiratorially.

Babe could make out his cologne—the new fragrance Arousal for Him by a hot British designer whose name escaped her. Hints of sangria, lavender, green tea, and vanilla. The combination was edgy, intoxicating, and seductive. In a word, Dean Paul's signature.

"You can blame me for *212* not getting the exclusive," he was saying. "I didn't want you working tonight. I wanted you to come as a guest."

If only you knew. Babe's bullshit alarm was blaring. She narrowed her gaze. "Come on. You can level with me. How much did *InStyle* offer?" A calculating glance around the room. "Did they pay for all of this?"

Dean Paul's smile was instantly disarming. "They could have rights to our first child for all I know." He shrugged helplessly. "Aspen's manager worked everything out. I didn't even get a say."

"Her *manager?*"

"Brian Monaco of Worldwide Talent. He handles the careers of most of the *Real World* vets."

Babe raised an eyebrow. "Interesting. I didn't realize that appearing on a reality show a year ago constituted a career. Stupid me. I spent a fortune on college."

Playfully, Dean Paul shook a scolding finger at her. "Careful. That's my wife you're talking about. She's been touring the country on the college lecture circuit ever since the show stopped, but that's beginning to wind down."

"Tell her not to worry. There's always *Big Brother.*"

He breezed past the insult. "Actually, she wants to get into broadcasting. Aspen loves politics. She watches the Fox News Channel all the time."

There could be no better opening. "My boyfriend works at MSNBC. I'll put in a word. Maybe she could intern." Babe savored what was coming next. "I'm sure Jake could find something for her."

The transformation on Dean Paul's face was total. "*Jake?*" You could almost see the TelePrompTer of his brain running the blind item from the "It Parade" column. He shut his eyes for a long second. "Please tell me you don't mean Jake James."

Babe grinned in confirmation. "You're not still carrying around that old grudge from college, are you?"

Dean Paul flashed a hot look of indignation. "*Old* grudge? That asshole uses his television show as a bully pulpit against me regularly. There's nothing old about it." He hesitated a moment. "I shouldn't care, though. He doesn't even register a full point in the ratings. The show's a joke."

"Don't be so sure," Babe said casually, careful not to come off as defensive. "Jake's numbers are steadily building. In fact, last week he edged out CNN. The network is thrilled."

Dean Paul just looked at her, silently fuming.

Babe moistened already moist lips, relishing his reaction.

For all practical comparisons, Jake James was a young, sexy, in-your-face and on-the-rise cable news yakker gunning for Bill O'Reilly credibility. His MSNBC talk show, *In the Ring with Jake James*, was building buzz on account of its infamous verbal sparring between the host and anyone who dared to go up against him. Sometimes, as in the case of Dean Paul and others on his personal hit list, Jake would simply shadowbox his opinions directly to the camera, the intent being to excoriate them to such a humiliating level that they would agree to guest on the program to defend themselves in person.

Like Babe, Jake had been an outsider at Brown. He was there on scholarship. The scrappy son of an uneducated single mother, he was hardwired to be hostile toward privileged rich kids. Given the campus environment, he spent his entire undergraduate career being pissed off. But girls still loved the pugnacious boy from the wrong side of the tracks. It helped that tales of his sexual prowess were legendary. Everything about him was the subject of rave reviews—the size of his endowment, his skill at cunnilingus, his phenomenal staying power during intercourse. What drove the coeds crazy was Jake's reverse snobbery. He had little interest in horny trust-fund girls. One of his oft-repeated cast-off lines: "Why would I want to sleep with a skinny bitch like you when I can have real legs and eggs anytime I want?"

Jake had been referring to the girls at the Foxy Lady, a local club. The dancers there loved him. He couldn't tip worth a damn, but after a long night of awkward groping from sexual inadequates and drunken boasts from college dorks who couldn't deliver, Jake became a popular after-the-shift party guest. He was fun, he treated the girls like real people, and he always made them come, usually more than once.

That he got regular free sex from hot strippers only polarized him more on the Brown campus. Women were intrigued. A true bad boy and a proven dynamo between the sheets? Those kind of guys definitely had their place. As for the men, they couldn't stand him. Jake was nothing but an arrogant, loudmouthed, poor son of a bitch. And it drove them insane that he had the looks, the athleticism, and the dick power to make any girl wonder . . . and sometimes wander.

The true campus rivalry had been between Jake and Dean Paul, though. Babe had never figured out exactly why Jake hated Dean Paul so much. But it was an animosity that seemed to feed on itself. Intellectually, they would square off in classes and at student protest events. Physically, they went toe-to-toe in intramural sports. And once, at five o'clock in the morning, after a particularly raucous party, the prince and the pauper had even gone fisticuffs at Ruby's, a local diner.

To Jake's credit, though, he was close to living up to his constant boasting about making it big. He left Brown and started out as a field reporter for an NBC affiliate in a small market. Great looks and a cocky attitude got him noticed. Cutting a swath through small, medium, and major markets, he eventually turned up as a correspondent on *Dateline* before being lured to MSNBC for his own show in an effort to punch up the network's younger demographics. Mission accomplished. *In the Ring with Jake James* had a core dedicated following of eighteen- to forty-nine-year-old females. They liked his brash, macho, the-bullshit-stops-here style. His media exposure attracted the interest of publishers, and his first book, *Put Up Your Dukes*, featuring a shirtless Jake in boxing trunks on the cover, was being prepped for a big launch and was already a top advance-order title on Amazon.

Dean Paul didn't have as much to brag about. His post-Brown years were unfocused at best. An aborted stint at law school. Flirtations with acting in Los Angeles. The ski bum years in Vail. An eighteen-month European adventure. His parents had revolted— and even threatened to cut him off—when he got cast to join the next season of *Survivor*. Dean Paul bowed out and hung around the L.A. scene, where he ultimately met Aspen. Throughout the years, enthusiastic rumors had persisted that Dean Paul might step into the political arena and run for a New York congressional seat, his incredible charisma superseding any lack of true achievement.

Jake had written about the media's love affair with Dean Paul Lockhart in his new book. Babe had read the passages in advance galley form. They were explosive. At the time, she had taken perverse delight in Jake's attack. But now, standing here with Dean Paul, she felt guilty for knowing about it. Goddammit! Why did her feelings for him have to be so complicated? With physical distance, she could hate him. For being the catalyst that ruined two great friendships. For breaking up too soon. For not staying in touch while he wasted time globe-trotting around the world. But here, face-to-face, she almost felt ready to forgive. But the key word there was *almost*.

"I just can't believe you're seeing that guy," Dean Paul was saying. "You could do so much better for yourself."

Babe's gaze cut to his new wife, close to being officially drunk, and whooping it up with her fellow *Real World* alums. "Right back at you."

Dean Paul parted his perfect lips in protest, but the words didn't come out. His eyes zeroed in on something or someone behind her. "Dean Paul Lockhart, this is your life," he murmured.

Babe turned to see for herself.

It wasn't Gabrielle Foster. That girl had been the pretty, articulate, Black American Princess from the Michigan Shore. This was Brown Sugar. The metamorphosis had been total. Like a caterpillar to a butterfly. From upper-class black society daughter to ubiquitous hip-hop diva. Daring. Sexy. Nasty when she wanted to be. The four-letter word was already being whispered about her by people who declared such things . . . *icon*.

Babe marveled at the way Brown Sugar's arrival instantly stopped the reception cold, as if someone had yelled "Anthrax!" in a crowded elevator. It was *Pimps Up, Hos Down* with an unlimited wardrobe budget. And one ballsy bitch dressed up to fill both roles.

She wore an open, full-length mink, a tube top that featured two distended nipples jutting out like baby bullets, hot pants, a wide belt with an enormous buckle that spelled out BLING in diamonds, thigh-high black leather boots, and enough jewelry to justify the 300-pound bodyguard scowling beside her.

The shock and awe on Dean Paul's face was priceless.

Babe couldn't resist capturing the magic moment. A brush of the hair. A turn of the wrist. A slight bracelet adjustment.

Click.

THE IT PARADE
BY JINX WIATT

Fill in the Blanks

Everybody knows that overexcited publicists can stretch the truth a bit when promoting the racehorses in their stable. Who hasn't heard Oscar buzz about a fall movie that turns out to be a real turkey? But the flacks at a certain record company have taken the practice entirely too far. They didn't just fudge the facts. They put out total fiction. How will the hard-core fans of a major rap priestess feel when they find out that she cut her teeth not in the slums of Detroit but in a mansion with five bathrooms?

3

Gabrielle

Yes, bitch, they're real.

Gabrielle Foster wanted to scream out the fact at the top of her lungs.

The custom-made Mimi So pink sapphire and diamond earrings dangling from her lobes were worth three million. Her Lorraine Schwartz sixty-two-carat diamond pinkie ring was another three million. P. Diddy had one, too. But his topped out at sixty carats. The value of the Damiani diamonds draped around her neck? She didn't know. The necklace was a gift from her producer, AKA Bomb Threat, to celebrate the number-one debut of her new CD, *Queen of Bling*.

Gabrielle stood there, impervious to the stares. She vibed on the band, moving her hips, digging the sound, as Rita Coolidge crooned her hit single from the mid-'80s. "Something said this is it . . . something said you can't miss . . . something said love . . ."

Her gaze was locked on to Dean Paul as the lilting music played, the lyrics an eerie poem for the way she had felt the first time he kissed her. That she even knew the song was a testament to how much she had changed. Rita Coolidge, Neil Diamond, and Barbra Streisand had all been favorites of her parents. Gabrielle remembered listening to their white-bread record collection growing up. The only black artists in the stack had been Roberta Flack and Diana Ross. It was all so hard to fathom . . . the cocooned childhood . . . the cosseted denial of her blackness and what that meant in the real, harsh, and sometimes cruel world. How could that existence have belonged to her?

Gabrielle tried to shake away the thought. Things were different now. Life was hard core. No coddling necessary. Her mantra: Bring it on, m.f. And yes, that stood for motherfucker. Straight up. No chaser.

Dean Paul strode in her direction, moving toward the Gabrielle of before, not the Brown Sugar of today. He approached with a wry smile.

Gabrielle worked hard to reveal nothing. The pampered white boy had no idea. No matter, it all came rushing back . . . how beautiful he was. There was no other word for it. She stood there, bewitched for a moment, temporarily losing her edge.

"This is some kind of evil plot," Dean Paul said.

Coolly, Gabrielle questioned him with a single raise of her brow. His famous baby blues were locked on to her emerald green eyes, which her makeup artist, J.J., enhanced with a dot of fuchsia shadow in the inner corner.

"My three favorite ex-girlfriends look drop-dead beautiful tonight," he explained, moving in for a kiss.

Before she could stop the inevitable, her bodyguard took a menacing step forward to manhandle Dean Paul's arm.

"It's okay, Baby Bear," Gabrielle assured him. "He's an old friend."

Shocked, and more than a little pissed off, Dean Paul twisted out of Baby Bear's grasp and shook his arm free. "Jesus, Gabby, do you really need this storm trooper? At my wedding?"

Gabby. He was the only person in the world who had ever called her that. Hearing it again unleashed a flood of bittersweet memories. She made a promise to keep that train of thought at bay, then whispered to Baby Bear, asking him to stay in sight but to give them some space.

With a dutiful nod, Baby Bear retreated.

As a peace offering, Gabrielle leaned forward and did precisely what Baby Bear had prevented Dean Paul from doing, planting a brief but intimate kiss on the lips. "I'm sorry. He travels with me everywhere. Sometimes the fan situation gets out of control. And lately there have been threats."

Dean Paul's forehead creased. "Death threats?"

Gabrielle nodded.

His focus was on her like a laser now. "There are security firms who can investigate situations like that."

She reached out to touch his forearm, her flashy pinkie ring clinking against his Tiffany and Co. cufflink. "It's being handled. There's an extreme right-wing group that thinks my lyrics are a danger to children. All bark, no bite. But still, you can't ignore these things entirely."

He stepped back to take all of her in, placing his hands on her upper arms, his long, perfectly manicured fingers digging into the luxurious pelts of her Louis Feraud mink. "Don't take this the wrong way. You look fantastic. But what happened to the girl I remember?"

"She's long gone," Gabrielle said. "This is the new and improved version." One beat. "Brown Sugar. And it tastes so sweet."

Dean Paul's eyes flashed with desire.

That's when Gabrielle gently flicked off his hands from her arms. "But you're a married man. Besides, I don't think you could handle it."

He laughed a little. "You're being a bad girl, Gabby. What are you trying to do to me? This is my wedding day."

Gabby. The sound of it played tricks with her mind again.

Dean Paul intercepted a passing waiter for a glass of champagne, which he gallantly offered to Gabrielle. "Here. Drink this. It's the expensive stuff, Queen Bling. You'll approve."

She accepted the crystal flute and drank deep, never averting her gaze, the slight smile on her lips matching his. Obviously, he was aware of her new CD.

Dean Paul shook his head. "I need a drink. You and your hot

box are too much for me. Cool down. We'll talk later." He gave her a final, sexually regretful once-over before swaggering off.

Gabrielle watched him go, letting the surprise sink in. Judging from his clever little reference, he was more aware of her than she ever imagined. "My Hot Box" was a smoking track on the new album. In fact, it was being geared up to follow "How Many Carats" and "Check His Credit" as the third single from *Queen of Bling*. AKA Bomb Threat was in the studio now, punching it up with a new remix that would feature a guest rap appearance by the ubiquitous 50 Cent. Next week, Gabrielle would meet with video directors to go over creative concepts.

"Too bad he's not a groomsman," Babe said, sidling up, watching Gabrielle watch Dean Paul. "It's so easy to get laid by one of them at these things."

Together, they stood silently, enjoying the view as Dean Paul kindly and gracefully engaged an effeminate teenage boy who was clearly smitten and starstruck.

"He's difficult to hate, isn't he?" Babe observed.

"Impossible," Gabrielle said.

Babe regarded her for a moment with a sweeping up-and-down glance. "You're not exactly trying to fly under the radar at this event."

Gabrielle cut her eyes to Babe's attention-getting art-deco leather pants. "Funny you should notice."

Babe grinned. "Touché." She tilted her head to the right. "I guess that makes three of us."

Gabrielle followed Babe's gaze to see a stunning Lara animatedly chatting up Sophia Mills, Dean Paul's mother. On further inspection, she noticed that Lara was tottering in her Armani heels. "How many drinks has she had?"

"Not enough," Babe said wryly. "She dated him for two years."

Since their college-drama meltdown, Gabrielle and Babe had been forced into a cautious civility by way of frequent encounters. Even if Gabrielle turned up at something random, like the opening for the new Jimmy Choo store on Madison Avenue, Babe was likely to be there, working the room for *212*'s night beat. There had been no choice but to get over the past and behave like sophisticated women. They often talked of meeting for drinks to properly catch up, but an actual planned date, as with so many of those anemic social promises, never materialized. It was the same scenario with Lara. Gabrielle saw her semi-regularly, but only as the hip-hop-star slot filler at one of the Regrets Only extravaganzas, where all of Lara's focus was concentrated on a smooth-running event. Could guests access the bar? Were VIPs caught in a logjam at the door?

Listening to Babe's smart-ass commentary and seeing Lara drowning her distress in champagne, it all of a sudden struck Gabrielle how much she missed them. There was nothing like deep, emotional, and uproarious female companionship. And she knew. Because, since college, she had been living without it . . .

Nobody knew what had happened the night Dean Paul broke up with her. Gabrielle preferred it that way. The incident was between her, God, and the bigoted lowlifes who had opened up her eyes to how evil the world could be.

Leaving Brown University had been easy. The campus had come to signify so many endings. Her friendship with Lara and Babe. Her relationship with Dean Paul. Her innocence about race in America. So it was time to find a place where she could find some beginnings.

Enter New York. Relocating there had been a no-brainer. Her tenure at WBRU, the campus radio station, all but secured her a job in the music business. The industry was chockablock full of Brown alumni, from artists like Mary Chapin Carpenter, Duncan Sheik, and Lisa Loeb, to scores of behind-the-scenes executives.

Gabrielle signed on with MTV as an assistant to the senior vice president of music and talent. It meant long hours, a crappy little cubicle, and an insulting salary, but she soaked up everything available to her. Still, as early as the first day, she knew that working behind the curtain would not satisfy her. Gabrielle wanted to be center stage.

She had been scouting potential new acts for *Everything But the Deal*, a pilot series in development about musicians who were talented, polished, and ready for the big time—but not yet signed to a major label. One night her search took her to Vibeology, an eclectic urban club known among the city's music insiders as *the* place to go to discover new black artists. Gabrielle had assumed that open mike night would mean acoustic sets from people who saw themselves as the next Babyface or Tracy Chapman.

But it had been something else entirely. No music. Only words. Fiery, passionate, provocative words. Poets had taken the mike and spoken their truth, wowing the crowd and inspiring Gabrielle. It was as if the world had opened up and shown her a pathway to emotional sanctuary. Deep down, she knew that this underground black poetry renaissance was her ticket. She had no interest in listening passively when she could be reciting actively. *Her words.* There was a reason why she had been filling notebooks and journals with her most intimate thoughts. This was it. Since the worst night of her life, it had been her private therapy. Now it could be her public training ground. She never worried about exposing herself emotionally, because that was the whole point. In a strange way, that mike, in that environment, represented one of the safest places she had ever known. It was a venue for being heard and understood.

Gabrielle had tried to pass on to the powers-that-be at MTV her excitement about this secret revolution. Each week at Vibeology, there were brilliant wordsmiths at work who deserved national attention. But the poetry factor generated little interest. "Find a bohemian rapper with good beats," her immediate boss had told her. "Sounds cool. But what we really need is the next Puff Daddy," another executive had said.

Gabrielle had returned to Vibeology to participate on her own terms. Her first slot was fifth from the top, and she received a warm introduction from Theory, the sexy master of ceremonies.

"Can I interest anybody out there in some *new* blood?" Theory had bellowed.

The crowd had erupted with wild approval.

"I don't know about you, but I want to hear what this sister has to say. And I have to be honest. I'm already crushing hard over her green, green eyes."

There had been whistles and catcalls from the audience.

Theory had flashed her a smile, his immaculate Chicklets teeth as blinding as alpine snow against his dark chocolate skin. He sported a white peasant shirt over tattered vintage jeans. A multi-colored do-rag covered a head of short dreadlocks, and dirty espadrilles adorned his feet. Despite the lack of effort, Theory was stop-and-look gorgeous, an antiestablishment Blair Underwood.

"If I do say so myself, she's beautiful," he had cooed to the crowd. "And this is her first time at the mike, so we already know the sister's brave. Make some noise for . . . *Gabrielle*."

With a strange mixture of terror and excitement, she had stepped into the bright spotlight on the small stage, taking her position in front of the microphone. Looking out, she had discovered a sea of black faces, dark-skinned, light-skinned, different styles, varied backgrounds, but everyone in that space shared one thing in common: They were all black.

In that moment, the realization had struck Gabrielle like a thunderbolt. Never in her life had she been in a room with so many of her own people. She had been raised in Grosse Pointe, Michigan, an enclave fifteen minutes from Detroit and nestled along the shores of Lake St. Clair. It was an elegant suburb for the well-heeled. Gabrielle's family home had been a five-thousand-square-foot Colonial with five bedrooms, five full baths, a finished basement that doubled as a recreational haven, and two garages. All for a family of just three. Her father was a high-level auto executive, her mother a full-time social butterfly and board president for the Edsel and Eleanor Ford House, the stately early-twentieth-century mansion that had been transformed into a premier community cultural center.

Growing up, she had never thought of herself as black. She was simply Gabrielle. Her house became the hub for all neighborhood play. The Fosters had a pool with a slide and a diving board. Their recreational room featured video games, a full-sized pool table, Ping-Pong, a kitchen stocked with junk food, a telephone with Mama Rosa's Pizzeria on speed dial, and a cookie jar stuffed with cash to pay the delivery driver. For Gabrielle's friends, the Foster house was a home away from home.

Looking back now, Gabrielle realized how her parents eschewed black culture. All of her mother's friends were white, and her father had gone further up the Ford Motor corporate chain than any black man in history. None of this had been a result of assimilation. It was simply who they were. Matthew and Diahann Foster lived in a white world. They just happened to be black.

Gabrielle had never questioned it. There had never been a reason to. Her childhood had been a plastic bubble of loving arms, safety, friends, and constant fun. The same held true for her adolescent years. She was among the most popular at Grosse Pointe Academy, involved in every conceivable activity and envied by many as the girl who had everything. That included one of the hottest guys. Morgan Atwood had been her boyfriend for three years. He was white, a star student and athlete, and from one of the area's oldest and most prominent families. Yet the issue of race was never raised. The union of Morgan and Gabrielle was not viewed as interracial. They were simply seen as a perfect couple. During the summer leading up to their freshman year in college, they sweetly parted company. He was on his way to Stanford in California; she, to Brown in Rhode Island. They were young. The distance was immense. To break up was sad but obvious.

In the beginning, Gabrielle's experience at Brown had continued more of the same. She immediately fell in with the elite crowd, bonding quickly with Lara. A bit later, the salty Babe joined the clique, adding a certain Rizzo factor to the mix. For over two years, it had been sisterly bliss. Until the Biltmore incident.

Babe had broken ranks. It was one thing to covet Dean Paul from afar, as practically every woman on campus—and certain men—openly did. But she had taken it to the nth degree, to the ultimate betrayal. Still, in her heart of hearts, Gabrielle found it difficult to judge Babe too harshly. Because she understood the temptation. If the circumstances had been reversed, and she was faced with the same opportunity, Gabrielle couldn't say with all certainty that she would walk away from it. Dean Paul was that desirable. And a few months later, she discovered for herself that he lived up to every bit of the hype.

"Speak on it, girl!" a female voice from the Vibeology crowd had shouted.

"That's right," another said. "Tell it!"

Gabrielle's smile had come from the deepest part of her. They were cheering her on, lifting her up with love and support, and she had yet to utter a single syllable. Even today, she could pinpoint the feeling that had come over her, and only one word could describe it: spiritual. Impulsively, she had left the printed words in her pocket, closed her eyes, and performed her piece from memory.

He Was

He was a god, a myth, an object of desire.
But he was hers, and she was a friend.
So I played like the girl in the candy store—
Baby can look, but baby can't touch.
He was so hot that all you could do was get burned.
And I wanted to be trapped in the fire,
He was blazing that much.
But he was hers, and she was a friend.
Until he belonged to another girl—
But he was hers, and she was a friend.
Until he belonged to me—
And he was more than the fantasy.
I went to the waterfall at the end of the world
Because he was that good, and I had it that bad.
And he was mine, and I was his girlfriend.
But all I did was wonder, am I enough?
Until he was gone.

And then I knew the answer—I wasn't
But he was.

The Vibeology crowd had erupted into a cacophony of applause, cheers, whistles, and standing ovations. Gabrielle was stunned. She merely stood there, frozen in shock. Theory had come to the rescue, piloting her out of the spotlight and into a cramped backstage office. He offered her water, secured her telephone number, and promised to call, then disappeared to finish out the rest of the night.

Open mike at the club became a weekly ritual, and Gabrielle gained more confidence and performance flair each time she took the stage. Though initially supportive, a growing faction of jealous poets began turning against her. Among their reasons: She had risen to audience favorite and featured attraction too quickly; she had a deep reservoir of material, each piece better than the last; and her relationship with Theory, which had blossomed into a hot romance, gave her an unfair advantage.

Gabrielle had trouble taking the Vibeology vipers seriously, and her condescending attitude only intensified their hostility. She wanted to parlay her spoken-word success into more than a social avocation. Her attempt to use her MTV clout went nowhere. Poetry recordings were dismal sellers. Every label rep told her that the interest level would be less than zero. When she queried literary agents about representation, they rebuked her as well, citing contemporary poetry collections as impossible contenders in the marketplace. And her own efforts to contact publishers directly only provoked more of the same discouraging news.

Theory had talked up his own industry contact, but the man turned out to be a smarmy sales executive for a vanity press. Gabrielle had no intention of *paying* a printing company to turn her poems into a book. This was not an ego trip for her. She wanted her poetry to work as a career. Gabrielle's instant dismissal of Theory's source triggered a major fight. He accused her of trying to sell out commercially, and lectured her about the artistic honor in struggling for financial rewards. She countered that he chose to stay in the small world of Vibeology because he was afraid of going after something bigger, and possibly failing. That night they broke up, and Gabrielle said good-bye to Theory and the club forever.

The man who would change her life called a few days later.

"I miss seeing you do your thing at the club. Where've you been?"

The voice had sounded vaguely familiar. But Gabrielle couldn't place it. "Who is this?"

A cocky laugh. "Answer my question first."

A gut thing told her not to be alarmed. This was no stalker. She knew the guy, and he knew her. The voice continued to tickle her brain. "Let's just say that due to creative differences I won't be going back to Vibeology. Now it's your turn. Who are you?"

"AKA Bomb Threat."

Gabrielle had almost dropped the phone. Here she was, hibernating in her cramped East Village apartment, reading a Terry McMillan novel, eating cheese popcorn, and picking up the phone to find one of the hottest music moguls in the business on the other end. Even though she worked for MTV and regularly encountered many music stars, this was surreal.

AKA Bomb Threat was a walking hip-hop cliche, his story tailor-made for VH1's God-I-Hope-I-Make-It *Driven* series. Born Curtis Ash to a single, welfare mother in the Coney Island projects, he had been on the fast track to prison—or worse, to pushing up daisies—before his twentieth birthday. He possessed the court skills to become a pro baller, but that meant college, and Curtis had dropped out of high school. Besides, wanting to be the next Michael Jordan was a starry-eyed punk's dream. Everybody knew that a black man stood a better chance of getting in on the action that was going to thug Trump types like Sean "Puff Daddy" Combs, Dr. Dre, and Snoop Dogg.

So Curtis began moonlighting as a party DJ. He wanted to soak up the reactions of end users, to find out what beats made the crowd move, to know which songs pumped them into a frenzy. Then he became the drug dealer of choice for guys who were already in the place he wanted to go. He made deliveries to recording studios, hung out, talked shit, and asked about the production process. It didn't take long before he was schooled enough to get started and teach himself the rest. After all, he was a fast learner. Curtis Ash had hot-wired his first car at twelve, fathered his first child at thirteen, and cooked up his first crack supply at fourteen.

He booked studio time and cut one track, a song he wrote called "My Bitch Pays for Everything." His rapping prowess was mediocre at best, but the music bed was a toe-tapping, booty-shaking, head-bobbing delight. And his lyrics hit straight to the heart of the misogyny and materialism taking over the hip-hop scene in the void left after the murders of Tupac Shakur and Biggie Smalls.

Curtis pressed a few thousand copies and slapped WRITTEN, PRODUCED, AND PERFORMED BY AKA BOMB THREAT onto the label. The first time he saw his moniker in print, he laughed his ass off. Calling in a bomb threat had been the reason for his last expulsion from school. His marketing plan was guerilla all the way—cold-calling area radio outlets, playing the track when he did his own DJ thing at parties, pushing the song into the hands of club spinners. But the results had been merely modest.

Until a station in Georgia got hold of the track. Suddenly, "My Bitch Pays for Everything" fever began to spread across the state. And then it infected Florida, and, ultimately, Alabama, Mississippi, Louisiana, and Arkansas. The Dirty South couldn't get enough of AKA Bomb Threat. And it wasn't just urban radio, either. Across the region, the song scorched top-forty playlists, too. That's when the major labels began paying attention.

The courting process was fast and furious, the executives thinking Curtis Ash was just another dumb nigger who would sign the first contract they put on the table. "You must be joking, bitch." That's what he told the first A&R guy, a white Jewish dude fresh from graduation at Brown University. And then AKA Bomb

Threat negotiated like a motherfucker from Harvard Law. In the end, he got a huge advance and his own label imprint, Riot Act.

"My Bitch Pays for Everything" went national and blew up everywhere. The video, featuring AKA Bomb Threat covered in white gold, platinum, and diamonds and surrounded by a throng of bikini-clad dancers, was quickly shot and serviced to all music channels. A full-length CD was rushed into stores. It went on to sell five million copies, and generated two more hits on the same theme, "Love Me a Ho with a Rich Daddy" and "I Swear That Bitch Didn't Ride in Your Mercedes."

He became the music industry's newest showman, front man, and idea man. What began as a vanity label imprint quickly became a powerful empire. AKA Bomb Threat built a stable of acts that soon surpassed his own success as an artist. Pretty Boy was a soulful ballad singer with the voice of a young Luther Vandross and the looks of a young Denzel Washington. The Sluts were three interchangeable teenage girls who performed in lingerie and cooed catchy ditties about sex. Chicken George was a bone-thin rapper and former pimp whose rhymes centered around his flashy style, his way with women, and his fat bank account.

AKA Bomb Threat stepped back as a performer but stepped up as a mogul, looking out for new talent, reviving stalled careers by bringing has-beens to Riot Act and reinventing them for a younger market, venturing into fashion with his own line of sportswear, partnering with Nike for a special edition sneaker emblazoned with his name, and throwing massive parties in Manhattan's most exclusive venues, a move which amped up his social profile and garnered him boldface status in all of the columns.

"Hello?"

Gabrielle realized that she'd fallen silent as AKA Bomb Threat's *E! True Hollywood Story* played out in her head. "I'm here."

"You've got style and skills. So check this—I'm looking to break a female solo artist on my label. I think it should be you."

Gabrielle had been stunned. "But every other label has told me that spoken word doesn't sell."

"They're right. It doesn't. I'm talking about you as a rapper. Punch up the rhymes. Throw down some beats. Show off that body. You'll be unstoppable."

Gabrielle had not jumped at the offer right away. Philosophically, she struggled with hip-hop's impact on the larger culture. On the plus side, the industry had empowered more young black people than perhaps the civil rights movement had in its day. And the golden era of the genre from the late eighties to early nineties had produced some truly consciousness-raising, gifted artists—Public Enemy, Queen Latifah, De La Soul. Back then, hip-hop truly was an urban folk art. But now it had evolved into little more than a modern-day minstrel show. Everything was about violence, sex, and material excess. When it came down to the image of black America, hip-hop was playing directly into the white, right-wing fantasy.

But Gabrielle had decided that she should try blazing her own trail. She would not hide her curves behind bulky clothes and spooky special effects like Missy Elliott. And she would not present herself as a glorified prostitute like Lil' Kim and Foxy Brown. No fucking way. Gabrielle vowed to be the kind of woman the rap world had never seen before. Breasts *and* brains. A feminine force of sexuality and intelligence. Like liquid lightning, the inspiration for her stage name struck down.

Come on, brown sugar. Give us some of that sweet chocolate.

The bigoted monsters had taunted her with those words on the most harrowing night of her life. Inside, the memory blistered and burned. But with a strange and instinctive notion, Gabrielle had known that this was her chance to turn misery into triumph, to go from weak to strong.

Brown Sugar. The next time someone called her by that name, it would be a positive and powerful experience.

The next day, Gabrielle quit the job at MTV and began working on her first CD. Collaborating with AKA Bomb Threat was alternately exhilarating and infuriating. He pushed her to mainstream her poetry for the record-buying youth. She fought against it. He refused to back down. She compromised.

The result was *Super Bitch*, a debut that *Rolling Stone* called "the most important new record of the year . . . Brown Sugar is a hip-hop revelation." With the critical praise came commercial success. Her first single, "He Was," stormed the charts, followed in short order by "Prince of My Pain" and "Monsters in the Night," each song climbing higher than the last.

What Gabrielle had never counted on was the image that would become her personal prison. Hip-hop artists were viewed as people pressed up against the windowpanes, looking in on lifestyles that had always rejected them. From the jump, AKA Bomb Threat had told her that being a Grosse Pointe princess with an Ivy League pedigree would keep her down. She had to be "real" for fans to embrace her.

All Riot Act artist publicity was handled by the umbrella label's PR office. A flack there scratched out a press kit bio that had Gabrielle growing up in the Detroit projects and being orphaned at fifteen when her single mother was killed in a gang-related drive-by shooting. At first, Gabrielle had been appalled and was prepared to revolt. But everything happened so fast. The first hit single, the second one, video shoots, promotional appearances, a slot on Riot Act's summer tour. Suddenly, it was too late. The media had played up the ghetto rags-to-riches story too much. Thankfully, more interest began to be paid to Gabrielle's fashion choices and whether or not she and AKA Bomb Threat were a couple. Still, in every story printed about her, there was always that single paragraph that perpetuated the big lie.

Rita Coolidge's band was rocking hard, seducing most of the guests at the reception to dance with abandon. "When I get you in my reach . . . I'll never let you go," she sang.

Gabrielle came hurtling back to the present. She shook her head, as if that alone could cast off the anxieties of the past.

"Look at her," Babe was saying, referring to the visibly tipsy

Lara, who had armed herself with yet another flute of Cristal. "Any minute now she's going to fall off those stupid heels and land flat on her face."

An impulsive idea sprang into Gabrielle's mind. She locked a serious gaze on to Babe. "Let's get out of here and have our own party."

Babe was hesitant.

"My producer has a house in East Hampton. He's working in L.A., so it's mine for the night. My driver can take you back to the city in the morning."

Suddenly, Babe grinned. "Okay . . . I'm game."

Gabrielle smiled. "Then let's rescue the drunk angel."

They headed straight for Lara, flanking her on either side.

"We're kidnapping you," Babe announced.

"What?" Lara slurred. "No . . ."

"I have full run of an incredible house not far from here," Gabrielle informed her.

Even in Lara's intoxicated state, she proved reluctant. "No . . . I have a car service waiting. I just want to go back to my—"

"This is no time for any of us to be alone," Babe snapped. "We're going to have a girls-only party, goddammit, and we're going to enjoy it! There are two things that we just need to accept and move on about. Number one, we've all touched Dean Paul's dick. Well, so what? And number two, he got married, and it wasn't to any of us. So fuck him!"

"How could he marry her?" Lara slurred. "She's not good enough for him."

Baby Bear hustled to get the white stretch limousine into position.

Gabrielle couldn't quite believe it. The three of them together after all these years. But she had to wonder. Would they be friends again? Or was this merely an isolated group therapy session for Dean Paul survivors?

THE IT PARADE
BY JINX WIATT

Fill in the Blanks

Now that America's dashing young prince has tied the knot (he's the golden son of a certain senator and a certain former movie star), it won't do for him to continue his playboy ways. That's right. He just might have to get a job like the rest of us. Talk has swirled for years that he would follow in Daddy's footsteps and enter the political fray. No trouble attracting volunteers to that campaign! But a rumor is rampant that Junior is mulling a job offer that has nothing to do with shaking hands and kissing babies. Prepare to be shocked. Mommy and Daddy sure will be.

4

Dean Paul

Aspen's giggle got hijacked by a loud belch as she clung to Dean Paul, bringing him toppling down onto the expansive bed with her. "Oops!" She giggled again. "Do you remember the first night we met?"

"Of course, I do," he whispered, kissing her forehead and gently brushing back her hair with his fingers, wishing she would just pass out. He had no desire to make love to his wife when she was drunk.

"You took me into the men's bathroom at Dolce, and I gave you a blow job in the third stall." More giggles. "Didn't your mother tell you not to marry girls like me?"

He put a hushing finger to her lips. "I rarely listen to my mother."

"Lucky me." Aspen attempted to pull him in for an open-mouthed kiss.

Dean Paul resisted. "Sweetheart, you should probably brush your teeth. You threw up in the helicopter, remember?"

Aspen covered her mouth with her hand. "Does my breath stink?"

"It just needs to be freshened up a bit," he murmured.

Her body went limp in concert with a heavy sigh. And she made no attempt to move. "Your mother spent more time at the reception with Lara Ward than she did with me." There was a sudden sulky expression on her face. "I bet she wishes you had married her."

Dean Paul tried to comfort his new bride with a triple-threat kiss, going from the center of her forehead, to the tip of her nose, and then to the curve of her chin, timing each peck with the delivery of his words. "Don't . . . be . . . silly."

"Did you see that necklace she was wearing?" Aspen snarled. "There's no way that belongs to her. She obviously borrowed it. I thought only stars could get away with that. I mean, why would any designer or jeweler think that there could be a PR benefit to her walking around in their stuff? Who cares what *Lara Ward* is wearing?"

"You're obviously giving it a lot of thought."

"I was just saying," Aspen snapped. "And what was up with Miss Gangsta Rap and the sumo wrestler bodyguard? It's not like anybody at a wedding like ours would try to steal her ghetto jewelry." She laughed a little. "I wish someone from PETA had been around to throw a bucket of blood on that fur coat of hers."

Dean Paul shook his head ruefully. Here they were, on their wedding night, ensconced in a deluxe city-view suite at the Four Seasons, ready to embark in the morning on a ten-day honeymoon trip to the Greek island of Santorini, yet all his new wife could think of to do was channel fashion monster Steven Cojocaru, with vomit breath no less.

"And don't get me started on that photographer. What's her name? *Babe?* I mean, what kind of a name is that? Wasn't there a movie once about a talking pig named Babe? Did you see those leather pants she was wearing? It looked like she was on her way to a Whitesnake concert or something." A wicked little laugh. "Sorry, *Babe*. Wrong decade. The eighties are over."

Dean Paul gave her a reproachful stare. "Do you have anything nice to say about anyone who attended our wedding?"

Aspen rolled her eyes. "I'll have to open all the gifts first. You know, I secretly wish Brian had given the exclusive to *212* instead of *InStyle*. Babe really does know how to shoot people at parties. She makes everyone look great. See, that's something nice. And more people in this city read *212* than *InStyle*. I told Brian that, but he kept telling me to think with a national mind-set." Aspen pulled a face. "Whatever. We live in Manhattan now. Who cares about people in Iowa?" She groaned. "Notice I didn't say live *and work,* since neither one of us has a job."

"Actually . . ."

Aspen propped herself up on her elbows, gazing at him expectantly.

"Your husband does have a job."

The look on her face was pure alarm. "Since when?"

"That call I took right before we cut the cake. It was official then."

"Well . . . what is it?"

"I'm joining *Hollywood Live* as a New York correspondent."

Aspen's lips formed a thin, tight line. "Did they say anything about me?"

Dean Paul gave her a curious look.

"The people who hired you," she explained. "Everybody knows that I want to get into broadcasting. Did they ask about me? Maybe we could do it together."

"Aspen, I've been in confidential talks with them for months. This started before we even—"

"What am I supposed to do? Just sit around our apartment until the next *Real World/Road Rules Challenge* comes along?"

"I thought you wanted to get away from the whole MTV thing."

"Yeah, but people write in and request me!"

Dean Paul shut his eyes for a moment. It was absurd that his wedding night had come to this. "I'm not doubting your popularity, but if you're serious about a career in broadcasting, then it might be time to distance yourself from the MTV reality franchise." He paused a beat. "What does Brian say?"

"He wants me to do a burlesque revue in Vegas. It's like the

Pussycat Dolls, except all the girls are from reality shows. Jerri Manthey is doing it. She was the bitch on the second *Survivor*."

"Again, not the best career move if you want to be the next Christiane Amanpour."

Aspen looked puzzled. "Who's she?"

Smiling, he whispered, "Put in some studying before you interview at CNN." Then he raised up just enough to take off his shirt and trousers, tossing them to the floor and rejoining Aspen in his socks, boxers, and ribbed cotton tank. He kissed her sweet, attention-hungry forehead.

All of a sudden, Aspen's eyes got wide. "I could do what Julie Chen does. Read the news and interview people who get kicked off *Big Brother*. How hard is that?"

"Maybe you could start out small," Dean Paul offered. "You could get on with one of the local affiliates as a lifestyle reporter."

"*Local affiliate?*" Aspen spat the suggestion back in his face. "That would be a step down. I already have a national reputation."

Dean Paul was too tired to explain the finer points. Impulsively flashing her breasts and routinely getting drunk on *The Real World* didn't translate to journalistic credibility. He thought about Babe and her snarky offer to put in a word for Aspen with Jake at MSNBC. No way. He'd rather see her slip on a thong and join the ranks of Jerri and company in Las Vegas.

"I don't have an ounce of energy to get up and brush my teeth." She reached out and threaded her fingers through his hand. "I should take off all this makeup, too, but I can't move." A dramatic yawn. "God, I'm so gross. I guess this means you won't get laid on your wedding night. Will you still love me?"

Dean Paul squeezed her hand in response. "We'll make up for it in Greece."

Aspen leaned her head against his shoulder and proceeded to pass out.

But Dean Paul was wide awake. Everybody thought he was crazy for marrying this girl—his parents, his friends, media pundits. The only thing that had shut up the naysayers was the ironclad prenuptial agreement. If it didn't work out, Aspen walked away with a few hundred thousand dollars and a gag order to never speak about the marriage publicly.

He released Aspen's hand and combed his fingers through his hair, thinking about his parents. What perfect timing. To be in the sky and on his way to Greece when they found out about his new career. The announcement would lead tomorrow's entertainment news. His parents would be angry, dismayed, disappointed—the usual crap. But this time Dean Paul didn't care. It still pissed him off that he'd caved in to their demands and given up his chance to be on *Survivor*. They were from a different generation. Everybody wanted a shot on a reality show these days. Shit. He'd never make them understand.

All they wanted him to do was finish law school and run for office. The mere thought of it gave him a tight fight-or-flight feeling in his chest. He could practically feel his heart constrict. Why couldn't his parents see the obvious? He wouldn't last five minutes shaking hands and listening to people complain about taxes.

His *Hollywood Live* gig would be a breeze. Easy work. Good money. The syndicated half-hour infotainment series was on the rise, having already supplanted *Extra* and *Access Hollywood* in the ratings race and gaining fast on *Entertainment Tonight*. Dean Paul would be issuing reports from parties and film premieres, and sitting down for flirty one-on-one chats with hot female stars. That sure beat a stump speech in a factory parking lot.

Both of his parents had grown up in normal, middle-class families. They lived in Protestant bubbles where working your ass off was the only sure way to success. What did they know about being famous before birth? That blessing/curse belonged to only a few. It was a crazy, heady way to come up in the world. People were constantly removing obstacles for you. In a natural way, Dean Paul had come to always expect things. An instant table in a packed restaurant. VIP status at the airport. Women who wanted to sleep with him upon eye contact. Basically, he counted on special treatment everywhere. And after almost thirty years of this, who wouldn't be

spoiled, lazy, and more than a little fucked up in the values department? The truth was, he hadn't gone through life like everyone
else. So why start now?

Aspen began to snore a little.

Dean Paul looked down on her. Suddenly, it dawned on him
that his wife of just a few hours had never uttered congratulations
on the new job. Her animal instinct had immediately pounced on
her own career crisis. A smile crept onto his lips. You had to love
her. And he did. Much to everyone's marvel. But Aspen was exactly
the kind of mate he needed—a woman even more self-absorbed
than he was.

He'd developed a crush on her watching *The Real World.* That
was an embarrassing secret. The big fight that erupted when the
fraternity boy from Alabama used Aspen's Sisley eye cream as a
masturbation lubricant had been classic television. Dean Paul was
three-quarters in love by the end of the episode. A few weeks later,
the season finale aired. That night he hit the cast party at Dolce
with a buddy from Brown, Kris Everhart, an actor celebrating his
first big part as Stabbing Victim Number Two on *ER.*

Dolce was the hot new restaurant/bar/place to be seen. Ashton
Kutcher, Adam Rodriguez of *CSI: Miami,* and Will Kirby, the last
man standing from *Big Brother 2* were among the backers. The vibe
for *The Real World* bash had been media desperation. At that point,
the whole cast had moved to L.A., ready to cash in on their
pseudo-fame. *I want to act. I'm ready for any opportunity that comes my
way. I've always dreamed of broadcasting.* All the typical cliches.

What they refused to acknowledge was that almost every reality rat from previous seasons of their own show, not to mention *Big
Brother, Survivor, Temptation Island,* and every other mind-numbing,
nonscripted show, had built the same castles in the air that went
splat. Still, everyone rented a U-Haul with the hope that they
might be the next Jenna Morasco who'd posed for *Playboy* or tomorrow's Kyle Brandt who'd turned up on *Days of Our Lives.*

There was something about Aspen, though. She treated the experience for the lark that it was. She vamped around—loud, drunk,

and flirtatious. Did he mention beautiful? Her blond, tanned, south Florida sex-kitten looks stood breast-to-breast against the California variety that populated Dolce every night. Dean Paul picked her out. They laughed about stupid things. She confessed her wish of having her own talk show one day. He encouraged the impossible dream. A few minutes later she was blowing him in the bathroom.

But in a quirky switcheroo, Dean Paul had pursued her. Aspen's innocent arrogance captivated him. She didn't think that the Lockhart name was such a big deal. So he was the son of a boring old senator and a movie star mother nobody could remember. Woop-dee-do. In fact, Aspen, basking in the afterglow of nanosecond MTV fame, actually believed that she was more famous. God, that was cute. And refreshing enough to hold his interest.

Weeks had turned to months. No fights, no hassles. Just great sex, big laughs, and nonstop fun. They became inseparable. The idea to get married had been a joke at first. But it stuck. And hell, it was serious now. She was Mrs. Dean Paul Lockhart. He actually had a wife.

Aspen was right about one thing, though. His mother didn't like her. *She's not substantial.* That's all Sophia Mills would say. But she rarely liked any woman he got serious about . . . except Lara. Everybody in his family approved of her.

Dean Paul lay there, exhausted but unable to sleep, thinking what a trip it had been to finally get hitched with his three most significant exes watching. The feelings it conjured up were tough to reconcile. But he made sense of them. At the end of the day, he knew why each woman was on the guest list and not the name after his on the invitation.

Lara seemed like a perfect match on paper: smart, beautiful, Ivy League–educated, prestigious family background. The thought that she would be the one he might marry had never left his mind. But deep down, there had always been that something . . . that something which made it easy for him to break up and stay away from her for all these years. It was difficult to pinpoint. But basically, she was too . . . perfect. Too intelligent. Too gorgeous. Too successful.

Too organized. Jesus. She was the only woman he'd ever been in-volved with who made him feel like a knucklehead.

As for Babe, she simply wasn't the marrying kind, at least not for him. A girl from a broken home who hated rich people? No, thanks. When it came down to bringing baggage into a relation-ship, Dean Paul only allowed two small carry-on items. If you had more than that, find another schmuck. That was his motto. Besides, sex with Babe had been too dirty for her to morph into the role of devoted wife. The things she did to him. The things he did to her. It brought a smile to his face even now. In fact, he felt the begin-ning of an erection coming on just thinking about it.

Aspen continued to snore.

Dean Paul tried to focus on nonsexual things to stave off any further arousal. He wasn't above a quick round of masturbation, in-volving, say, a Lucy Liu fantasy, but not on his freaking wedding night. That would be too pathetic. He thought of the interminable openmouthed kiss between Liza Minnelli and David Guest at their wedding. Just as quickly, he went as limp as a wet noodle.

But a vision of Gabrielle in that hip-hop Barbarella outfit flashed into his mind, competing with Liza and David, ultimately winning the battle. Great. Now he was hard again. Suddenly, he started to laugh as he imagined the look on his mother's face after she got an eyeful of Gabrielle, or rather . . . *Brown Sugar*. It had been classic Sophia Mills disapproval. Nothing tickled him more.

Gabrielle's transformation from good girl to bad gyrl still puz-zled him, especially the bit about growing up in the Detroit ghetto. Dean Paul's parents had shipped him off for a week of mis-sionary work every summer. He knew more about the poor than Gabrielle. But who could argue? She was taking her act straight to the bank. Still, very little about her resembled the woman he'd known at Brown. Back then, all that hard-core sass had been soft-core sweetness. The way she used to look into his eyes frightened him sometimes. There had been so much reverence in her gaze. Whatever she thought he was, Dean Paul had known he could never quite be. That made it easy to leave her.

He felt his eyelids begin to grow heavy. By now, Aspen's snoring had become a soothing white noise. Sleep was closing in. If the tabloids ever got the tip that Dean Paul Lockhart did not get laid on his wedding night, they would never print the story. Too unbelievable. He grinned. Then he leaned over to kiss Aspen's cheek and to cover her bare shoulders with as much blanket as he could stretch out without disturbing her. "Good night, Mrs. Lockhart," he whispered, content in the knowledge that this woman suited him so perfectly.

But a tiny realization prevented him from giving in to slumber completely. There had been a moment tonight at the reception. A brief but powerful one. It made him question everything. What had he done? What was he doing? Why had he been such a fool back in college?

Oh, yes, he'd felt it. And as he finally drifted off to sleep, Dean Paul could only wonder . . . *Had she felt it, too?*

THE IT PARADE
BY JINX WIATT

Fill in the Blanks

If you thought the Hilton sisters were trouble, then brace yourself for a monster import of something similar straight from Tokyo. These girls make Paris and Nicky resemble Laura and Mary Ingalls from *Little House on the Prairie.* Here's the proof: Was there ever talk about the hotel heiresses engaging in a three-way with a certain polo-playing stud? Those sisters never went that far! And it can only get worse. Rumor has it that these Japanese Olsen twins are pitting PR girls against each other for the right to plan their birthday party. Not just any mud will do for this kind of wrestling. These women are high maintenance. Borghese Fango mud only.

5

Lara

She didn't know what made her feel worse—the combination of the headache and nausea, or the look of consternation on Privi's face. Lara braced herself for another wave of almost sickness. It came on fast, nearly did her in, then faded. If only she could just throw up and get it over with.

"I'll make you a cup of herbal tea with milk and honey," Privi said tightly.

Lara raised a halting hand. Barely. This sapped her of much-needed strength. She would need everything she could muster to deal with the Kometani twins in a few hours. "It's no use, Privi," Lara murmured weakly. "I won't be able to keep it down. I just know it."

Privi shook her head. "A young lady should only have one glass of champagne at a wedding. Anything more is disgraceful." She sighed, then, having made her point, softened a little as she stepped toward Lara's bed and adjusted her pillow for greater comfort. "I suppose you'll just have to sleep it off."

"Not today," Lara croaked. "I have a client meeting."

Privi tossed up her hands in a pantomime of disgust. "Get as much rest as you can. If you need anything, I'll be watching my story."

Lara managed a faint smile as the tiny woman made a quiet exit.

Privi stood no taller than four-foot-nine. The Dominican woman was rotund but graceful. She had started with the Wards when Lara came home from the hospital as a newborn. A live-in housekeeper and cook, Privi had filled in as baby-sitter, too. The only years that Privi had not been a daily presence in Lara's life were those at Brown. But her parents' graduation present set into motion a surprising reunion.

Just minutes after parading in cap and gown to accept her diploma, Lara's parents had presented her with keys to an eleven-room condominium on New York's Upper East Side (the seventies to be exact). Located in an elegant, full-service building on a quiet, tree-lined street, the place was magnificent. High ceilings. A Juliet balcony off the expansive living room. A formal dining area. An eat-in gourmet kitchen with laundry facilities. Three bedrooms and three full baths. A maid's quarters with a private kitchen and bath. For a single career girl just starting out in the city, it was beyond ridiculous.

And more indulgence was to come. The palace came complete with Privi, who had been anxious to relocate to New York to be closer to her sister, Yari, who was reeling from her husband's sudden death. At first, Lara had balked. It was all just too much. In the end, though, she realized that her parents were unstoppable. She was their only child and had never given them a moment's worth of rebellion. Plus, their dual careers as surgeons had generated enormous wealth. They had the money to spend, and it gave them great pleasure to reward Lara for significant achievements.

Privi was in her early sixties and not in the best of health, fighting both high blood pressure and diabetes. She managed all the cooking, cleaning, laundry duties, and day-to-day pet care. With just Lara and her little Maltese, Queenie, as charges, it was a light workload that gave her purpose and kept her busy, yet proved untaxing.

By Manhattan standards, Lara's lifestyle was pure fantasy. A huge condo. A live-in housekeeper. A glamorous career. Many people dismissed her as a spoiled princess. Okay, maybe she was. But she also worked hard. Getting Regrets Only up and running had been a job that required the strength and fortitude of an Amazon. With the deed to her condo in her name, she borrowed against it to raise the up-front capital for the business. Within eighteen months, she had closed out the loan. Exquisite details, high-profile connections, and smooth running events were her claim to fame, but Lara also possessed a precise head for numbers that routinely enhanced her profit margins.

She lay there, willing herself to sleep. But it was hopeless. The constant throbbing at her temples just wouldn't subside. She regretted all of it. Going to the wedding. Seeing Dean Paul. Encountering Aspen. Dancing with Joaquin. Drinking the champagne.

Oy. Especially the champagne. Privi was absolutely right. Not even if Dean Paul announced his annulment would more than one glass of the bubbly ever pass her lips again.

She put a hand to her unsteady stomach as the room dipped and swayed in another tumult of nausea. *Whoa.* How on earth was she going to rise up from the prone position, take a shower, get dressed, put herself in a car to the Mercer Hotel, and listen to the Kometani twins blather on about their party wishes, without dying in the process? It just didn't seem possible.

Privi padded back into the room with a steaming cup of beef bouillon and a glass of cold whole milk.

Lara raised up a hand in silent protest.

Queenie rose from underneath the comforter with great interest.

"You—put that hand down. And you—go back to sleep," Privi scolded both of them. "An old hangover cure. My sister Yari got her husband off to work after his all-night poker games for years with this same trick. Get every bit of it down. No matter how hard it may be."

"But—"

"Every drop," Privi cut in. "It's your only hope of getting to that meeting. I don't think you'll make it downstairs otherwise."

Lara sighed in defeat and raised the bouillon to her lips. The aroma sent her reeling.

A stern Privi stood by the bed, daring her not to obey.

The first sip was the hardest. It seemed incongruous that Lara could feel so horrible this morning when only last night she had experienced the time of her life. Ironically, the champagne had been the reason for that, too. . . .

It was only because of her altered state that she had agreed to join Babe and Gabrielle at AKA Bomb Threat's East Hampton home. But it was a safer bet than another dance with Joaquin Cruz. After tumbling into the white stretch limousine, the three of them rode the whole way standing up through the open sunroof, laughing hysterically, tasting the sharp tang of the air from the Atlantic.

Gabrielle had ordered the driver to pump up the volume on the music—her own, of course. It was a highly danceable track from Brown Sugar's first CD called "Super Bitch."

Yes, that's my Mercedes
No, you can't contain me
Cuz I make my own gravy
If my bling makes you feel less a man
Poor baby, this I understand
It takes a big star to say he can
Cuz I'm a Super Bitch
Rhymes with rich
One taste of me
Will scratch that itch
Yeah I'm a Super Bitch
You'll beg for more
I can be virgin sweet
Or a nasty whore

Against all normal impulses, Lara had found herself singing along to the vulgar lyrics. But the beat was infectious, the melody instantly catching. What a sight it had been—the three of them jutting out from the roof of the limo from their waists up, dancing and rapping a song called "Super Bitch."

Babe and Gabrielle had wasted no time in catching up with Lara, taking full advantage of the stocked bar. Not to be outdone, Lara had squealed in excitement at the discovery of a bottle of Cristal, and popped it open. And thus began the final infusion that had rendered her disabled a few hours later.

But before that, there were toasts. To Dean Paul's marriage. To Dean Paul's annulment. To Dean Paul's divorce. Done in the snarky way that only three ex-girlfriends could manage. Even in Lara's loopy state, she had been in awe as the limousine turned onto a narrow, dark gravel road that looked to be a dead end. It went on for more than a mile, providing refuge for about twenty houses.

She knew it well. West End Road. Some called it the street of dreams. On one side was Steven Spielberg's property; on another, a Gothic home that had once been the sanctuary of Jackie Kennedy's maternal aunt.

AKA Bomb Threat's place was a beautiful Greek Revival—deep green shutters, an old-fashioned porch, an American flag snapping in the night wind. She knew the view must be spectacular in the light of day. Georgica Beach was right there, arguably one of the best ocean spots in the world. Just beyond it she could make out the lights of houseboats and mansions.

The minimalist interior surprised her. Given AKA Bomb Threat's flashy lifestyle, Lara had expected a lavish, almost tasteless decor. Instead, the entire home had been outfitted with smooth restraint—everything in white or muted shades of sand and gray. Huge living, dining, and kitchen areas fed into each other seamlessly, anchored by four bedrooms, and flanked by an outside deck with a large terraced pool and a sunken hot tub.

Gabrielle had flung off her fur and started up the music and the hot tub right away. Babe had wasted no time in raiding the house bar. And Lara merely tried to remain upright on her Armani heels. The drinking in the limo had sent her over the edge. In fact, she had just stood there, tottering and weaving, as Gabrielle and Babe stripped to their undies and stepped down into the steamy, bubbling jets of the hot tub, screaming for her to get in.

Lara had wanted to. The water looked so inviting. But it seemed outrageous to just casually sling her Michael Kors number over a pool chair as if it were a blouse from Banana Republic. Oh, well. The day was already spilling over with outrageous moments. Off went the dress. People could buy one of those economy cars for less. Whatever. She was feeling no pain. So in her strapless bra, thong underwear, and sparkling diamonds, she slipped out of her dangerous stilettos and joined them.

She moaned out loud as she sank down. It felt so good to be away from those people at the reception, to be out of those shoes, to have Dean Paul's nuptials behind her. For a moment, she had closed her eyes, head bobbing, mere seconds away from passing out.

"No!" Babe shouted. "You are not fading away on us!" She jumped out and raced inside, dripping wet, returning moments later with a slim can of Red Bull, which she promptly pushed into Lara's hand. "Here. Drink this. It'll keep you going."

Lara had trouble flicking the tab on the can.

Babe took it back and did the honors.

Gabrielle laughed and drank up. It was a brown liquid, and she took it straight from the bottle, like a rebel gunslinger in a hot saloon.

Lara forced down the Red Bull. It seemed to do the trick. At least she could keep her head up and participate in the conversation. The subject was Dean Paul. What else?

"It's every girl's rite of passage to date an asshole in her twenties," Babe had been saying.

Even drunk, Lara had known how stupid this was. Babe Mancini was barely out of her twenties herself, and here she was holding court like a veteran of forty. "But Dean Paul isn't one," Lara argued. And she really believed that.

"Isn't what?" Babe asked pointedly.

Lara hesitated. "What you said."

"Princess, you're drunk, half-naked in a hot tub, and bonding with two other girls who got fucked over by the same guy. You can say 'asshole.' 'Page Six' won't get wind of it and confuse you with Courtney Love."

"Forgive me for being able to get my point across without using profanity," Lara said primly.

Babe kicked the water, splashing Lara in the face. "So how long did the doctor say that stick would be lodged in your ass?" And then she started to laugh. Hysterically.

Gabrielle had joined in with obvious reluctance. But she just couldn't help it.

Lara wiped the water from her eyes and glared at Babe. "If a guy like Dean Paul is an unfortunate rite of passage, then you're a very slow learner. Aren't you with Jake James now? He's much worse."

Babe's face registered the strong comeback. She paused a beat, then grinned. "It could be worse. I could be single and still pining away for my first college boyfriend."

Lara didn't back down. "I'd rather be pathetic and alone than end up with Jake James. What's wrong? Couldn't you tempt Geraldo away from his fifth wife?"

Gabrielle moved fast to defuse the ticking bomb. "Okay, that is enough! We're not here to claw each other's eyes out! We're here to forgive and move past the bullshit. Dean Paul is married. He made his choice. That bitch at the altar didn't look like any of us. Why can't we have five minutes of solidarity, mutual consolation, whatever?"

"Consolation? I didn't want to marry him," Babe snapped.

"Bitch, please," Gabrielle fired back. "If you were seriously over that man, you wouldn't be with Jake James, knowing full well that Dean Paul hates that motherfucker. You expect us to believe that's a coincidence? Baby girl, you're not in a hot tub with two crackheads."

Lara and Babe traded puzzled glances, then zeroed in on Gabrielle curiously.

"Sorry," Gabrielle said. "That was Brown Sugar talking. Sometimes I can't help it."

Everybody laughed.

"It's like the Incredible Hulk," Babe said. "Only instead of turning green, you turn into a ghetto girl."

Gabrielle shook her head and negotiated another swig from the bottle.

Babe started to say something else, then halted, suddenly pensive for a moment. "Maybe that's the thing," she said with philosophical directness. "He's *not* an asshole. That's what makes it so hard to get over him. But he is an asshole for not being an asshole. Does that make any sense?"

Lara finished her Red Bull, feeling a surge of energy. She looked at Babe as if to say she understood. And she did. "Yes, it does."

"I didn't think I would still be in this emotional place about him at this point in my life," Babe went on. "I should be more evolved. All those underwhelming but trustworthy guys I've been ignoring should look good to me now. They've learned how to dress. They're successful. Some of them are actually *hot*." She shook her head. "But there's no interest. I don't even want to go out to dinner with one of them. What did that son of a bitch do to me?"

Gabrielle skated a bejeweled hand through the bubbling water. "Whatever it was, honey, he did it to all of us."

Lara cleared her throat. It was all coming back to her. How good this could be. To have girlfriends you poured out your heart to. Ever since college, work had absorbed masses of Lara's time. Regrets Only was all-consuming. It took devotion, a certain kind of fidelity, even competitive camaraderie with her peers in the same business. Basically, total human energy. But without the return of warmth, without the comfort of the sisterly society she had clung to in college.

Lara parted her lips to speak. Babe had shared something heartfelt. Now it was her turn. "A few years ago, I spent a small fortune on a first edition of his favorite novel—*The Great Gatsby*. And I just put it on the shelf. I don't know why. I guess I thought it would be nice to have around in case we got back together."

Babe laughed. "You kill me, Lara. That's your best self-destructive story? All you did was invest in a literary masterpiece."

Gabrielle laughed.

Lara shrugged helplessly. This time she didn't take offense. There was genuine affection in Babe's ribbing.

"I made a mix tape of his favorite songs and played it whenever I screwed another guy," Babe announced. "There's a certain power in recycling music like that."

"My first two singles were about him," Gabrielle put in. " 'He Was' and 'Prince of My Pain.' " She laughed a little. "It was cathartic, and I'm still earning royalties."

Babe's rapidly reddening eyes flashed with a quickly lit anger. "Does he even acknowledge what he did to us?" she demanded hotly.

Lara and Gabrielle merely looked at her.

The expression on Babe's face was furious and expectant. "I don't mean what he did to us as individual women. I mean what he did to us as a group."

Her announcement was punctuated by the hot tub jets going dead. A pregnant silence boomed.

Babe thundered on. "We were tight. Before college, I never had girlfriends like the two of you. I haven't since. Jesus, I don't even know how to make friends with another woman. You know? I've turned into the enemy. When I'm at a party, I usually ignore other women and talk entirely to men. Yet I call myself a feminist. It's so fucked up."

Lara felt compelled to speak next. "Everyone thinks I live this glamorous life." She tilted up her chin airily and trilled, "*The city's social diva.* That's what *New York* magazine said once." She rolled her eyes. "But it's work for me. It's my business. And on the odd chance that I don't have an event on a Saturday night, you'll find me home alone in sweatpants watching *Trading Spaces* with my maid."

Babe looked uncertain. "I can't picture you in sweatpants."

"Okay, I only wear Juicy Couture," Lara admitted. "But you get the point."

"I do, girl," Gabrielle said. "In my case, I don't think there's anyone in my life who isn't on my payroll. Producers, A&R guys, publicists, stylists, personal assistants. These are the only people I interact with. And if the hits stopped tomorrow, they wouldn't give a damn about me."

"At least you both come from decent families," Babe said. "My parents are worthless."

Lara said nothing. Her relationship with her own mother and father was pure gold. She couldn't imagine not having that to fall back on.

Gabrielle sighed. "Mine are unhappy about this Brown Sugar thing. We've been at an impasse for a long time." Her tone was somber, the look in her eyes faraway. "They just don't understand."

Lara gazed at Gabrielle for a long moment. "Frankly, I don't either," she said finally. "Why did you have to make up an image that's not anything close to who you are?"

Gabrielle shook her head. "It's a complicated story, baby girl. I'm too drunk to tell it, and you're too drunk to hear it." She stood up, a little unsteadily. "How cold do you think that pool is?"

Lara shivered at the thought.

"Why don't you dive in and tell us all about it." Babe smiled. "I dare you."

That's all Gabrielle needed to hear. She stepped out of the hot tub and made a daring dash for the pool. There was a big splash. Seconds after that, a scream. "Oh, my God! It's freezing! This feels so great!"

Babe needed no more prompting. She was out of the hot tub, off and running, and into the deep end within moments.

Now both of them were calling for Lara to take the plunge.

Slowly, she stood up, wrapping her arms around herself to brace against the cold. The night air was so chilly. This was insane. Here it was in the wee hours. She was drunk, practically naked, and under peer pressure to leap into a pool of ice water.

If only Dean Paul could see her now. That boy would never believe it. He always chided her for being so straitlaced and dignified. In bed, he made love to her so slowly and with such tenderness, as if she were a porcelain doll that might shatter under the roughness of too much passion. Out of bed, he would nuzzle her neck and whisper, "My perfect little princess. I'm not good enough for you." Lara was more than that, though. He just didn't take the time to find out.

"Come on!" Babe taunted. "Don't just stand there!"

"You'll love it!" Gabrielle assured her.

Lara sprinted to the edge of the pool. She stopped. She held her nose. She jumped. And it was exhilarating . . .

"Just a little bit more," Privi was saying.

The bouillon was already history. Now Lara finished the milk.

Privi smiled and took the empty glass. "That was much easier than I anticipated."

Lara put a hand to her stomach. "I can't believe that I got it all down. And I think I'm starting to feel better."

Privi smiled. "Yari swears by it. Carlos put away much more liquor than you did. It worked for him every time."

Lara glanced at the clock on the bedside table and felt a flash of guilt. "You're missing *All My Children*, Privi. This is awful. I'm fine. Really. No more tending to me."

The telephone jangled.

Lara grimaced as the shrill sound arrowed straight between her temples.

Privi noticed this and picked up the receiver. "Hello? I'm fine, Mr. Robards. And you? That's good. Lara's feeling under the weather. I'll let her know that you called . . . It's urgent?" Privi glanced at Lara.

She felt a tremor of alarm and took the phone. "Finn? What's wrong?"

"I thought you would've called me by now."

Lara's brow furrowed. "About what?"

"Dean Paul."

Lara rolled her eyes to assure Privi that no real crisis was afoot. She waved the sweet lady back to her soap opera. Then she sighed into the mouthpiece. "A recap of yesterday is hardly urgent, Finn."

"I'm not talking about his wedding. That's old news. I'm talking about his new job."

Lara's heart lurched. Her interest was piqued to the maximum. "What job?"

"He's joined *Hollywood Live* as a New York correspondent. It's all over the columns. Haven't you read the papers yet?"

"I've been too sick," Lara explained. "I'm in bed, half dead." She glanced at the clock again, even though she knew what time it was. The appointment with the Kometani twins loomed like a torture sentence.

"So what do you think?" Finn pressed.

"I'm surprised," Lara admitted, still processing the news. "I thought his parents would ultimately get their way."

"Meaning?"

"That he would finish law school and run for a congressional seat." Lara's mind began to drift to Jennifer Goldblum, her producer contact at *Hollywood Live*. The show routinely covered Regrets Only events, which thrilled her clients and all the boldface names in attendance. Jennifer always seemed to be way ahead on delicious gossip. How had this development slipped past her radar?

"His parents need to get over it," Finn was saying. "Their son has slept with too many women to run for office, and his new wife is no consultant's idea of a political asset. That's for sure."

"I know," Lara agreed. But she was barely listening. "Finn, I'm going to be late. Can we deconstruct this later?"

"I'll call you when I get back to the city."

Lara sat up, bracing herself for her body's revolt. None came.

With a hint of confidence, she moved to stand up. "You're still in the Hamptons?"

"Yes," Finn grumbled. "I ended up going home with a bartender. He calls it an apartment, but it's actually someone's garage. There's a microwave and a little refrigerator. Does that count for a kitchen these days?"

"Finn, don't be mean. What if he hears you?"

"He's already at work. Jerry Seinfeld's wife is having a luncheon. That's the great thing about one-night stands with service people. They always have someplace to go."

"You're terrible," Lara scolded, laughing in spite of her disapproval. "Call me later."

She hung up and ventured toward the master bath, surprised to find herself opening the shower door and turning on the hot water without having suffered an attack of the dry heaves. Privi's little recipe was amazing.

As she stepped under the steaming jets, the realization of Dean Paul's new career began to sink in. It was one thing to read about him in the columns, but it would be quite another to see him in the flesh and on television every night. Lara's TiVo recorded every episode of *Hollywood Live*, and her nightly ritual was to watch it before bed.

She went to work with the blow-dryer, completely forgetting about her hangover state. Maybe it was over. She did feel like one of the living again. God bless Privi. More than usual, the loose curl in Lara's hair seemed out of control. Only Yoshi at Oscar Blandi could ever manage to straighten it to Jennifer Aniston–level perfection. No time for that today. She let it fly. A good thing, because makeup took longer than usual. Most days she could simply apply Bobbi Brown mascara, add a Guerlain bronzer to her cheeks, and swipe on her favorite lip gloss, Pink Sugar Rush by Jacqueline. But today she required a serious session of under-eye concealer, foundation, and blusher to mask a night of little sleep.

Surveying her walk-in closet, Lara decided quickly on clothing, throwing on a vintage Arnold Scaasi blouse with huge sleeves over white toreador pants, accessorizing with a massive Cartier tank timepiece. Men's watches were much more chic and better designed than the female variety. It always cost more, but it was worth it. She grabbed her file on the Kometanis to scan on the way over, snatched her Hermes kelly bag, said her good-byes to Privi and Queenie, and shuffled out the door.

As always, Lara felt a tingle of guilt when the driver opened the door to the backseat of the Lincoln Town Car. She scooted inside and sank into the rich leather. An obscene indulgence, yes, but better than the alternative. Lara hated cabs. Why should she arrive at her destination smelling like curry, or flustered from an argument with the driver because she didn't know the cross streets for an address? Life was too short. It was so much easier to arrange a car service. Finn ridiculed her savagely about this, but she didn't care.

"The Mercer Hotel, ma'am?"

"Yes," Lara answered. She checked her watch. A half hour to get there. Her stomach knotted. Lara was punctual to a fault and hated to be late or wait for anyone who was. "I need to be there in thirty minutes. How's traffic today?"

The driver pulled out from the curb and stepped on the accelerator.

Lara dipped back as the sedan zoomed forward.

"Don't worry, ma'am. You'll make it."

Lara smiled faintly. No doubt. She opened the file on her potential new clients to refresh her mind on what Regrets Only might be getting involved in. If nothing else, it would be . . . interesting.

Mio and Mako Kometani were perhaps the most celebrated women in Japan. Born to a billionaire industrialist father, the twins were modern-day princesses famous for being, well, famous. It was a notoriety they had parlayed into all things commercial. Mio had been crowned Miss Japan one year, Mako the very next. Their image had been branded, paving the way for best-selling product launches like Mio & Mako Noodles, Mio & Mako Beauty Vitamins, even Mio & Mako Bust Cream, which promised to keep a woman's cleavage smooth and beautiful. The girls commanded six figures to show up at parties and look pretty, filled banquet halls at three hundred dollars a ticket to deliver musings about their lives, and posed for provocative photo-essays that were produced into rich, glossy, and expensive coffee-table books. The most recent, *Mio & Mako in Love*, which featured the sisters in various states of seminude, sensual embrace, had broken all first-week sales records for any book in Japanese history.

But like so many international icons, the Kometanis yearned to conquer the American market. It was, after all, the Mount Everest of stardom. They craved the kind of gossipy heat that Paris and Nicky Hilton generated. They dreamed about the mass-merchandising dominance of Mary-Kate and Ashley Olsen. Would the Mio and Mako cosmology interest people Stateside? Lara had her doubts, but stranger things had happened in the culture. The right incident at the right moment could so easily sweep the Asian twins on a magic carpet ride of media devotion.

The Lincoln arrived with a smooth stop at the intersection of Mercer and Prince. Lara checked her watch again. Ten minutes early. Perfect. She asked the driver to wait for her and swung out onto the trendy SoHo street, making a beeline for the Mercer, a luxury boutique hotel well known for its romantic bathtubs and showers that easily accommodated two. The Romanesque Revival had been completely redone by French interior designer Christian Liaigre. The lobby-cum-library was intimate and understated—pale leather screens, Turkish carpet, leather banquettes, low oval coffee tables, and shelves of books.

Lara sat there until fifteen minutes after three. Still no sign of the Kometanis. Annoyed, she approached the front desk and asked the attendant to ring their suite and remind the girls that they had an appointment waiting downstairs.

He nodded dutifully, his expression transmuting into something close to weariness at the mere mention of their names.

Lara managed an empathetic grin and returned to her perch.

A half hour later, Mio and Mako Kometani turned in an ap-

pearance. They were extravagantly cheap-looking—surgically enhanced breasts spilling out of skimpy tops, expertly pillowed wet
lips, and insignificant jewelry adorning their necks, wrists, and too
many fingers. Except for the enormous, purple-stoned rings. At
first, Lara had thought it was silly costume jewelry. But up close,
she could tell it was alexandrite, a rare gemstone discovered in
Czarist Russia in 1830.

Putting their unfortunate style aside for a moment, the Kometanis
were astonishingly beautiful girls. Wide-set, almond-shaped eyes,
flawless alabaster skin, and lithe, curvaceous bodies. They introduced
themselves in perfect English, offering no explanation for the
forty-five-minute wait.

Lara moved past her irritation. "I think it's wonderful that
you've decided to celebrate your birthday in New York. Have you
given any thought to what kind of party you want to have?"

"We want a big party," Mio said.

"Yes," Mako seconded. "With lots of stars."

Mio nodded. "And photographers from all the magazines."

Mako presented Lara with a single sheet of paper.

Lara studied it. A preliminary guest list handwritten in wavy,
girlish cursive on pink paper ghosted with the image of Mio and
Mako. She recognized only a few of the names. Obviously, a large
contingent would be flying over from Tokyo. Suddenly, her eyes
zeroed in on one particular name on the roster. Joaquin Cruz. She
looked up. "Do you know Joaquin?"

Mio and Mako traded knowing looks, then giggled in concert,
offering teasing nods in answer.

Lara felt a brief stab of anger. She didn't know why. As if
Joaquin had anything at all to do with her. He was free to do whatever with whomever. But the possibilities of what had transpired in
that dressing room at Tennis East rampaged through her mind. She
pushed the thoughts away, ignoring the slight stirring in her loins.
As she straightened her spine and turned her head to adjust her
hair, Lara noticed Bizzie Gruzart clomping through the Mercer
entrance with all the grace of a camel loaded up on Vicodin.

Bizzie Gruzart ran Bizzie Gruzart Public Relations, a boutique firm notorious for charging sizable retainers and delivering minimal results. But Bizzie was a big name, with bigger connections. Her father, Gordon Gruzart, produced blockbuster films, mostly megabudget action fare and mediocre sequels. His most recent conquest was the small screen. *The Complex* had become a ratings powerhouse and reality television's answer to *Melrose Place*.

Ironically, Bizzie shot to fame when she became her own PR crisis after crashing a Vespa straight into outdoor diners at Pastis in the meatpacking district. Nobody had been killed, but at least half a dozen turned up with semiserious injuries. Bizzie walked away unhurt, and disappeared until the next day, erasing any chance of nailing her for operating the scooter while intoxicated, which at least one member of her inner circle admitted she was. In the end, though, Bizzie just went through the media-scandal grinder, then her father wrote a few big checks, and the matter eventually disappeared from memory.

The incident only served to enhance Bizzie's business, as her every move stirred up attention. She taught sold-out seminars at the Learning Annex, where her inside tips for aspiring PR professionals ranged from "Google is a great tool, and it's free," to "Get a list of your parents' friends, and call them for help." It disturbed Lara that Bizzie had become such a major player. She was rude, pushy, sniping, and a borderline fraud. And her homeliness only added to her unpleasant nature. She had hard, unyielding, close-set eyes, a bulbous nose, thin lips, and big teeth that were stained from constant smoking. Add to that the stocky build of a butchy softball player.

Bizzie's eyes were clocking the lobby. She located Mio and Mako right away and beamed brightly. Then she noticed Lara and scowled, pausing a moment before stomping over to greet them. "Are you finishing up here? It's time for *our* meeting to start." Bizzie directed this at Lara.

Lara gave her a cool glance. "Actually, we just sat down."

Bizzie looked to Mio and Mako. "I think I'll have a drink in the bar while you wrap things up with her."

The Kometani twins merely grinned. They obviously enjoyed holding court and having a ringside seat as two PR mavens duked it out for the honor of their business.

Bizzie started to leave, then halted. "Oh, Lara, how was Dean Paul's wedding? I couldn't go. Britney had a thing at Bungalow."

"It was lovely," Lara said evenly, knowing full well that Bizzie was aware of her romantic history with Dean Paul and was simply probing for a weak spot.

"I met Aspen in L.A. a few months ago. She's an awesome girl. I think they're perfect for each other."

"They seem very happy together." Suddenly, Lara rose up to give Bizzie the full benefit of her height, her slender frame, and her power of style. Plus, it always helped to be standing eye to eye when you issued a proper dismissal. "It's great to see you, Bizzie. We'd better get back to it, so you're not kept waiting long."

Bizzie took the cue huffily and stalked away in a hideous pair of brown pumps. The story was that Bizzie Gruzart had been born with such odd-shaped feet that her shoes had to be specially made. It was a source of great humiliation that she could never wear Manolo Blahniks and Jimmy Choos.

Lara banished Bizzie from her thoughts and returned to the matter at hand, sitting back down to directly face Mio and Mako. "Have you had a chance to view the electronic press kit I messengered over?"

The girls nodded in unison.

"Then you know the caliber of event that Regrets Only is capable of producing. I can't discuss specific themes for your party until a contract is signed. I've run into the problem of other event planners poaching ideas from preliminary meetings like this one. But I would like to point out that my firm employs a staff of thirty and maintains three warehouses throughout the city. Regrets Only is about illusion. For example, last week I did a fund-raiser for breast cancer research and transformed a hotel lobby into a Venetian streetscape." Lara paused to glance at the handwritten guest list. "This is a good start, but to pull off a major event, you need a better mix. Social, junior social, media elite, politicos, sports figures, entertainers, models. They're all in my database, and with the right theme and buildup, I can deliver them to your party." Abruptly, she stood up.

Mio and Mako appeared stunned.

Lara didn't play the please-choose-me game with anyone. If the Kometanis wanted Bizzie Gruzart, then they could have her. "Let me know what you decide. My calendar is open to commitment now, but that could change." With that, she nodded politely and walked out of the Mercer and into the waiting Town Car.

Her kelly bag started to ring. She fished out the cellular and saw Jennifer Goldblum's name on the ID screen. A tremor of dread raced through her as Dean Paul's new job crashed back into her thoughts. Jennifer was a producer at *Hollywood Live*. She would be able to fill in the blanks. Lara picked up eagerly. "Were you holding out on me?"

Jennifer's voice was perpetually hoarse. "I'm sorry, Lara. I was *dying* to tell you, but they were threatening to fire anyone who leaked it before the deal was signed."

Lara laughed. "So you *were* holding out."

"Only at gunpoint."

"For a minute there I thought you were out of the loop, and I rely on you for the best dish, so this is a relief, I suppose," Lara said easily.

"I just hope this won't be awkward for you," Jennifer said.

Lara was puzzled. "I don't understand."

"Dean Paul will be the show's primary New York correspondent. He'll be covering all of your events."

Lara fell silent.

"But that's ancient history, right?" Jennifer asked. "I mean, you went to his wedding. You must be *so* over him."

"It's not a problem, Jennifer," Lara lied. "I think Dean Paul will be a great asset to the show. Viewers will love him. I hate to cut this short, but I got a late start today, just left a meeting, and have a million phone calls to make."

She signed off and put a hand over her rapidly beating heart. Damn him. Lara had worked so hard to create her own world without Dean Paul Lockhart, and now he was invading it like some third-world marauding conqueror.

On impulse, Lara dug through her purse until she found the business card Babe had given her last night. She dialed the cell number listed. The act alone provided a modicum of relief. It felt good to have a friend who would truly understand . . .

THE IT PARADE
BY JINX WIATT

Fill in the Blanks

Don't you just know the powers-that-be at *InStyle* are fist-shaking, boot-stomping mad. The magazine paid a fortune (yours truly heard a million plus!) for exclusive photo rights to the recent "I Do" bash between Mr. Gorgeous and Ms. Real World (yeah, right—that girl has gone straight to fantasyland). Anyway, a certain tabloid has the pictures they didn't want you to see. Like the one of the "beautiful" bride with a salmon wrap spilling out of her mouth. Yuck! After seeing that, no one may ever eat fish again.

6

Babe

"Go Jake! Take it to the limit, man! Oh, yeah! Give her what she wants!"

Babe clamped her legs around Jake James, holding him vise tight as he pumped away like a madman. She knew he was close. Whenever he began referring to himself in the third person, he was ready to explode.

"You love it! Don't you, baby? I bet that punk Dean Paul never made you feel this good! Go Jake! Go Jake! Oh, fuck, yeah!" He shuddered and expelled a deep, satisfied sigh.

Babe pushed him off her body. "Jesus Christ! Why do you have to be such a pig?"

He rolled over, wiped the sweat from his brow, and tweaked one of her nipples, laughing.

She slapped his hand away. "I'm serious, Jake! That's your idea of pillow talk?"

"What? I was just talking shit. You know me. I'm not responsible for anything I say right before I come." He jumped out of bed and started for the shower.

Babe glared at the sculpted muscles of his back and ass. "You're a sick fuck."

Jake shook his head, then turned around to face her, completely naked, waving his index finger at her. "I knew you shouldn't have gone to that wedding." One beat. "It got you feeling all senti-mental." He said this in a mocking female voice.

Sometimes Babe hated him. Like right now. "You're an idiot."

His smile was smug. "But I'm right, aren't I?"

If he only knew how wrong he was. A sentimental girl didn't sell bootleg photos of her ex-boyfriend's wedding for two hundred thousand dollars. That's what Babe had negotiated even before Jake had left for his early morning gym workout. But he didn't need to know this. It was Babe's secret. So let the jerk believe whatever he wanted.

"I thought so," Jake muttered arrogantly. He disappeared into the shower.

"Asshole," Babe hissed.

He was always impossible in the last hours that led up to him leaving for the studio to tape *In the Ring with Jake James*. Horny. Full of himself. Pugnacious. And those were the better qualities.

Babe slipped on one of his T-shirts and grinned to herself. Jake could put on that macho game face, but she knew he was still smarting from the announcement about Dean Paul's new job. Most notably the part about salary. His college rival would be waltzing into his first broadcasting gig earning more than Jake. And it fucking burned him up.

It occurred to Babe how unhealthy this relationship was. Besides an active sex life, they rarely enjoyed each other. Sometimes she felt like Jake was just using her to mark his territory on one of Dean Paul's exes. Shit. Could she blame him? After all, Babe was using him for the same reason. Dean Paul hated the fact that she had hooked up with Jake.

Babe looked around the cramped, cluttered Union Square apartment. Jake had the bucks to live better now but just hadn't taken the time. He insisted that they meet here because it was con-venient for him. Everything always operated on his terms.

Jake stepped back into the bedroom. There was a short towel tied around his slim hips. Droplets of water trailed down his tanned and defined six-pack abs. Even without the benefit of an erection, the imprint of his cock was impressive.

Babe experienced a tiny rush of desire. Sex with Jake had become a drug. But it wasn't good for her anymore. She needed to detox.

He shook the water from his hair with both hands, flexing his big, boxer-perfect arms in the process. "Still pissed at me?"

Babe could feel herself thawing out . . . and heating up. "I'm always pissed at you, Jake. It's our thing. Didn't you know?"

His lips curled into a half smile. "I want you to watch my Shadow Boxing segment tonight."

"Let me guess," Babe said. "You have an opinion on Dean Paul's career direction."

Jake moved toward her, placing his hands on the top of her thighs and moving up and under the T-shirt to cup her buttocks. "You can bet your ass on it." He squeezed.

"Why do you care so much, Jake? Why can't you just let it go? At least I have the excuse of having been in love with him." She paused a beat. "What's yours?"

He shrugged. "You wouldn't understand. It's a guy thing."

"Oh, really?" Babe let out a tinkling little laugh that filled the air with ridicule. "Are you sure it's not a homoerotic thing?"

Jake stiffened. There was an instantaneous angry glint in his eyes. She was pushing his buttons.

"Maybe you should talk to a therapist," Babe went on silkily. "It could be a latent homosexual obsession that's manifesting itself in animosity. I don't know. I'm just a girl throwing out a theory."

His right hand skated around her hip and across to her inner thigh, stopping just short of its intended target.

Babe took in a little breath. She felt a hot anticipation.

"If there was an ounce of fag in me, I'd need more than two fingers in a crowded restaurant to make you come." His hand journeyed up. It was right there . . . at her opening.

Babe remembered their first frenzied weeks together. She had snapped his photo with Tim Russert at a MSNBC anniversary party. They met for a drink a few days later and caught up on their post-college lives and their mutual hatred for guess who. The wild sex started that night. In the days that followed he asked her not to wear underwear. No matter where they were—a restaurant, a bar, a taxi—he would find a way to bring her to climax. And two fingers and two minutes was all that it took.

Jake kissed her roughly, pushing his thick tongue into her mouth and pulling back just as she started to respond.

Babe moaned out loud as he trapped her lower lip between his teeth, nipping playfully, as those two magic fingers dipped into her very core.

"I know you pictured yourself in that girl's place," Jake whispered.

Babe glared at him. She knew her eyes were mere slits.

"Walking down the aisle to the wedding march . . ."

She attempted to push him away, but Jake was as solid as a brick wall. "He told me that I could do better than you," Babe hissed.

"Oh, yeah?" Jake taunted her, his fingers still doing their work. "Why haven't you, then?"

Babe's emotions were at the boiling point. She wanted him to throw her out and tell her never to come back. She wanted him to push her onto the bed and ravish her. The bastard repulsed her emotionally but enslaved her physically. Desperately, she lashed out against the carnal longing. "He still thinks you're a nobody, Jake. You can make a fool of yourself on that little TV show that doesn't even register a full ratings point." She laughed in his face. "You might as well be on fucking cable access. And you can write your stupid book, the one you had to pose half-naked on the cover for to get anybody's attention." She jabbed at his chest with her index finger. "But no matter what you do, you'll always be a poor, scrappy nobody in the eyes of Dean Paul Lockhart and everybody like him. You'll always be a joke."

Jake's eyes flashed with such fury that Babe experienced a

nanosecond of fear that he might strike her. But then he gave her a hint of a secret smile and angled his fingers up to the spot that drove her crazy every time. Suddenly, he withdrew, tossed off his towel, and brought her hand down to his hard, throbbing cock. "Is this a joke to you?"

The sigh of pleasure that came next was involuntary. In that moment, Babe wanted Jake so badly that it felt like a psychotic compulsion. She peeled the T-shirt off her body, slid onto the bed, and opened her legs.

"I didn't think so," Jake said. And then he mounted her with passionate aggression. . . .

A half hour later, Babe was searching for her bra and itching to get out of the grungy apartment when her cellular rang. She followed the noise and found the phone underneath a stack of cover flats for Jake's new book. The number on the ID screen didn't look familiar. "Hello?"

"Babe, it's Lara. Have I caught you at a bad time?"

"I'm at Jake's place, so I'm not sure how to answer that. Part of me wants to say yes."

Lara hesitated. "I'm sorry. I'll—"

"No, it's fine," Babe assured her. "Jake's not here. He just left for the studio. I'm trying to find my clothes and what's left of my dignity."

"Have you heard about Dean Paul?"

Babe laughed. "Shit, that's all I've heard. Jake's having a field day with it."

"He didn't mention a single word about it yesterday," Lara remarked crisply. "And now he's in Greece. I just heard from one of the *Hollywood Live* producers that he's going to be covering all my events."

Babe found a bra. An expensive one in a size not her own. She threw it down. "Son of a bitch," she muttered.

"What?" Lara asked.

"Where are you?" Babe countered.

"In SoHo. Why?"

"Meet me for a drink. We'll hash all of this out. I like the bar at the St. Regis. It's classy. Nobody will hit on us. Are you game?"

"I can't drink, Babe. Seriously. Not today. I'm lucky to be alive after last night."

"So nurse a club soda. I'll drink for both of us."

Lara considered the offer for a moment. "Okay. I'll meet you there. What time?"

Babe spotted the strap of her bra peeking out from underneath the bed. "One hour."

"Perfect."

She hung up and finished dressing, taking in the surroundings. Boxing gloves, sweat clothes, and athletic shoes were littered throughout. The pitiful excuse for a kitchen was filthy. Basically, the whole place gave off college jock vibrations.

She scanned the room for stray items. Once more, her eyes fell on the mystery bra. Impulsively, Babe stuffed it into her purse. Ha! Maybe she'd figure out whom it belonged to and return it with a personal note suggesting that the bitch should know a cheap bastard like Jake James wasn't worth nice lingerie.

Babe had just enough time to stop by her own crappy apartment to shower and change clothes. It wouldn't do to show up freshly fucked to meet a woman like Lara Ward at a place like the St. Regis. The fact that Lara had sought her out filled Babe with a sense of pride, and she realized how much she really missed her dignified friend. Lara's regal manner had the potential to inspire. A little bit could rub off in positively influential ways. Maybe the rupture between them had been repaired. Last night's reunion had gone a long way toward forgiveness.

Was time the only factor? Babe began to wonder. Or did Lara actually understand why Dean Paul had stayed with Babe at the Biltmore that night instead of driving back to campus to be with her. He was a highly sexual being, and there was obviously a limit to how much Lara's cool sophisticated reserve could satisfy him. Early in the urgent hours of their first coupling, Babe surmised what it must have been like between them—sweet, respectful, properly passionate. Dean Paul didn't kiss Lara like a demon lover. He didn't push her head down when he wanted to feel her mouth around him. He didn't take her vigorously from behind. He didn't plunge his tongue between her legs and inside her ass until she writhed in ecstasy. But with Babe, it had been all of that and more.

Back then she had been stupid, arrogant, and naive, thinking her sexual freedom gave her the upper hand. Keeping him happy in bed was not the secret to keeping him happy in the relationship. It just kept him happy in bed. Part of her felt manipulated, too. It was the reason her resentment toward him—and even Lara, to a lesser degree—had maintained a steady, radioactive hum over the years. Babe had never experienced the tender side of Dean Paul's ardor. It was as if he had continually tested her sexual limits. Would she go that far? And when she did, he seemed both pleased and disappointed. There was no way to win.

Babe pushed away that train of thought the moment she hit the moldy stairwell. Suddenly, it struck her as odd that her tabloid sale hadn't triggered—at the very least—a full day's worth of satisfaction. The two hundred grand was a hefty addition to her savings account. If only the deal had come through a few weeks ago.

That's when Babe had fallen in love with an apartment just hitting the market. It was an amazing art-deco pied-à-terre in a prewar building on Central Park West, with beamed ceilings, an open dining area, two baths, and a remodeled kitchen with all-new appliances. God, it had been everything she wanted. And out of her price range. Of course, it wasn't now. But the unit had sold within a few days of her touring it. That disappointment had cemented her decision to take full advantage of her invitation to Dean Paul's wedding.

But now the rogue photo sales were an addiction. The risk had become a thrill, the easy money a passport to a better life. She didn't want to stop. There was always one more monster yet to go after. Why settle for a pied-à-terre when she could keep going and buy a loft or a penthouse? And deep down, Babe knew that it wouldn't end there. More square footage. A better view. A hotter location. A car. A weekend home. The temptations could run on forever.

It was a dirty business, but how else was Babe supposed to get what she wanted? There were no rich parents to hand over the keys to a dream home lock, stock, and walk-in closet. She thought of Lara. Now there was a girl who had it easy. But even Babe had to admit that she had the work ethic of an Olympian.

The event-planning industry could chew up and spit out the lazy and ambivalent. The party circuit kicked into high gear in September and maintained a steady hum through the holidays. New Year's could be particularly brutal. Babe had heard that it was nothing for event producers to work forty-two hours straight at that time. It cranked up all over again in February and went non-stop through May. Summer months were lighter. That's when all the high-profile types migrated to the Hamptons and other play-grounds for the well-heeled.

Babe braved the fifteen-minute walk to her apartment. She scrubbed herself free of Jake James, then dressed quickly in snug-fitting Seven jeans and a vintage Billy Squier rock tee, finishing off with a pair of Gucci boots that she'd scored at a sample sale.

The cab ride to the hotel was interminable. All she could do was sit helplessly as the car plodded through bumper-to-bumper traffic, its driver yammering on a cell phone headset in Arabic from pickup to drop-off. She arrived twenty minutes late, and remembering how Lara could be about such things, raced up the steps.

Lara sat at the bar considering a cup of hot tea. Even with a nasty hangover, the girl had most women beat. She looked like a stylish television star ready to sashay onto the Regis and Kelly set for a chat.

Babe got the bartender going on two tequila shots to start. "Sorry to keep you waiting. Traffic was murder."

Her drinks turned up in record time.

Lara glanced at them. "Your stomach must be lined with steel."

Babe shrugged. "I've always been able to hold my liquor." She knocked down both in quick succession, feeling a warm burn down her chest, followed by a tingle in her brain.

Meanwhile, Lara sipped demurely on her tea.

"I'm glad you called," Babe said.

Lara smiled faintly in reply. "Finn called me on the way over here. He read Jinx Wiatt's on-line column out loud. A photographer has already sold unauthorized pictures from the wedding. Apparently, there's a hideous one of Aspen with a salmon roll stuffed in her mouth. Can you believe that?"

Babe marveled at how fast gossip could circulate. It was only hours ago that she had uploaded the images. Now it was water-cooler conversation. "That's awful." She signaled the bartender for one more. "I hope someone notifies the new Mrs. Lockhart about this news. I'd hate for her to come home to unexpected humiliation." Babe fought to keep a straight face but couldn't hold it. Then she started to laugh.

Lara caught the bug, covering her mouth. She took in the other patrons with a cautious circular glance, as if they were listening to every word. "We should be ashamed of ourselves. This isn't funny. It's terrible."

"Correction. It's terribly funny. That bitch deserves it."

"But what about Dean Paul?"

"Don't worry about him," Babe assured her. "He can't take an unflattering picture. It's impossible." She was grateful for the arrival of the third shot. All this talk about the photographs was making her nervous. Sending number three down the hatch, she looked at Lara seriously. "Does this *Hollywood Live* business upset you?"

"I'm not happy about it," Lara said matter-of-factly. "Part of the reason I went to the wedding was because I thought it would give me closure. And today I find out that he'll be back in my life with perhaps more regularity than he was at Brown. I knew how to avoid him there. But I can't very well stay away from a Regrets Only event just because he'll be there with a microphone and a camera crew."

"I wouldn't worry," Babe told her. "We both know he won't stick with it very long. It's Dean Paul, remember? He has the attention span of a three-year-old."

Lara managed a wan smile. "I'm not so sure about that. This could be his calling." She sighed. "Sometimes I wish I had handled the breakup differently. Maybe I wouldn't be so paralyzed where he's concerned."

"Have you had a serious relationship since Dean Paul?" Babe asked.

Lara paused a beat and stared into her tea. "Not really. I've dated some men, but nobody who really held my interest." She looked at Babe curiously. "How are things with Jake?"

Babe picked up one of the empty shot glasses. "I'll need three more of these to tackle that. Mind if we skip that subject?"

Lara nodded. "You know, I've watched other girls ritualize their failed relationships. They burn pictures, or they host a back-on-the-market party. Do you think it's too late for me to do that?" She shook her head in disbelief. "And do you want to hear something embarrassing? I still have my Dean Paul scrapbook from college. Every picture. Every letter. Even silly mementos like ticket stubs from concerts and a parking citation we got on our first date in Providence."

Babe could feel the buzz from the tequila, but her mind was still clear. Something Lara had said tripped her into a deep distraction. *Pictures from college.* Jesus Christ, Babe hadn't thought about those in years. But she still had them. In fact, she could visualize the black archival box on the shelf in her storage closet. Even better, she could visualize the handwritten adhesive label stickered onto the box's cover: D.P. LOCKHART—BROWN U.

Babe felt a ripple of awareness race through her body. How could she have forgotten? That rainy day when Dean Paul had modeled for her on the steep incline of College Hill. He had been so quick to strip down for the unabashedly sexy and impromptu photo shoot. She had her Nikon FM2. He had a bold exhibitionist streak. Together they had made beautiful, erotic art.

Lara was still talking.

Babe had stopped listening. What she possessed could be the stuff of bidding wars. But it was different. No anonymity this time. She couldn't throw a rock and hide her hand with these pictures. The moment they hit, Dean Paul would know exactly where they had come from. It would mean selling him out completely. It would mean crossing a line that he might never forgive her for. Still, only one question percolated in Babe's mind. It had nothing to do with emotions. It had everything to do with money.

How much could she get?

THE IT PARADE
BY JINX WIATT

Fill in the Blanks

Everybody thought a certain hip-hop diva (hint—her name is very sweet) was sitting pretty with Mr. Thug Mogul (hint—his name reeks of terrorism). That is, until he turned up at The Ivy in Los Angeles with her archrival (hint—her name buzzes with royalty). According to spies, the two looked very cozy. This could get very awkward. Especially when diva number one hears how badly diva number two slams her on a new song. Why say it in person when you can sing it over the radio?

7

Gabrielle

The bitch was back.

That unmistakable voice bounced off the walls of the Waldorf-Astoria penthouse suite. In disbelief, Gabrielle stopped to stare at the speakers of her Bang & Olufsen BeoSound 1.

"What's up, New York? Yo, yo, yo! Shaniqua's in the house! Shaniqua's in the house! Go Niqua! Go Niqua! Go Niqua! Go Niqua! It's your birthday! It's your birthday!" A cackling stream of self-amused laughter. "I know, I know. Y'all are probably sitting there thinking, 'That bitch is so damn country.' But that's okay. This sister ain't offended. I'm from the Dirty South, baby. That's why y'all love me so much. Because I bring a different flava to the concrete jungle. And let me tell you, it's *good* to be back. I want to thank Hot Jams 97 for having the balls to put Shaniqua Jackson back on the mike where she belongs. Y'all know it took a set of steel ones to do that. All those haters out there. It ain't easy being Shaniqua. You know what I'm saying?"

Gabrielle pushed aside the room service tray, her appetite suddenly gone. So this was the big surprise that her favorite radio station had been promoting for weeks. The return of prodigal DJ-diva Shaniqua Jackson.

A year ago, the Yazoo City, Mississippi, native had been suspended from her top-rated show on The Beat 101.7. Stories varied on what exactly pushed her out. Was it her gossipy revelation about the sighting of a powerful hip-hop star in a gay leather bar? Her announcement that a young television sitcom actress was recovering from a botched abortion? The curious manner in which she secured new music and played it weeks before the official add date?

No matter the reason, Shaniqua Jackson had been effectively silenced. The station management had suspended her indefinitely but refused to release her from the remainder of her contract, preventing her from seeking employment within New York's five boroughs. But now a year had passed, Shaniqua Jackson had become a free agent, and Hot Jams 97 had paved the way for her return. No doubt the audience would be rejoicing. Listeners loved her dirt-dishing, bad-girl antics.

"It's been a year, so y'all know I'm chomping at the bit to get in the game again, right?" Shaniqua bellowed. "And I ain't about half-stepping on my first day. I'm coming back hard and in charge. That's why I got royalty in the house."

Gabrielle experienced a momentary tingle of dread. She reached for the remote control and ticked up the volume.

"Queen Bee, welcome to *Down and Dirty with Shaniqua Jackson.*" Another arrogant laugh. "I'll be doing it nice and rough every afternoon from two to six. Now whatcha think about that?"

"It's all good, girl," Queen Bee answered. "It's all good. And you know I got something hot for you. I ain't about bumping in here just to say, 'What's up?' "

"I know that's right," Shaniqua said. "Y'all, the Queen has brought her subjects a little taste of her new CD. A smoking track called 'The Sting.' And it's a message to a certain somebody. Now my mama always told me, 'Don't start no mess, won't be no mess.' But Queen Bee don't live like that. Sister girl says what's on her mind. Listen up, y'all. We'll trip over this on the other side."

The opening guitar riff from the Rolling Stones' "Start Me Up" arrowed straight into Gabrielle's heart, igniting an inferno of anger. Instantly, she knew. The bitch had stolen the sample track from the remix of her upcoming single, "My Hot Box." And now that Queen Bee had hit the airwaves first, there was no way Gabrielle could release it. Goddamn her!

Queen Bee was a minor talent at best. Born Quantika Williams, she had grown up in Brooklyn's notorious Marcy Projects and used her body as a ticket out, working as a stripper, sometime prostitute, and a booty dancer in rap videos before taking a turn at the mike. A regular john who also happened to be an executive at a major record label had given the green light for her first effort, "Size Matters." The song had enjoyed marginal success, setting the stage for a full-length CD, *Bigger Is Better*, and the cheap notoriety of Queen Bee's in-your-face sexuality.

Though she possessed little natural beauty, Queen Bee put her enhanced charms to exhaustive work. With double-D-cup breasts, fake eyelashes, big, candy red lips, elaborate hair weaves, and a penchant for enormous feathers and tiaras, she was equal parts circus diva and fagged-out drag queen.

Gabrielle listened with ferocious interest as Queen Bee delivered the rap lyrics in her grunting, melodically challenged style . . .

There's a fake-ass ho—who shall remain nameless
Calls herself Queen of Bling—and that's shameless
It gets worse—she thinks she's a Super Bitch
Drop the prefix—and I'll be down with this
Buzz Buzz, Sting Sting
There's only one royal
Queen Bee—That's me
My first real fight—tenth grade
Girl pulls a punch—I pull a blade
I got a bruise—but she got forty stitches
Now she's workin' drive-thru—and I'm here countin' riches
Buzz Buzz, Sting Sting
There's only one royal
Queen Bee—That's me
I tell you this cuz Queen Bee always brings it real

I don't hide, I don't lie, I don't cheat, I don't steal
I grew up gangsta hard—bangers shootin' straight at me
Didn't know shit about private schools and fancy things
Buzz Buzz, Sting Sting
There's only one royal
Queen Bee—That's me
Didn't have to make up ghetto life—baby, I lived it
So I dare that imitation sweetener to come with it
Name the time, Name the place, Let's go, Let's rock
We'll see how tough you are—staring down my glock
Buzz Buzz, Sting Sting
There's only one royal
Queen Bee—That's me

Gabrielle merely stood there in stoic, simmering silence.

"Queen Bee!" Shaniqua exclaimed dramatically. "My girl! I got one word for this—*damn!*" She strung out the one syllable into two. "You are not playing with this new track!"

"That's because Queen Bee don't play. Trix are for kids, okay? I bring it on the level. I don't hide behind nothing. You know where I came up."

"The Marcy Projects," Shaniqua said knowingly. "That's a hard life, girl."

"You know it. Ain't no Chuck E. Cheese where I'm from. We got liquor stores and check-cashing joints. My best friend got shot because she didn't have a watermelon Jolly Rancher in her pocket when her strung-out cousin wanted one. Girl was twelve years old. You didn't hear about that on the news, did you?"

"That's a nightmare walking, girl," Shaniqua said quietly. "But you got out."

"Hell, yeah, I got out. I shook my ass. I sold my tail. I did whatever I had to do. Ain't no shame to my game. Other bitches try to look down at me and call me a ho. I'm like, 'No, no, no. Think twice. A ho meets a brother at a club and gives up her stuff later the same night. *That's a ho.* I charged green paper for my coochie to get me what I needed. *That's a businesswoman.* Okay?"

"No, you didn't just go there," Shaniqua said with devilish glee.

"Yes, I did," Queen Bee replied with a proud smack of her lips.

"Okay, girl, let's continue being real," Shaniqua began.

"I'm *always* real," Queen Bee snapped.

"Then let me get real right back at you," Shaniqua countered. "Your last CD did a little bit of business, but you didn't see any platinum, am I right?"

"No, but it went gold. You got a gold CD, Niqua?"

"Ain't trying to get one. We're talking about your career, sweetheart."

"Don't talk about my shit like it's raggedy just because it didn't go fucking platinum. Gold is some serious shit, too. That's all I'm saying."

"Well, what *I'm* saying is this—up until now you've been trying to do your thing while Brown Sugar, Lil' Kim, Eve, and Missy Elliott have taken all the rays and left you in the shade. You might call yourself Queen Bee, but all you've been is a little gnat."

"Bitch, who you calling a gnat?" Queen Bee demanded hotly. "Can a fucking gnat run you down in a Bentley?" She jangled a set of keys.

But Shaniqua didn't back down. "I have my spies and sources," she responded confidently. "I hear that the Bentley is on lease from your record company, that they can take it back whenever they feel like it, and that you're just a broke bitch."

Gabrielle howled with laughter. Queen Bee's expletives were being bleeped, but you could clearly make out the intended words. This was shock radio at its finest.

"Now wait a minute. You low-down stanky ho! Follow my motherfucking ass to the ATM to check my balance. I'll prove that I ain't no broke bitch. I got serious cheddar in the bank."

Living up to her reputation, Shaniqua Jackson proved relentless. "I don't care what that little slip of paper says. My sources tell me that you're all tapped out on advances from your record label. I hear it's only a matter of time before you file for bankruptcy."

"Bitch, your *sources* don't know what the fuck they're talking about!"

"Quit calling me outside my name, girl." There was a severe warning in Shaniqua's tone. "I'm just presenting stories that I've heard. If you ain't a broke bitch, then there's no reason to be upset."

"Let me make it crystal clear then—I ain't no broke bitch. I ain't no *fake* bitch, either."

Shaniqua laughed. "Okay, girlfriend's got promotional skills. She knows how to bring it full circle and back to the product. So let's talk about that new track, 'The Sting.' It's fierce, girl. I have to give you props. That's a hit."

"It was a song I had to write. The shit came straight from the heart."

"This ain't just a song, girl. What I hear is a declaration of war. You're calling out Brown Sugar as a pretender."

Queen Bee grunted. "You said it. I didn't. The name Brown Sugar ain't in my song."

"Come on, sweetheart. Let me go over what you mentioned in the track, okay? Queen of Bling, Super Bitch, imitation sweetener. Now who's not being real?" Shaniqua paused a beat. "Flat out, are you telling me that Brown Sugar is a phony?"

"Why don't you ask her that question?" Queen Bee said.

"Because she's not here right now. And you are."

Queen Bee hesitated. "I'll say this much—my song speaks for itself."

"So you stand behind it?" Shaniqua challenged.

"You know it," Queen Bee said tightly.

Gabrielle felt the urge to call the radio station and blast Queen Bee live on the air. But she resisted. No need to draw attention to this. It had the potential to develop into a big scandal and possibly damage her career. Better to take the high road.

"Everybody knows that Brown Sugar is AKA Bomb Threat's girl," Shaniqua went on. "He molded her into a star. Does he know that she's fronting like this?"

Queen Bee didn't bite. "You'll have to ask him that."

"Why can't I ask you?" Shaniqua asked teasingly. "You had dinner with him at The Ivy in Los Angeles the other night. What did the two of you talk about?"

"That's personal."

"So is the fact that you were a teenage hooker, but you shared that with no problem. Spill it, girl. Everybody knows that the two of you hooked up in L.A. That piece of business is out. My sources told me. It's even in the papers."

Gabrielle rushed to find the latest edition of the *New York Examiner*, the new tabloid of choice, ripping through it to find Jinx Wiatt's column. She scanned the gossipy blind items until she found the one so clearly about AKA Bomb Threat and Queen Bee. The realization smoked inside her brain.

Without thinking about what she might say, Gabrielle dialed his private cell number.

AKA Bomb Threat answered on the second ring.

In the background, she heard music, loud voices, and laughter. "Where the fuck are you?"

"In my skin."

Gabrielle was shaking with rage. "It sounds like you're in a strip club!"

"I'm in L.A. getting a lap dance at the Wild Goose. Amber's riding my jock right now. Wanna say hi?"

"Go to hell!"

"Who the fuck do you think you're talking to?"

"I just heard Queen Bee's new song! Using the Stones' 'Start Me Up' for the remix was *my* idea! But she's stolen it! And now I find out that the two of you have been hanging out together in L.A. I suppose you're going to tell me that this is a coincidence!"

"So I tossed the track in her direction," he admitted easily. "Big deal. I came up with a new killer beat for 'My Hot Box.' It's wicked, baby. Even better than the sample. You'll hear it when I get back. Trust me. You'll love it."

"Queen Bee is out to get me, Bomb," Gabrielle said urgently. "Have you heard this track? It's blowing up on Hot Jams 97 right now. Shaniqua Jackson's all over it. This could get ugly for me."

"Ah . . . oh, yeah, baby . . . grind it good . . . work it, girl . . . work it."

Gabrielle sat on the edge of the bed, a cauldron of anger, fear, and frustration as her producer/Svengali/lover/whatever ignored her and spoke in thick, broken whispers to the stripper. "Bomb!" Gabrielle screamed.

"Calm down, baby. Queen Bee's just making a little noise. Nothing will come of it. Don't worry. I can handle her."

"Who do you think I am, Bomb? You can't fuck around with Queen Bee in public, hang out in strip bars, and expect me to keep your bed warm in New York like some clueless housewife! This is bullshit!"

"Damn right, it's bullshit!" he shouted back. "No woman tells me what I can't do! I run this fucking show! You know that! Queen Bee was a little side thing for me. We had some fun. I tossed her a bone. And that's my fucking business. Not yours!"

"I think it is my business," Gabrielle said savagely. "Especially if you want to keep me in your bed and on your label."

There was a long, intense silence.

"Baby, you better hang up this phone and pull yourself to-gether," AKA Bomb Threat advised. There was a sinister edge to his words. "I created Brown Sugar. But I'll tear her down, too."

And then the line went dead.

Whatever instinct she possessed to play this thing cool van-ished. Gabrielle dressed quickly in velour Sean John pants, a pair of brown Timberland boots, and a tight white shirt emblazoned with the phrase TOO MUCH, TOO LOUD, TOO FAST in a red, lipstick-like scrawl.

Baby Bear was hanging in the outer seating area, eating pizza and watching *Scarface* on a portable DVD player. The moment he saw Gabrielle, he jumped to attention.

"Get the limo," she said.

"Where are we going?" Baby Bear asked.

Gabrielle could feel the adrenaline rising, the blood pumping. "On a bitch hunt. So stay close. There could be serious trouble tonight."

THE IT PARADE
BY JINX WIATT

Fill in the Blanks

It just doesn't seem fair that a certain party-planning sophisticate should get her pick of the hottest guys around. First it was the ultimate golden boy and America's favorite prince. Now it's a man with international flavor, a certain polo player who's got women in Manhattan suffering from fainting spells (yes—that age-old condition). Don't be too jealous, though. A rumor is swirling that Mr. Heartthrob is hiding a dirty little secret.

8

Lara

Lara slipped under the covers, content in the knowledge that her day had ended with a few notable successes. She had whipped a nasty hangover. There was the sweet satisfaction in knowing that Bizzie Gruzart would soon be informed that Mio and Mako Kometani had elected Regrets Only to plan their birthday party. And her drinking date with Babe had been surprisingly pleasant, free of awkward silences and unspoken resentments.

Just as she shut her eyes, the telephone jangled to life.

Startled, Lara checked the ID screen, not recognizing the number. She glanced at the clock, noted the after-midnight hour, and answered sharply. "Hello?"

"You're awake." It was the thick and richly accented voice of Joaquin Cruz.

"How did you get this number?" Lara hissed. "And why are you calling at such an indecent hour?"

"A mutual acquaintance gave me your number."

"And who might that be?" Lara demanded.

"I'll never tell," Joaquin teased. "As for the indecent hour, it's only appropriate, since I'm having indecent thoughts." One beat. "About you."

Lara felt a warmth take over her body. She let out a sigh of what she hoped sounded like exasperation. "If this is an obscene phone call—"

"Just say the word. It can be."

"It's after midnight. This is rude and disrespectful."

"I'm sorry. Perhaps I can try again tomorrow. What time do you prefer obscene calls?"

Against all urges to do otherwise, Lara found herself responding to his little joke.

"I made you laugh," Joaquin said. "This is promising."

"It's been a long day. I'm delirious," Lara countered.

"Deliriously horny, I hope."

Lara experienced a tingle between her legs. Feeling hot all of a sudden, she pushed away the covers. "Are you sure you have the right number? You're talking like I'm some barmaid who served you a beer last week."

He pretended to be shocked. "You mean this isn't Angie, the Hooters waitress?"

She laughed again.

"My offer still stands," Joaquin said.

"And what offer would that be?" Lara inquired. She already knew what it was, but she wanted to hear him say it again.

"To fuck you properly and make you forget Dean Paul Lockhart."

Though every instinct told her to hang up, Lara held on. A meaningful silence loomed. Her heart quickened. Finally, she spoke. "Even a Hooters girl deserves a better line than that."

"That's disappointing to hear," Joaquin murmured. "I thought it was a good line. Very confident and full of exciting possibility."

"Try blind arrogance," Lara said.

"You don't believe I can deliver on the promise?"

This time she sighed wearily. The conversation was titillating, but she knew that nothing would ever come of it. "It's late, Joaquin. Too late for games."

"I'm not playing a game," he said earnestly.

"Try your luck at a bar. Good night." She moved to break the connection.

"I bet you've never received one of these before," Joaquin said. "Or placed one, either."

Lara hesitated. Now he had her curious. She put the phone back to her ear. "What are you talking about?"

"I believe the American phrase is . . . *booty call.*"

She smiled at his pronunciation. He made it sound so formal and respectable. "You're right on both counts."

"When you go to bed alone, don't you ever wish someone was there with you? Not to hold you. But to please you. To leave you so spent and satisfied that you sleep like a baby until the next morning. Don't you ever crave that?"

Lara didn't quite know how to respond. Because she was craving it right now. "I'm only human," she whispered frankly. "Of course I have those occasional desires. And if I find myself alone with them, I just imagine George Clooney, and then I fall asleep with a smile on my face."

Joaquin laughed. "I'm better than George Clooney."

"You really are full of yourself, aren't you?"

"I'm just being honest."

"That's the excuse of every narcissist."

"How can George Clooney be better than me? He's somewhere in California, on location for a film, or at his villa in Italy." Joaquin paused dramatically. "And I'm standing right outside your building."

Lara bolted upright and dashed to the window, the cordless firmly planted against her ear. Slowly, she parted the heavy curtains.

Joaquin stood under a streetlight, looking up at her. "Turn on a light. I can't see what you're wearing. Or not wearing for that matter."

Lara didn't move. She just stared at him in the darkness. After several long seconds, she spoke. "I think you have a problem."

"Invite me up. We can talk about it."

"*Invite you up?*" Lara didn't have to try for her incredulous tone. It spilled out naturally. "I barely know you, and you're calling me in the middle of the night from outside my building. I should be dialing the police."

"To report a stalker?"

"Exactly."

"They'll just advise you not to talk so long next time. That tends to encourage stalkers."

Lara's smile was reluctant. But it was there. "Go home, Joaquin. Don't you ever sleep?"

"I'm restless tonight. I was hoping you were, too." He peered up at her.

She peered down at him.

"One kiss."

"What?" She pretended not to understand. But she did. And even worse, a vital part of her wanted to oblige him.

"You can't send me home like this. Just one kiss. After that, I'll leave. I promise."

"This is insane."

"You know what they say. Desire has a mind all its own."

"Who says that?"

"People who act on it," Joaquin said matter-of-factly.

Lara bit down on her lower lip. She was perilously close to buzzing him up. Right away, the potential obstacles started tumbling over themselves in her mind. Queenie would bark up a storm. Then Privi would wake up and ask a million questions. There was also the matter of the overnight moisture mask slathered across Lara's face. She would have to rinse that off before any kissing could commence. So much for spontaneity. Real life was not a scene from a Catherine Zeta-Jones movie.

A taxi stopped in front of the building. Alex Gilbert, a stockbroker and her neighbor on the seventh floor, tumbled out of the backseat holding the hand of a cheap-looking date.

She watched as Joaquin covered the cellular mouthpiece with his palm and engaged them in quick conversation, pointing up at Lara.

Alex glanced upward, waving excitedly.

Lara raised a tentative hand. What on earth was Joaquin saying? And then they all disappeared toward the entrance.

Suddenly, she understood his plan. Lara experienced a mounting panic.

"Joaquin! Don't you dare!"

He returned to the line. "What was that?"

"I know what you're doing! Don't come up here! You're not invited!"

"I'm having a hard time hearing you. Damn cell phones. Must be the elevator. It's unit 703, right? Alex told me. Nice guy. Have you met Michelle? They just started seeing each other, but I think she's a keeper."

Lara felt a helpless horror mixed with a sensual excitement. "Don't press the buzzer! You'll wake up my maid!" She hung up, tossed the phone onto the bed, and dashed into the bathroom to wash off the treatment mask. Covering her pink babydoll-tee and panties set with a white terry-cloth robe, she stared into the mirror. Her long hair was freshly shampooed and pulled back in a scrunchie. She looked scrubbed clean and golden.

Queenie pranced into the bathroom and licked her ankle.

Lara glanced down, feeling a wave of guilt over Queenie's obvious consternation. The Maltese wanted Lara back in bed pronto. Lovingly, she scooped up Queenie and carried her back to her favorite spot, bunching up the pillows and covers to maximize her comfort, hoping to mollify her high-maintenance pet.

But seconds after Lara closed the bedroom door, she heard Queenie scratching on the other side.

"It's okay, angel. Go to sleep."

Queenie began to bark.

"Queenie, stop!" Lara hissed, more sharply than she intended. "You'll wake up Privi."

More scratching. A slight whine. But at least the barking stopped.

Lara sighed. Then she breathlessly ran to the front door and opened it.

Joaquin just stood there, leaning against the frame.

For a moment, Lara simply drank him in. Wearing a tight black turtleneck and snug but broken-in jeans, he looked more gorgeous than any man had a right to be. She narrowed her gaze, playing up an anger that strangely wasn't there. "Alex should have never let you in the building or told you where I live. Tomorrow morning I'm reporting him to the co-op board."

Joaquin reached for the tie on Lara's robe and tugged her closer. "I'm only interested in what you plan to do to me."

The breath caught in Lara's throat. Just as well, because she didn't know what to say. The way he had come here tonight— unannounced, after hours, full of no-nonsense come-ons and crude promises—she found it exceedingly sexy. It was so against her nature. But he brought out something dormant in her.

Queenie cranked up the barking again.

Lara groaned, knowing that Privi would be out here at any moment unless she did something fast. Impulsively, she yanked Joaquin inside and pulled him into the bedroom.

His introduction to Queenie proved awkward. She growled at him, then sought refuge underneath the bed. But the barking stopped. Thank God.

Lara laughed softly, a nervous reaction to the hidden part of her that was glad she had Joaquin Cruz all alone right now.

"What's so funny?" he asked.

"Nothing . . . I . . . I just can't believe I'm doing this."

He smiled, inching closer, trapping her against the lingerie chest. "Doing what?"

"You said one kiss," Lara reminded him.

"I lied." And then Joaquin's mouth was on hers, his tongue darting in and out, his breath quickening, his hands moving under her robe, skating up her legs, her thighs, her torso, then around the outline of her breasts.

Lara stared at him, eyes widening, mind and body in revolutionary war. To stop him or to let him go on? That was the question. Deep down, she knew that the solution to her general ambivalence about sex stood right here, pressed against her. Sure, there had been other men since Dean Paul. Alan, the distinguished art dealer, old enough to be her father. Miles, the legal analyst for the cable network, with the wandering eye. Garrett, the dark, brooding professional tennis player who routinely made it to the finals but could never win a Grand Slam title.

None of them had commanded her arousal. Not like this. With them it had been merely pleasant ardor. But right now she felt naked need. Joaquin's hands were brushing across the soft cotton of her top, his thumbs playing a vibrato across the erect, tender buds of her nipples.

He moved closer and held it there, letting her feel the growing erection in his jeans, tracing the outline of her lips with his tongue.

As thick as a man's wrist. Finn's gossip played in her mind. Where there's smoke, there's fire. The old adage proved true again. Even confined by jeans, it seemed to have a life of its own. It was larger, thicker, and harder than anything she had ever felt.

Lara clung to him, arrowing her body up to experience more, every layer of societal hang-up stripping away. It was practically the middle of the night. He had come to her like a phantom lover. She could take this delicious journey in secret. Nobody would ever know. Suddenly only aware of ravenous impulse, she pushed up his turtleneck, marveling at the dark hairs that gathered in impossible thickness on the path that led to his . . . Oh, God, she could barely think it, much less say it.

Joaquin pulled the shirt over his head and tossed it to the floor. Those brief seconds that his mouth left hers felt like an eternity. But he was back now, lips against lips, hands busy divesting her robe, pelvis grinding against her.

Every prudish inhibition disappeared. Nothing else mattered. Nothing else existed.

His fingers were working on his five-button fly.

She glanced down, instantly amazed. The stories didn't do him justice. It was superb. Like a monster, his penis sprang from its denim cage, straining and twitching in anticipation, veins pulsating.

Joaquin watched her take in the eighth wonder of the world.

The act of going down on a man had always repelled her to a degree. Sometimes she acquiesced, but never with much enthusiasm. Even with Dean Paul she preferred making love. Yet right now she was not only considering the act, she actually *wanted* to do it.

As if reading her thoughts, Joaquin placed his hands on her shoulders and gently guided Lara to her knees, where she promptly tugged his jeans down to his ankles, her lips parting of their own volition.

For a fraction of a second, she knelt, statue-still, feeling the delicious sensation as he played with her hair, sensing the silky tendrils move between his fingers. His hands were on the back of her head now, pushing forward.

Lara needed no more prompting than that. Her mouth locked itself around him, and greedily, she feasted on the flesh, the sensation shooting erogenous pulses throughout her body.

It was shameful. It was delicious. And it was the last time she intended to see Joaquin Cruz. She would give him the chance to live up to his bold assertions. Just this one time . . .

THE IT PARADE
BY JINX WIATT

Fill in the Blanks

How sacred are *your* previous relationships? Would you reveal everything and more about past intimacies to the highest bidder? A very glam shutterbug for the society set is doing just that. And the auction is expected to hit the sky. Why? Because her ex is a just-married famous name whose every move becomes the stuff of headlines. She even has naughty personal photos to ratchet up the offers from panting publishers. Some girls have all the luck.

9

Babe

Once upon a time it had been the Mercantile Exchange. Now it was Chanterelle, a refined French restaurant in the heart of TriBeCa on Harrison Street.

Babe stepped into the elegant space with the soaring ceilings. She noticed the spiderlike brass chandeliers, the warm wood columns, and the Chippendale chairs. It was more private party in an exquisite house than public eatery. A pretty hostess made a religiously dedicated effort to guide her to the table.

Linda Konner sat there waiting with raven hair, Chanel red lips, a porcelain complexion, and a welcoming smile. "You made it. I was beginning to worry."

Babe checked her watch. She was almost twenty minutes late. Probably because her decision to show up had been finalized at the last possible moment. "I'm sorry." She felt a flush of heat and used the menu to fan herself, wondering if it was just her.

"It's too warm in here," Linda announced, as if reading her mind. She complained to a waiter.

He passed this on to a fastidious-looking woman. Then another server joined the fray. When a fourth person entered the mix, there was a hushed miniconference about the temperature.

Linda laughed at the display. "Between the four of them I hope they can adjust the thermostat."

Babe smiled as she kept a possessive hand on the archival photo box.

Linda gave it a covetous glance. "I see you brought the pictures."

Babe nodded noncommittally.

"May I have a look?" Linda asked.

Babe hesitated. "I'm still not sure about this." But she slid the box to the other side of the table anyway.

Linda began sifting through the images. "I placed a few calls after we talked. There's already a great deal of interest." She stopped and looked at Babe. "These are incredible shots. Better than I imagined. Please tell me you have a signed model release."

"Back in college, a department store in Providence used one of my images for a newspaper ad. Dean Paul was one of the models, and he signed a general release. The language is very broad. It covers all of my images of him. Not the most ethical approach, but it's lawsuit-proof."

"That settles the legal obstacle. What about your personal one?"

Babe paused to drink down a few sips of water. She flagged the waiter and ordered a glass of wine identical to Linda's. "If I do this book, it's going to cost me a few relationships."

Linda returned a diffident shrug. "How important are they?"

Babe was silent.

"You're not doing anything wrong." Linda closed the box and tapped the cover with her knuckle. "These are your pictures. And they're not cheap and pornographic and meant to embarrass. They're artistic and erotic. Dean Paul looks like an Adonis, and that's all anybody will be talking about. Trust me, a man like that won't stay angry long."

"A man like what?" Babe asked. The wine arrived. She was grateful.

"Come on, Babe. Dean Paul's an exhibitionist. He exploits himself. Why shouldn't you get in on the act? There's nothing damaging here. So he posed for some sexy pictures. It will only deepen the mass love of the women and gay men already fawning over him. Are you afraid it will hurt his career?" She didn't wait for an answer. "The brass at *Hollywood Live* better hope they locked him into a long-term deal, because when this book comes out, his price will skyrocket."

Babe could sense her reluctance fading.

Linda Konner was a savvy literary agent and the obvious conduit between Babe, the Dean Paul photographs, and megabucks. A former colleague at *212* had passed along her name. Paige Sheridan was now swimming in cash thanks to Linda's aggressive and enterprising negotiation of *The Class Reunion Diet*. The book had mushroomed into a merchandising phenomenon—calendars, journals, meal-replacement bars and shakes, even a reality show on cable.

Babe stared at the wispy calligraphy on the menu, but found it hard to concentrate.

"The pictures are enough for a good deal, but there's a way to juice it up to guarantee a bigger advance," Linda said.

Babe's eyebrows perked to attention.

Linda leaned forward to make her pitch. "The accompanying text should be as intimate as the pictures. Dean Paul is a fantasy icon. The people who buy this book will want to know what it's like to date him. How he smells, how he makes love, what his secret personality traits are—everything an ex-girlfriend would know. You're obviously a talented photographer. Can you write?"

"I graduated from Brown."

"So? I had a client once who finished at Penn State. She didn't know the difference between 'there' and 'their' or what the hell to do with an apostrophe. Her favorite word was 'amazing.' She used it a million times. I had to bring in a ghostwriter."

"I can write," Babe assured her. "And I promise to go easy on the number of 'amazings.'"

Linda smiled. "I thank you in advance for that." She scanned the menu. "How soon can you write a sample chapter?"

Babe drank the rest of her wine and instantly wanted more. "Not long. I kept a journal during that time, and I still have it."

Linda looked up. "The photographs are so personal. You really feel like you're seeing him through the eyes of a lover. Maybe that's the way to approach the text. Instead of chapters, you could present your memories as expanded journal entries."

A goateed waiter in a crisp, white oxford appeared to present a taste sample of one of the chef's new creations—lobster mousse.

Babe fell silent until he disappeared. Then she regarded Linda. "How important is the journal text? I'm not sure if reliving the past that way is the best thing. It was a complicated time. There are other people's lives to consider."

Linda stared at her for a moment, unflinching. "The lowball price for this book will be one million dollars."

Babe experienced an adrenaline rush. All her reservations faded into oblivion. She had lived without Lara and Gabrielle since college. She could live without them again. And as for Dean Paul, it was high time she got paid for that broken heart. "Give me a week to write the sample."

Linda Konner smiled.

Babe turned her attention to the menu, ordering the striped bass with red butter and fresh sage, and indulging in a sinful dessert—molten chocolate walnut cake.

The meal was delicious. The wine flowed. And the celebratory toast echoed in her brain. *To becoming a millionaire . . .*

An hour later she was back at her apartment, gathering voice messages and e-mails that detailed her gauntlet for the night. There was a club opening, a ribbon-cutting for a new designer's boutique, the premiere of a Sundance-winning film, and a book launch for a former secretary of state who called himself a novelist now.

Shit. Tonight's agenda was really going to be a bitch. She couldn't wait to leave this rat race. And if Linda Konner got a good enough offer, Babe could do it. Oh, yes. She would leave *212* before the ink dried on the publishing contract.

Three fast knocks startled her. Peering through the peephole, she saw a sweaty Jake standing there in his boxing workout gear. She unhooked the security chain and opened the door. "What are you doing here?"

He pushed himself inside and flattened her against the wall with a bruising kiss, his breathing labored. "I just had a sparring match with a super middleweight. The guy's a pro, but I kicked his ass. Goddamn, what a rush. I felt ten feet tall. It made me so fucking horny. All I could think about on the way over here was your sweet pussy." Jake grinded into her, his mouth traveling down her neck, his hands kneading her breasts.

Even as she felt herself beginning to respond, Babe tried to push him away. "Jake, stop. You're all sweaty and gross. And I've got work to do."

He silenced her with another kiss, angling his pelvis upward. "Come on, Babe. Be a sport. You can feel how hard I am. I need it so bad it hurts."

Babe thought about the mystery bra from Jake's apartment. She twisted away from him and snatched it from her bag, then threw it down to the floor as evidence. "Go see whoever this belongs to. Maybe she'll help you out."

Jake didn't pretend to be ignorant about it. "She lives in Brooklyn. Too far for a quickie. That's why I came here."

"You're a pig. Get out."

"Christ, Babe, what is this? Are we an exclusive item now? Because I didn't get the memo."

"You can't just show up at my door without notice and expect me to take off my clothes like some bimbo on Cinemax."

"Why not?" Jake demanded. "It's hot. From what I hear, a lot of men aren't that interested in sex anymore. I know women who would love for a guy to be spontaneous like this. Your typical man can barely get it up. I'm like a college dude on spring break seven days a week. You don't know how lucky you have it."

Babe laughed in his face. "This is luck? You barging in smelling like a locker room and reciting bad porn dialogue?"

"This is bullshit."

Babe splayed out her hands. "Finally! Something we can both agree on." She rolled her eyes. "Next time, call first."

"I tried your cell three times."

"I forgot to charge it last night." She threw a glance to her regular phone. "You didn't try this number."

"I couldn't remember it."

Babe pointed at the bra. "Do you have her number committed to memory?"

"718-857-6453."

"You son of a bitch."

He stepped closer. "Surprised?"

"Not in the least."

And closer. "She's just a girl. A college intern. I've banged her a few times. It's nothing."

"What a relief." Babe could smell him now, and she had to admit that he really didn't stink. There was an intoxicating salty musk emanating from his sweat-soaked body.

Jake leaned in and flickered his tongue across her earlobe.

Babe shivered.

"We always have the best sex when we fight," he whispered. "That's why we never break up."

"You know what they say. There's a first time for everything."

He sank down to his knees and gazed up. "Do you want me to leave, or do you want me to stay and eat you all the way to heaven?" His fingers started on the buttons of her pants.

This time she didn't stop him.

They never made it to the bed. He took her right there on the hard floor. All the rumors from college were true. Jake James was a champ at cunnilingus, his tongue thick, strong, and probing, every flick and whorl leaving her paralyzed.

Babe just closed her eyes and lay there, a willing, pliant vessel, the world light-years away. When he slid up his middle finger to work in concert with his mouth, she let out a soft mewl of breathless appreciation.

Jake handled her with such authority. He knew the machinery like a prized mechanic. Every move he made was the right one, sending a thrumming sweetness throughout her body. She loved him for it. She hated him for it, too.

Ultimately, they ended up in her bedroom for the final act. Like always, Babe clung to him in a jailer's grip, amazed at the steady voltage of Jake's energy. He hammered into her with steadily increasing amperage just as the chant began.

"Go Jake! Go Jake! Oh, fuck, yeah!" And with an arch of his back, a cry of release, and a convulsive body shudder, he collapsed on top of her, an inert tangle of muscled limbs.

Babe could almost hear their mutual hearts pounding against each other. It should feel so much better than this.

"Goddamn. That was great." Jake rolled off her and sighed, perfectly content. He placed a hand on the inside of her thigh. "Aren't you glad I didn't go to Brooklyn?"

"Thrilled." Babe jumped out of bed and took the top sheet with her to cover her body. The postcoital feelings were typical. Physically satisfied. Emotionally empty. Borderline shameful. Something had to give.

"I thought we could go out for dinner after I finish the show tonight," Jake said. "My producer loves Town. It's in the Chambers Hotel. We've never tried it. What do you think?"

"I've got four events to shoot tonight."

"Don't say I never try."

Babe looked at him, noticing the body-length sweat stain that had formed on the fitted sheet. When she went to sleep at three in the morning, his scent would still be all over the bed. "A lame dinner invitation passes for effort now?"

He shook his head and threaded his hands behind his head, displaying the full power of his biceps. "I can't win." One beat. "Do you have any beer?"

"I need you to leave, Jake. I have to get ready for a long work night, and I want my privacy."

"One beer and a twenty-minute nap. Then I'll split. Promise."

Babe groaned wearily and started for the refrigerator. "Import or domestic?"

"A lite beer's fine," Jake called out.

She grabbed a bottle of Michelob Light, popped the cap, and set it down with a bang on the nightstand. "I'm going to take a shower. I want you gone by the time I get out."

Jake put on an exaggerated pout. "You make me feel so used."

A reluctant grin crept onto Babe's lips.

Jake caught it right away. "I believe that was a smile. See, Babe, I'm a stand-up guy. How many men out there tell the truth about their screwing around? At least I put my cards on the table."

Babe left to turn on the shower. Before shutting the bathroom door, she said, "Jake, it's admirable that you're honest about being an asshole. But it doesn't make you any less of one."

She let the hot jets wash away her frustration, taking her time, applying a tea tree oil treatment to her hair and Tracie Martyn Enzyme Exfoliant to her face.

"Nice work," Jake said. "When you're head over heels for a subject, it really shows."

The sound of his voice jolted her. She hadn't heard him come in. "What are you talking about?" Babe peeled back the shower curtain. And then she knew.

The expression on Jake's face explained everything. He had found the photographs of Dean Paul.

She silently cursed herself for being so careless, then smiled, trying to appear nonchalant. "That was a long time ago. I was filing away some negatives that had piled up, and found those in storage."

Jake took a quick hit of Listerine, gargled for a few seconds, and spit into the sink. "What are your plans for them?"

"I don't know," Babe said casually, laughing a little. "I didn't take a gift to the wedding. Maybe that's the solution."

He gave her a strange look. "You're lying."

"Well, Matlock, what do you think my plans are?"

Jake didn't answer. He wiped a circle of fog off the mirror and inspected his face, smoothing a hand down his beard growth. "Those pictures are ripe for *Playgirl*. I knew the guy was a punk."

A defensive impulse kicked in. Babe couldn't stop herself. "Kind of like your own book cover, huh? I don't remember David Brinkley ever posing in a jockstrap."

His eyes blazed with anger. "Tape the show tonight. Watch it when you get home." And then he walked out, closing the door behind him.

Babe experienced a terrible sense of dread. She rinsed quickly, draped a towel around her body, and dashed out of the bathroom, dripping wet with each step.

But Jake was gone.

Her gaze shot to the chipped draft table.

And so were the photographs.

THE IT PARADE
BY JINX WIATT

Fill in the Blanks

You can take the girl out of the ghetto, but can you take the ghetto out of the girl? More than fake nails and hairpieces went flying when two rap divas got down and dirty outside one of New York's top radio stations. Arrests were made. Bless you, NYPD! There was no boy in blue in sight when yours truly became the victim of a purse-snatching a few weeks back, but I'm glad they were around to put these hellcats in the pokey. Sorry, readers. No luck on sneaking one of those lovely mug shots out of the precinct. Another scandalmonger got there first. Wonder where they will turn up? Are you humming that old Carly Simon chestnut, too? It's called "Anticipation."

10

Gabrielle

Gabrielle was handcuffed to a bench and sobbing uncontrollably, her makeup smeared by tears.

A police officer approached and asked for her autograph. "For my daughter," he said, smiling. "She's thirteen. Her name's Misty."

Shaking, she reached for the pen and scribbled her name on the scrap of paper, wishing her writing hand had been shackled.

"It's routine to detain everyone until all the statements are taken," he explained kindly. "You'll be free to go soon. Don't worry." He stepped away and returned with several tissues.

Gabrielle tried gamely to wipe her eyes and blow her nose with her free hand. She finished and stared in horror at her fingertips. They were still stained with printing ink.

The officer sat down beside her. "It'll come off easy with soap and water. You just have to scrub."

She glanced at her new friend.

He seemed too young to have a teenager. With his unlined skin, neatly trimmed goatee, deep tan, and green eyes, the man with the name badge that pronounced him Kris Kirby looked late twenties, tops.

"I don't understand what's going on. I've been here since last night."

Kris shrugged. "It's procedure. You were involved in a shooting."

Gabrielle started to sob again. This had been the second-longest night of her life . . .

It all began in the domain of Shaniqua Jackson, fifty stories above the roar of Park Avenue in the skyscraper jungle. Gabrielle had arrived just minutes before six. She had been a guest on Hot Jams 97 before, and knew exactly where to go.

Inside the small studio, Shaniqua reigned supreme, aromatherapy candles burning, overhead lights dimmed to a faint glow. A short, bald black man—the producer, no doubt—sat opposite her, manning the phones and monitoring e-mails.

A hard-charging track by DMX boomed over the airwaves as Shaniqua studied a wire-service report and chomped on a strawberry Twizzler like a girl from the block. She took one look at Gabrielle and broke into a I-just-won-the-lottery smile, then motioned to her colleague.

They seemed to speak a silent language all their own.

DMX went down.

Shaniqua Jackson went up. "Sorry, DMX. I'll make it up to you, baby. You know that. Y'all aren't gonna believe who just walked into my studio. *Brown Sugar.* That's right. I said *Brown Sugar.* I know she's steady tripping about Queen Bee going off, and she came to the right place to set things straight. We're coming up on a station break, so don't touch that dial. Brown Sugar is next. You're listening to *Down and Dirty with Shaniqua Jackson.* I'm serious now. Hands off the dial. I'm watching you."

The DJ diva threw down her headphones and rushed to the glass door. "Girl, I wish you would've called instead of wasting all that time in traffic. We've only got about ninety seconds left in the show. Will you come back tomorrow?"

Gabrielle iced her down with a cold glare. "No, thanks. That's all the time I need to say what I have to say."

Shaniqua turned to her studio mate. "Nathan, get that mike ready. Brown Sugar's about to swat a bee, baby!"

The man rose to a full five-feet-two. He offered his little hand. "Nathan Quinn. I'm Shaniqua's producer."

Gabrielle rebuffed his gesture. "Let's just get this over with."

The advertisements rambled on. Vanilla Coke. The new Ice Cube movie. UPN's Monday night lineup. And then Shaniqua Jackson commanded the airwaves again.

"I'm back, y'all. Fixing to hit the streets, but I've got one more little something something before I peace out. Brown Sugar is in the house. And I believe she's got a message for Queen Bee. We're almost out of time, so I'm going to let you close it down, girl."

Gabrielle gripped the mike. "When I was a child, my mama told me that if you can't say something nice about somebody, then don't say anything at all. Obviously, Queen Bee didn't get that home training. My heart goes out to rappers who have so little to say that they waste their time tearing down other artists. Listen to any song on my new CD. You won't hear a single mention of Queen Bee. No reason to. I've got important subjects to write about. This sister doesn't need controversy to bring attention to her records. Because Brown Sugar fans come to the party for the music. 'Nuff said."

Blazing a look of disgust at Shaniqua, Gabrielle released the mike and started for the door.

Baby Bear stood waiting. Silently, they headed for the elevator.

She could hear the radio host scrambling to wrap up her show, then rushing out to catch them. "Girl, you need to come correct and sit down for a real interview. That golden rule shit ain't going to cut it."

Gabrielle spun angrily. "You don't deserve your platform, Shaniqua."

Nothing in Shaniqua's eyes revealed a propensity to back down. "Maybe you don't deserve yours. Why don't you prove it? Come on my show and answer the allegations."

"I have no plans to sink to Queen Bee's level—or yours."

"You sink to AKA Bomb Threat's level every night, and he didn't mind getting down with Queen Bee." Shaniqua Jackson smacked her lips triumphantly. "He didn't mind getting down with me, either."

Gabrielle struggled to edit her surprise.

"Don't worry. He was just a baby back then. A little thug plugging his first record, station by station," Shaniqua said. "But, yeah, I let him hit it."

"That doesn't surprise me. Those were desperate times. He was willing to do almost anything for airplay."

"Well, Miss Priss, if Queen Bee's right, not much has changed. Now he's fronting a rich bitch as a ghetto girl for the same thing."

Gabrielle swallowed hard.

"You better hope your story checks out," Shaniqua said menacingly. "Hip-hop fans don't like fakers. Just ask Vanilla Ice."

The elevator doors opened.

Baby Bear stepped inside to hold their position.

Gabrielle stood frozen, feeling a frightening sense of life spiraling out of control. Finally, she joined Baby Bear and nodded for him to take them down.

Shaniqua got her last lick in mere seconds before the doors closed. "Be sure and listen to the show tomorrow, girl. An old friend of yours is my special guest. I'm sure you remember him. The name's Theory."

With each descending floor, Gabrielle's stomach knotted tighter and tighter. She didn't imagine that Theory would have many nice things to say about her. Their relationship had ended bitterly, and nothing had changed for him. He was still holding court at Vibeology, doing the same starving poet routine.

Baby Bear regarded her seriously. "Is there anything I can do, Sugar? Maybe I could pay this Theory cat a visit. You know, convince him to stay at home tomorrow."

Gabrielle reached out and touched his massive forearm. "I don't think so, Baby Bear. It's out of our control now." She sighed wistfully. "And I'm afraid it's going to get real ugly."

"I don't care what they say. I've got your back, Sugar. Anytime. Anyplace."

Gabrielle was moved by his expression of loyalty. She felt her eyes mist with tears.

"You're not just a paycheck to me. Whatever goes down, I'm your dawg. You know that, right?"

Gabrielle embraced him warmly. "Yeah, Baby Bear, I know."

They exited the building and made a beeline for the limousine.

"Shit!" Baby Bear exclaimed, lumbering over to remove a traffic ticket slapped on the windshield.

Gabrielle laughed. "What do you expect? An illegally parked white limo stands out like neon. How many does that make this month? Thirty? Forty?"

"Twenty-seven," Baby Bear grumbled.

"If you weren't such a sweetheart, I'd have to think about deducting it from your earnings." Suddenly, she noticed a black Cadillac Escalade with dark-tinted windows speeding in their direction.

Baby Bear picked up on this, too. He watched it closely.

The luxury SUV screeched to a stop, blocking the limousine's path.

"Get in the car, Sugar," Baby Bear said.

Before Gabrielle could make the move, Queen Bee swung out from the vehicle's passenger side. "Bitch, what do you know about home training? Your own mama taught you how to be a lying-ass ho!"

For a moment, Gabrielle stood there, stunned, until the immediacy of live radio crystallized in her mind. Then she stepped around the limousine to face down her nemesis directly, raising up her hand. "I've said all that needs to be said. You're not going to provoke a feud out of me. Maybe you need it for your career, but I don't need it for mine."

"Wait a minute, bitch!" Queen Bee rolled her neck and waved a hand of long, extravagantly painted acrylic nails. "Don't try to play me out like some nobody."

"If the shoe fits . . ."

Queen Bee was steaming now. "Yeah, bitch, it's Gucci. Of course it fits. Keep talking. Any minute now it might be fitting straight up your ass!"

Baby Bear shot a stern look at Gabrielle. "I'll handle this, Sugar. Get in the car."

But Gabrielle didn't move.

And Queen Bee thundered on. "What's this shit about me not being important enough to write about?"

"That's between you, your publicist, and the media coverage you don't get," Gabrielle said. "It's really none of my business."

Queen Bee pushed out her big breasts and smiled with a cool comeuppance. "Is AKA Bomb Threat your business?"

Gabrielle smiled savagely. "He's more my business than he is yours."

Queen Bee twisted around to share a secret grin with her driver.

He cackled.

Queen Bee cackled, too. "Are you sure about that?"

"Absolutely. Bomb is old school. You know how men like that can be. Sometimes they just like to take out trash."

Queen Bee's nostrils flared. She eyed Gabrielle up and down scornfully. "That's something he used to do. Now he's taking out me."

Baby Bear had made his way around to the driver's side of the Cadillac. Suddenly, he slapped the hood with the palm of his hand. "Move your ride, man. It's blocking me in."

Queen Bee's driver jumped out, displaying the kind of youthful aggression that signals stupidity and nothing to lose. "Yo! Fat-ass motherfucker! Keep your hands off the car!"

Baby Bear raised up both arms in mock surrender. "Not looking for trouble, man. Just move so we can go. Simple as that."

The driver dipped back into the SUV.

Without warning, Queen Bee lurched toward Gabrielle and pushed her violently, slamming her against the limo. "You want to take me on, bitch? You want to take me on?"

An uncontrollable rage surged through Gabrielle. She swung with one arm and yanked with the other, making hard contact with Queen Bee's face and ripping out an expensive hairpiece at the same time.

Queen Bee lost her balance and went down fast, crying out in agony as four acrylic nails scraped the pavement and broke off.

The driver reappeared.

Gabrielle saw a flash of metal.

A gun!

"Goddammit, Sugar, get in the car!" Baby Bear shouted.

This time, Gabrielle obeyed him to the letter, diving into the rear cabin of the limousine.

"Shoot that bitch!" Queen Bee screeched.

Gabrielle experienced a moment of total fear.

The first shot rang out like a clap of thunder.

Gabrielle closed her eyes.

The second shot shattered the windshield.

There was a rumbling inside her chest. She wondered if it would all end right here, right now. A senseless fight in the street. Over a stupid song. And a man she cared nothing about. The irony burned in her brain. In the end, she would have lived the phony life story the record label had made up for her.

The next few minutes played out like a blurry montage in a movie she didn't want to see.

Blistering sirens.

Cops hitting the scene.

Bystanders gawking.

The hotheaded driver facedown on the limousine, two officers working hard to restrain him.

Queen Bee resisting arrest with a steady stream of, "Get your hands off me, motherfucker!"

Baby Bear looking dazed on the sidewalk as blood pumped from his right arm.

In the distance, a man with a camcorder, beaming with glee as he recorded every horrible moment . . .

It had been fourteen hours, and she was still manacled to this goddamn station-house bench. *Oh, God! How much longer?* The metal cutting into her wrist hurt like hell.

Gabrielle was exhausted, hungry, and thirsty. Her mouth was dry, her lips cracked and longing for moisture. She just wanted to be set free. Despite her pleas, nobody would give her any information about Baby Bear. They just wanted her to relay her version of events over and over again.

Fuck! She felt as if she had told it a million times. And each recall was exactly the same. Gabrielle had remembered things with unflinching clarity. They tried to trip her up with their endless questions, but she never changed her story. It had been the truth. The first time and the millionth time.

She watched the detectives who conducted her interview resurface.

The lead interrogator motioned for Kris Kirby.

The officer jumped to attention.

There was a brief conference.

Kris returned with a smile on his face and promptly removed the handcuffs.

Gabrielle gazed at him gratefully, massaging her sore wrist. There was a question in her eyes.

"You're free to go," Kris said. "But please be careful. Those were some rough riders you tangled with. They had two more firearms hidden in the car. It could've been much worse. Your friend was taken to Mount Sinai. He's going to be fine. His injuries were minor."

"Gabrielle!"

She spun quickly to see Lara standing in the precinct entrance, then thanked Kris for his kindness and rushed to embrace her, taken aback by how good it felt to have a friend right there when you needed one.

Lara withdrew to give Gabrielle a once-over. "Thank God you're okay."

"I'm fine," Gabrielle assured her. "Baby Bear—my body-guard—he was shot."

Lara nodded. "I know. It's all over the news."

Gabrielle put a hand to her heart, experiencing a sudden panic. All of her belongings—her purse, her cellular. And then she remembered. They were in the limousine, which had been impounded. "Can I borrow your phone?"

"Of course," Lara said, reaching into a sleek leather bag to hand it over.

Gabrielle struggled to recall Baby Bear's mobile number. Finally, it came to her. Waiting for the connection was torture.

He picked up right away, sounding groggy.

"Baby Bear!"

"Sugar!" More energy now.

"Where are you?" she demanded.

"In the hospital."

Gabrielle started to cry.

Lara reached for her hand and squeezed tight.

"I'm okay, Sugar. I just got it in the arm." He laughed a little. "It takes more than one bullet to knock out my big ass."

Gabrielle smiled through her tears. "It's all my fault. You told me to get in the car, and I didn't listen. If only—"

"Sugar, stop. Those cats were looking for trouble. Queen Bee and that punk-ass driver are the only ones to blame."

"The police just released me. I'm coming to see you."

"Get some rest. You've been in that station all night long. I'm cool here. Got my whole crew with me—my mom, my brother, two of my cousins, some of my boys. Don't worry about me. Just take care of yourself."

Gabrielle signed off.

"I have a car and driver out front," Lara announced. "You're coming home with me."

Gabrielle started to protest.

"You're a woman in crisis. Nothing would please Privi more

than to pamper you for a day. She'll run you a glorious bath and cook you a fabulous meal." Lara grinned. "Of course, you'll have to endure a good scolding from her, too. But that's all part of it."

Gabrielle smiled. She remembered going home with Lara for Thanksgiving during their sophomore year at Brown. Privi had been a highlight of the visit, so warm and comforting.

Lara took her hand. "There. It's settled then. Now come with me." She sought out a rest room and, once there, proceeded to pull out anything Gabrielle might need from a bottomless Louis Vuitton duffel bag—Evian water, hand sanitizer, a toothbrush, toothpaste, a washcloth and towel, La Prairie foaming facial cleanser, a hydrating Chanel lipstick, Hermès scarf, D&G sunglasses, and a Burberry trench coat.

Gabrielle laughed. "You're a lifesaver!"

Lara sparkled with pride. "Just brushing your teeth and washing your face will make you feel like a new person."

Gabrielle indulged. The sink was dirty, the hot water nonexistent, but the simple acts of cleanliness felt marvelous. With a few giggles, she swiped on the lipstick and donned her disguise, the scarf over her head, dark shades, and long coat completely transforming her.

She surveyed her reflection in the mirror. "I look like one of those celebrities hoping to leave a plastic surgeon's office undetected."

All of a sudden, a distinct shadow of dread clouded Lara's face.

Gabrielle titled up the sunglasses to gaze at her directly. "There's something you haven't told me, Lara. What is it?"

Lara paused a beat. "Have you ever heard of 'The Smoking Gun'?"

Gabrielle's heart sank. "The Web site that digs up dirt on people," she said quietly, already aware of where this was heading.

"They posted your mug shot this morning."

Gabrielle let out a deep sigh. "Well . . . I've looked better."

Whatever Lara was about to say next, it appeared to be the

most troubling news of all. "They also made the connection between Brown Sugar and Gabrielle Foster."

She said nothing.

"They even scrounged up your senior prom picture."

It was worse than she imagined. Now Morgan Atwood would
be drawn into this. Gabrielle flipped down her sunglasses again.
Stoically, she stared at Lara. "Okay. How bad is it?"

"I won't lie to you, Gabrielle. This won't be easy. As far as scandals go, it already has a life of its own."

THE IT PARADE
BY JINX WIATT

Fill in the Blanks

The new union between Mr. Everything and Missy Reality Star has whipped the matrimonial record of Zsa Zsa Gabor and Mexican playboy Felipe De Alba (in the early '80s, those two called it quits after one day!). But this observer finds it curious that an extended honeymoon in Greece was abruptly cut short. Airport spies say the just-married lovebirds barely spoke to each other throughout the transatlantic flight back home. Could there be trouble in paradise already?

11

Dean Paul

They were on the cable car to Fira, Santorini's capital, when Dean Paul made the announcement.

"I've made arrangements for us to leave tomorrow."

Aspen didn't look at him. "That's five days early. I'm surprised you made it this long."

"What does that mean?"

She turned on him hotly. "This was supposed to be *our* honeymoon, and you haven't focused on me at all. First, it's your stupid job, and then day after day you've worried about one of your ex-girlfriends. Why didn't you just marry one of those bitches? Hell, why didn't you marry *all* of them? Then you could move to Idaho or Utah and live in a commune."

"It's not about that, Aspen." He reached for her, but she pulled away. "This shitstorm about those pictures won't die down. My parents are freaking out."

Aspen rolled her eyes. "Oh, it's your parents now. So I'm not even in the top five."

"It's not a contest."

"Not a fair one anyway. I can't compete."

Dean Paul sat silently for a moment. "We'll go on another honeymoon. Soon. I promise."

"I want to finish this one."

He could feel his patience eroding. His wife was just being petulant now. "Since when? You've complained about everything. The shopping sucks. The sun is too intense. The mule drivers are rude. We've had sex twice. You're either not in the mood or too sensitive from sunburn. I honestly thought you'd be relieved to go home."

"*Home?* New York is your home, not mine. My opportunities are on the West Coast."

"How many times have we gone back and forth on this? We're starting a new life together."

"Correction—*you're* starting a new life. What am I supposed to do?"

He didn't answer.

"I don't see why you can't talk to the *Hollywood Live* people about hiring me, too. We could do it together. As a couple. That's how we should approach everything. Why should Nick Lachey and Jessica Simpson get all the glory when we're smarter and better looking?"

He gave her a strange look. "So that's what this is really about. Your jealousy about my new job."

"I'm not jealous. I just can't believe you're being so selfish. It could be *our* job."

"Aspen, come on! This is supposed to be a marriage, not some kind of act that we take on the road. We need to establish separate professional identities. Anyway, I thought you wanted to report on politics."

"I do." There was a slight whine to her voice. "Why can't I have a show like Greta Van Susteren? I'm prettier. All she does is sit there and ask people questions about whatever lawsuit is in the news. I can do that."

"It's not that simple. As I understand it, she has an extensive legal background."

"Oh, please. I've got friends who went to law school, and I know more than they do just from watching Court TV. It's my second-favorite channel after Fox News."

Wearily, Dean Paul stared at the magnificent view. Santorini's famous volcano was right there, its mysterious beauty and multi-colored rocks breathtaking. The sky and water were a perfect peri-winkle blue. This should be the happiest week of his life.

But Aspen could be so frustrating. Moments like this triggered a sense of panic. Had it really been love that made him go all the way to the altar? Or merely some superpowered infatuation? Finally, he spoke. "If that's what you see yourself doing, then the last job you should want is *Hollywood Live*. Overcoming *The Real World* will be enough of a battle."

"Do you have a problem with *The Real World?*"

He shook his head. "Of course not. It's how we met. But I don't see any of the show's alumni behind the desk at CNN. Choose your next job very carefully. That's all I'm saying. Make sure it will take you in the right direction."

Aspen rolled her eyes again. "What are you—some kind of life coach all of a sudden?"

Dean Paul sighed deeply, accepting the fact that nothing he said would be taken in the context intended. At least not now. He would try again later. Threading his hand through hers, he squeezed tightly. "No, I'm not a life coach, sweetheart. I'm just your husband."

Aspen took in the scenery, scowling, as if the incredible beauty of this small Greek island on the south end of the Cyclades com-plex was completely lost on her.

They made it back to the Santorini Palace Hotel. He tried to interest her in dressing to the nines and going out for a fabulous dinner, but she declined. Instead, Aspen swallowed enough Ambien to knock her out long before bedtime. Miserably, Dean Paul spent most of the night packing their things.

The journey back home was an endurance test. A private jet to Athens. A flight to Paris. Another plane to Boston. And now the final leg into New York's LaGuardia. They were heading into their seventeenth hour of travel, and so far they had exchanged maybe a dozen words.

In Boston, Dean Paul stocked up on every New York news-paper and tabloid to assess the damage. The photographs were still Topic A. Jake James had succeeded in piling on the embarrassment this time. His little cable show had started a brushfire that was evolving into a torching blaze.

And the son of a bitch had been smart as hell about it, this ac-cording to one fawning media critic. Jake had held court at his an-chor desk and presented the pictures one by one with his own hands, ensuring that any outside coverage of the scandal would in-clude him. It had been his master stroke.

Every outlet covered the story. Jake James bubbling under be-came Jake James boiling over. Ratings for his nightly program spiked. Advance orders for his new book doubled. The asshole had even succeeded in turning the story into a morality argument. Why were men like Dean Paul Lockhart objects of idolatry? What had they given back to society to deserve such worship? God, it was such hypocritical bullshit. But the debate raged on.

He scanned one story and saw where his parents had issued a terse "no comment." But there was no chance that Mom and Dad would be so tight-lipped with him. Dean Paul rubbed his tired eyes, dreading the confrontation. He was frustrated, jet-lagged, and pissed off.

Flipping through *212*, he noticed Babe Mancini's photo credit on a VIP candid spread. The name seemed to pulsate on the page like a blinking cursor. He still couldn't believe she was selling him out like this. Sneaking those private pictures to her pit bull boyfriend. Shopping around a trashy book deal.

He remembered the day of that shoot. A lazy Sunday. Raining off and on. It always rained at Brown. There was even a popular poster in the dorms that read IT RAINS TWO OUT OF EVERY THREE DAYS, EXCEPT DURING THE RAINY SEASON, WHEN IT SNOWS LIKE A BITCH.

Nobody had been around. They were just bored college lovers avoiding schoolwork. It started off innocently enough with Babe snapping pictures like she always did. But then he took off his shirt.

And she kept clicking away. Pretty soon she was daring him to show her the full monty. He didn't need to think about it. Shyness about his body had never been one of his traits. He worked out regularly. He did five hundred crunches every night. He was well hung. So off went the khakis and the boxers.

Babe had shot him from odd angles. And he used his hands and legs strategically. Every inch of his ass was in frame, but the lens only captured part of his dick. Still, for all practical purposes, he had been a nude model. And how the hell was he going to explain that to his parents?

Dean Paul shrugged in defeat, flipping through the pages of *212*, checking out a hot layout of those Japanese twins, Mio and Mako Kometani. The girls had no talent. But when you looked like that, it didn't matter.

He smiled ruefully as he wondered if Babe had picked out the color of her Porsche yet. She'd better hold off on leasing that perfect parking space. His family's lawyers would be in full attack mode, and any interested publishers would likely be scared away. So what if he'd signed a model release? Big deal. He planned to tell his parents that Babe forged it. Yeah. That would keep the attorneys busy.

Finished with *212*, Dean Paul tossed it down and picked up the *New York Post*. Poor Gabrielle. The Brown Sugar scandal seemed to be gaining momentum each day. His heart went out to her. The anger was ferocious. People were calling her the ultimate fraud, and crying sacrilege over a Black American Princess adopting a ghetto-girl persona to make inroads on the hip-hop scene. Radio stations had dropped her cold from their playlists, and there were reports of public events where the entertainment was mass destruction of her CDs.

"Page Six" caught his attention next. The day's column led with a photograph of Joaquin Cruz at some benefit the polo player probably knew nothing about. What an operator. No doubt the dude had just shown up in hopes of making it into "Page Six." Mission accomplished. Dean Paul shook his head, baffled. No matter how hard he tried, he could not picture Lara giving this guy the time of day. But Jinx Wiatt and her "It Parade" column were rarely off the mark.

It suddenly dawned on him. Who needed phones, e-mail, and get-togethers? This crew lived out their whole lives in the fucking columns. He laughed a little. All you had to do to stay informed was keep up on current events. Still, this Lara business with that Cruz character had Dean Paul worried. He needed to warn her about him. She had no idea what kind of games he played with women.

The shuttle touched down on the LaGuardia runway.

Aspen stirred from her semi-sleep.

Dean Paul grinned warmly and stroked her leg. "You feel okay?"

"Since when do my feelings matter?"

"I underestimated you."

She gave him a quizzical look. "How?"

"I thought for sure that bitchy resolve would fade somewhere between Paris and Boston."

Aspen glared at him. "You have no idea how long it can last."

And he believed her.

It was back to the same dreary silence as the happy newlyweds waited to file out. They were passing a newsstand in the airport terminal when Aspen screamed. And not just any scream. This was Jamie Lee Curtis in *Halloween*–worthy.

A brand-new edition of a tabloid mocked them. Shit, the issue must have just hit the stands, because he'd picked up last week's rag ninety minutes ago in Boston. But there it was. Front and center. Stacked high. With a headline that shouted THE WEDDING PIC-TURES THEY DIDN'T WANT YOU TO SEE.

Well, Dean Paul couldn't actually accuse the editors of spreading lies. He didn't want to see the photos. Especially if they looked anything like the cover sample—Aspen, eyes closed, mouth open, eating something of unknown origin. Jesus Christ. It was beyond ghastly.

Aspen dropped her carry-on and snatched up the offending tabloid, tearing through it only to see more of the same. The bride at the altar from an unfortunate profile angle, the caption reading OINK, OINK, ASPEN—THE DOUBLE CHIN SHOULD START A FEW YEARS AFTER THE WEDDING. And under a close-up of Dean Paul with a lusty expression on his face, HORNY HUBBY CHECKING OUT BROWN SUGAR AT THE RECEPTION. A SEVEN YEAR ITCH ALREADY?

The psychic damage went on and on. Brown Sugar's street-walker costume. That washed-out Broadway tramp getting felt up by her loser husband. Finn Robards in the last stages of a trick-of-the-night pickup with some bartender. The spread made the affair look like a gathering of cheap freaks.

Aspen started to cry. "Who took these pictures?" she wailed. "*InStyle* had the exclusive!"

Dean Paul put his arm around her, drawing her close and kissing the side of her head. "It's terrible, sweetheart. But it's all part of the game. This will be off the stands in a week, and everybody will forget about it."

A young female traveler stopped next to them to eyeball the cover. She glanced up and did a double take. "Oh, my God! What are you guys doing in the airport?"

Dean Paul smiled kindly. Even in their grungy travel clothes and baseball caps, they were still recognizable to some. "Coming back from our honeymoon."

The woman stared at the tabloid again. "That's gross!" She turned to Aspen. "What are you eating in that picture?"

"Leave us alone!" Aspen yelled.

"Fuck you!" the woman snapped. "By the way, everybody I know hated you on *The Real World*. You were a bitch!" And then the stranger disappeared.

Aspen sobbed into Dean Paul's shoulder.

He threw down some cash for the tabloid, managed to add her carry-on to his own haul, and gently but firmly led her away from the scene. "People don't realize what they're saying, baby. You're just this person on television to them."

"I don't give a shit about that stupid girl!" Aspen cried. "She's just jealous and wants my life!"

Dean Paul surmised that it would be easier to go along with this. "Of course she does."

Aspen's crying jag began to subside. "I want to sue! The magazine! The photographer! Everybody!"

Dean Paul said nothing. It just didn't seem worth the effort. In a week, all this drama would be a stale joke. But for the moment, he had to mollify her. "I'll have our family lawyers look into it."

Aspen clung to him all the way down to baggage claim. They waited around for their luggage without incident, then tumbled into a cab and began the somber ride home. She cried quietly, and he stroked her hair, sinking down against the torn leather seat, thinking about the complications that lay ahead.

It was important that he talk to Lara.

A confrontation with Babe was inevitable.

And he wanted to see Gabrielle.

After all these years, they were back in his life. God, it was ironic. That marrying another woman had been the catalyst to bring them together again. Dean Paul glanced down at Aspen. A stinging regret seized him.

Who was he kidding?

THE IT PARADE
BY JINX WIATT

Fill in the Blanks

All it takes is one bad boy to make a good girl go the same way. Yours truly is a staunch advocate for getting this out of the way in high school. Remember that hot guy who never came to class, totaled his parents' car, and hated your popular jock boyfriend? Well, here's hoping you went out with him at least once. Otherwise, trouble lies ahead. Don't believe moi? Take a look at the too-perfect event planner. You know the one. By comparison, she makes Miss Manners seem uncouth. Not anymore. Her sizzling new romance with that scrumptious polo player has her making major faux pas in the etiquette department.

12

Lara

Lara seemed to be operating on autopilot. Here she was, back in the lobby of the Mercer Hotel, scarcely paying attention as Mio and Mako Kometani yammered on about their birthday party.

"We want our pictures on the invitations," Mio said.

Lara nodded vaguely.

"We think it would be best to show off our pussies," Mako put in.

"I think you're right," Lara said automatically. All of a sudden she stopped. *Rewind.* "Hold on. What did you just say?"

"We want to show off our pussies," Mako said. She stood up, forming a triangle over her crotch with her hands.

"The woman who does our bikini wax is an artist," Mio explained. "She shaved our hair into the shape of the astrological symbol for Libra."

Lara paused. She waited for the laughter. But it never came. These girls were actually serious. "So you want to send out invitations to your birthday party with an image of yourselves that displays full frontal nudity?"

Mio and Mako nodded brightly.

"This party is a very important social event," Lara began carefully, trying valiantly to get back on board. "It's a presentation of the Kometani twins to New York society. Certainly we want people to get to know you. But it's essential that you hold something in reserve. An air of mystery. And letting everyone see your . . . private areas . . . well, that could dispel it."

Mio and Mako frowned.

Lara attempted to bulldoze ahead.

Mako gestured for her to stop. "But we really want to show off our pussies."

Lara leaned in confidentially. "I think it's great that you want to share that part of yourself with so many noteworthy people in this city, but it's just not a good idea. Trust me."

Reluctantly, Mio and Mako conceded.

Lara moved on to a more useful topic—the atmosphere. She had been anxious to attempt a romantic Venice theme, and finally, she had clients with the budget and the moxie to go ahead with it.

She talked up her plan. The full-scale gondolas made of wood. The huge ornamental columns of cardboard and polystyrene. The welded metal centerpieces. An elaborate stage with an extended catwalk. The hand-painted Venetian murals. The black-and-white checkered linens. She assured the twins that the warehouse in the meatpacking district would be magically transformed and that their party would be the talk of the season.

Mio and Mako cut the meeting short. They were meeting La Mode New York fashion stylist Dex Dexter for a day of shopping later in the afternoon. The girls wanted to relax with a warm stone massage and manicure before their lunch with a realtor at Le Cirque 2000. There was also something about a consultation with a meditation specialist, but by that point, Lara had tuned them out.

She stood up to leave, and as luck would have it, Bizzie Gruzart came crashing through the door and clomped toward the bar in her special shoes. Lara held back a moment, hoping to avoid an encounter.

But Bizzie swept the area with a circular gaze, captured Lara, put on a plastic smile, and switched directions. "Lara, how are you? Isn't it awful about those pictures of Dean Paul? I can't believe one of his exes is doing this. You're friends with her, right? Somebody told me she saw the two of you having drinks at the St. Regis. It's Baby, isn't it? Like the girl in *Dirty Dancing?*"

"*Babe,*" Lara corrected.

"Oh, like the pig. That's fitting. I hear her agent wants a million dollars for the project. Is that true?"

"I wouldn't know. I wasn't aware of the book, and I haven't spoken to her since the story broke."

Bizzie put on a show of distress. "Dean Paul must feel so betrayed. I can't imagine an ex-boyfriend of mine writing a book about me."

"That would mean a man coming forward to admit dating you," Lara said. "Don't lose any sleep over it." She started to leave.

Bizzie stepped in her path. "Who has time for sleep? Random House just hired me out to do Jake James's book party. I wonder if Dean Paul will cover it for *Hollywood Live.* Wouldn't that be fun? Oh, by the way, how's the party coming along for the Kometani twins? Did I hear that you're doing an Egyptian theme?"

"Venetian," Lara answered tightly.

"That's what I love about your little parties, Lara. The right people rarely show up, but you make the event seem bigger than it is with your trick themes. It's brilliant."

Lara managed to smile, even though she was quietly fuming. "It's not brilliance by a long shot, Bizzie. When a woman isn't relying exclusively on her father's connections, it's amazing how resourceful she can be."

The jingle of Lara's cellular played like a symphony.

She waved off Bizzie, recognized Finn's number, and answered right way, turning her back to the beast. "You've got so-so timing. If only you had called five minutes ago."

"What did I almost save you from?" Finn asked.

"Bizzie Gruzart," Lara hissed.

"Please tell me she's found a doctor to fix her feet."

"I'm afraid not."

"I'll never understand medical science. They can clone a sheep, but Bizzie will always have to wear those awful shoes. Why, darling, why?"

"I don't know. Karmic balance?"

"Perhaps. Can you meet me for lunch?"

"No," Lara lied. "I have a meeting." She checked her watch. Then she glanced at her ID screen just in case another call might be coming through.

"Oh, push it back. Please. I beg you. Guess what I have? The tabloid with Dean Paul's wedding pictures." His voice went down an octave. "*The ones he didn't want us to see.* There's a picture of me with that bartender. He's actually very cute. It's days later, and I'm not pretending it didn't happen. This is practically a relationship. And if his reading taste is as poor as mine, he'll find out my real name. Then it will be serious."

Lara hated herself for hesitating. She was starving. Lunch with Finn would be wild fun. What if Joaquin called, though? She sounded like some high school girl now. Since when did she wait around for unreliable men? After all, he had her home, office, and cellular numbers, and it had been three days without a word. Forget Joaquin Cruz.

But she couldn't. How many times in the last seventy-two hours had she pretended to soldier on with disregard, only to be slavishly yearning for him minutes later? The truth was, Lara didn't care about anything else.

She didn't care about gossiping with Finn. She didn't care about Babe's quest for money at the expense of friendship and dignity. She didn't care about Gabrielle's public relations nightmare. She didn't care about the Kometani twins' party or any other Regrets Only event at this moment.

All Lara cared about was Joaquin Cruz. His voice. His body. His lips. His tongue. His hands. His fingers. His . . . Oh, God, how could she be thinking this? Okay, why not admit it? His cock. Yes, his cock! His big, beautiful, hard cock. There! That was all she cared about. And it was positively shameful. What had this man done to her?

"Have I convinced you yet?" It was Finn, wanting an answer. "I'm dying for seafood. How does Blue Water Grill sound?"

"Fine," Lara agreed. Her heart constricted. What if Joaquin wanted to see her? "But my next meeting is still up in the air," she added. "If I get a call, I might have to ditch you at the last minute."

"I'll chance it," Finn said easily. "It'll be worth it to see your face when you see Aspen on this cover. By the way, I hope you don't have a craving for salmon."

Lara signed off and stepped out onto the SoHo street. Her car service was right there, the driver on his feet and opening the back door. She stood on the sidewalk and took in a deep breath. It dawned on her that she had no idea where Joaquin lived. She wanted to find out. Mechanically, she slipped into the Town Car and announced her next destination.

Her cellular jingled again.

The sound filled her with a tiny hope. Just as every telephone ring had in the last three days. This time she didn't check the screen. She just closed her eyes and said a little prayer. "Hello?"

"Do you miss me yet?"

Lara's body flooded with relief. *Oh, thank God!* It was him. That voice was instantly soothing. Like balm for the soul. She was already smiling. "Maybe." Her tone was silky.

"Maybe?" His voice was sharp, yet playful. "I should stay away longer then."

"No!" Lara blurted, alarmed at her own instant desperation. "I miss you. I've been missing you for three days."

"That's more like it." He paused a beat. "Where are you now?"

"On my way to meet a friend for lunch. Finn. He was my escort to the wedding."

"Yeah, the fag. I remember."

The protective instinct rose up to correct him, but she said nothing.

"Which restaurant?"

"Blue Water Grill. It's on Union—"

"I know where it is," Joaquin cut in. He yawned.

Lara could hear him stretching. She imagined him sprawled out in bed. Naked. The image sent her heart racing. "Are you just now getting up?"

"A perfect day for me is to sleep until the crack of noon and then fuck until three."

She swallowed hard.

"But you've got other plans."

"I'll cancel them."

Joaquin laughed. "You're a dirty girl."

She fell silent.

"Aren't you?"

"Yes." It croaked out in a whisper.

"You're ready to bail on everything. You want it that bad, don't you?"

"Tell me where you live. I'll come meet you."

He called out an address on Second Street between Avenues A and B. "It's a sublet," he told her. "Run-down building. No doorman. No elevator. There's not even a sink in the bathroom. Just a tiny number in the kitchen. The whole apartment is about the size of your bedroom. It's filthy, too. I'm hardly ever here, and I keep forgetting to hire a maid service. You'll hate it."

"I don't care," Lara said.

"What if I told you there was no bed?" Joaquin asked. "Just a mattress on the floor?"

"I said I didn't care," Lara insisted, afraid that he might change his mind and want to rendezvous at her apartment. She could just see herself trying to explain any of this to Privi. Covering the receiver with her palm, she announced her new destination to the driver.

"This probably isn't a good idea. Go on to your lunch. I'll—"

"Joaquin, please. I said I didn't care. It's a lousy sublet. You travel all the time. It's no reflection on you."

There was a long stretch of silence.

Lara shut her eyes and gripped the phone tightly. At this moment, she wanted him so bad that it felt like a sickness.

"Okay."

She breathed a sigh of relief.

"I'll unlock the door. Come inside and take off your clothes. Quietly. I don't want to hear your voice until I make you come. Do you understand?"

"Yes."

"Good girl." And then he hung up.

Lara stayed on the line long after Joaquin had gone. She felt like Kim Basinger to his Mickey Rourke. The motivation in *9½ Weeks* had always been lost on her. But Lara understood it now.

She called Finn and broke the news, citing a client meeting.

He sounded disappointed.

Lara made noises about doing something later but kept the specifics vague. Until she knew about Joaquin's plans, she didn't want to schedule anything.

The Town Car grinded through traffic. To travel a few yards took minutes. They even sat in one honking, halting snarl while a light changed three times. It was slow murder.

Lara wanted to scream. She was practically itching to feel Joaquin inside her. Just hearing him give voice to his intentions triggered a secret wetness. The only thing keeping her sane right now was the realization that every passing second led her closer . . . to him. To the dirty apartment with the mattress on the floor. To the feel of his smooth skin and firm touch and forceful kisses.

Another ring of the cellular.

A sudden fright seized her. And for a moment, it was the greatest fear she could ever imagine. That Joaquin had changed his mind. But traffic had started to move at a rapid clip. She was almost there. He couldn't deny her . . .

"Hello?"

"Lara?" It was Dean Paul. "Are you okay? You don't sound like yourself."

"I'm fine," she murmured. "Just rushing from one appointment to another." It dawned on Lara how many times she had longed to hear from him out of the blue like this. Right now it was happening. Yet she felt nothing. Just a mild sense of annoyance. "Are you calling from Greece?"

"No." He paused meaningfully. "We came back early."

The Town Car pulled up to Joaquin's building.

It seemed an impossible turn of events. That Dean Paul Lockhart could ever become a nuisance to her. Someone she just wanted to get rid of. But that's exactly how she felt about him now.

"There's something I want you to know, Lara."

What a loaded statement. How many castles in the air would the old Lara have built upon that? It was amazing. She honestly didn't care to hear anything that he had to say. Everything Lara wanted was six flights up.

"I can't talk right now. I just arrived at my next appointment."

"What—another meeting with Joaquin Cruz?"

Lara was shocked. And more than a little angry. "That's none of your business."

"Stay away from him, Lara. He's bad news. I could tell you stories."

"I'm not interested in your stories."

"Meet me for a drink. Hear me out. I don't want to see you get hurt."

Lara laughed bitterly. "Do you have any idea how ridiculous that sounds coming from you?" She stepped inside the building and started up the stairs.

"I've done a lot of stupid things—"

"That's the understatement of the century. Add this phone call to the list." And then she hung up.

When Lara walked into Joaquin's apartment, she followed his instructions to the letter. She stripped silently. She joined him on the floor. She submitted to his eager embraces. And she remained quiet. The first sound out of her mouth came when she did.

By then, Dean Paul was a distant memory.

Joaquin had been right all along. . . .

THE IT PARADE
BY JINX WIATT

Fill in the Blanks

Everyone knows that two actors in a relationship is a certain recipe for disaster. Do you think two aspiring authors stand a better chance? Don't bet on it. He's the rising cable star who knows how to throw a punch with his new tome. She's the slinky shutterbug causing a stir in publishing circles with a tell-all proposal about her very famous ex. But his book is just hitting stores, while her deal is stuck in legal barbed wire. In fact, spies are reporting back that it's dead in the water. Professional jealousy can be napalm to a new romance. Translation: Don't book the church yet, darlings.

13

Babe

"Nobody wants this proposal. All the editors are sending it back to me," Linda Konner said. "I'm sorry, Babe. This would've been a great book. But his family is more powerful than I ever imagined."

Babe, shocked and crestfallen, just held the receiver. "I don't understand."

"He's saying you forged the release."

"That's a fucking lie!" Babe shouted. "Aren't there handwriting experts who can prove it?"

"Yes, but every legal maneuver costs money, and publishing is about the bottom line." Linda sighed. "And there's more."

"I'm listening."

"Dean Paul's mother is involved now. I don't think it's a coincidence that Sophia Mills's agent has chauffeured her around to every big house over the last few days. There's been interest in her memoirs for years. The implicit message is that anyone who takes on your book won't stand a chance at landing hers. So the complications are just piling up."

"Does that mean it's over? I should just put these pictures in a goddamn scrapbook?"

Linda hesitated. "A small publisher from the West Coast called this morning. To be honest, I didn't get a good feeling from the editor. My guess is that he's just curious and wants to pretend to be in play. I don't think he's even worth the postage."

"So it *is* over."

"A lot is working against us. And your boyfriend's stunt sure didn't help matters. I hear it did wonders for his book, though."

"He's not my boyfriend," Babe snapped.

"See? There's a silver lining. Out of this experience you developed better taste in men. It's not a total loss."

Babe was silent. She wouldn't claim the bastard as her boyfriend, but here she sat having this conversation in his apartment. How fucked up could a girl get?

"I'm not writing you off, Babe. I like you. And I think you're a very talented photographer. Who knows? Maybe there's a project we can work on together sometime in the future."

"That would be great," Babe murmured.

"I'll be in touch if anything changes. Stranger things have happened. But for your own peace of mind, I would just move on."

"Thanks for trying." She slammed down the receiver.

Goddamn Jake.

Goddamn the Lockharts.

Goddamn Dean Paul.

This book could've been her ticket out. No more late nights flashbulbing New York's social animals. No more paparazzi cat-and-mouse games to earn an extra buck. But now it was back to square one.

Her gaze fell on the hot-off-the-presses tabloid Jake had left on the kitchen counter. The money shot of Aspen Bauer-Lockhart stuffing her face with a salmon wrap stared back at her. Proof positive that the Lockharts couldn't win every battle. Babe smiled. Score one for the girl with middle-class roots.

She checked the clock. Jake would be back soon from the gym. She had to get out of here. The last thing she needed today was to hear him bragging about his fucking book.

But just as Babe started to gather her things, she heard him click over the dead bolt. *Shit.*

Jake walked inside and headed straight for the fridge to grab one of his homemade post-workout power smoothies. He drained it to the halfway mark, then stopped to look at her. "I thought you were going to the gym, too."

"I'll go later." She zipped up her overnight bag. "Why the sudden interest in my exercise routine?"

He shrugged. "Just making conversation."

"It's not your passive-aggressive way of suggesting that I'm getting fat?"

"Don't worry. If I have a problem with the way you look, you won't have to crack a code. I'll just tell you."

His gaze darted to the file folder near the phone. "Any news on the book?"

"No. Thanks to you." She snatched the folder, stuffed it into her bag, and tried to move past him.

But Jake held her arm. "You look a little deflated. Want to talk about it?"

"I just got off the phone with my agent. The deal is dead. Congratulations."

"What happened?"

"Don't play dumb, you son of a bitch."

"You're blaming me? That's rich. My show put your little project on the map. You went from a few blind items to fucking headline news."

Babe twisted out of his grasp. "Exactly! My deal was happening under the radar until you hijacked my photographs, did your grandstanding routine, and shined the klieg lights all over it. That's when the Lockhart family got involved. And now it's DOA."

Jake put down his drink and reached for her.

She pushed him away. "Fuck you, Jake! I hate you right now! You ruined this for me! But it worked out great for you, didn't it? Your ratings are up, it's contract renegotiating time at the network, and the print run for *your* book doubled!"

"Come on, Babe—"

"No, Jake, this isn't something you can fuck your way out of this time. God, I'm such an idiot! I can't believe I came here last night. Every time I swear to myself that it will be the last one. But this is it. We're over."

"You want to lay all of this on me? Go ahead. But that's bull-shit, and you know it. If you stopped blaming me for five minutes, maybe you'd realize that this is a blessing in disguise."

Babe shook her head. "I want nothing more than to get the hell away from you, but I think I'll stay just to hear this. I could use a good laugh."

"You're better than that book, Babe. You might not believe that about yourself, but it's true."

Babe stared at him. Jake Asshole had metamorphosed into Jake Sincere.

"A cheap tell-all by an ex-lover?" he went on. "I thought you were above bad cliches. Fast-forward a year, Babe. If you sold that book, you'd be the It Bimbo for a week, maybe two. Every talk show. Every radio show. Every weekly magazine. Howard Stern asking if you let Dean Paul give it to you up the ass. Is that how you want to be defined? Because that's the journey for women who cash in like that. Nobody cares about them. America just wants the gory details. And once those are spilled, you're out like yesterday's garbage. On to the next. I know. I've interviewed these women. I've sat in on the production meetings that ridicule them. I've seen the focus-group research that rips them apart. Don't be that woman, Babe. You don't have to be. You've got real talent."

"It's not just a tell—"

Jake cut her off. "Don't fool yourself into believing that the pictures make it art. Sure, they're great photographs. Technically sound. Interesting composition. Even back then you were a pro. But that jazz is lost on the crowd your publisher would go after. Have you seen the message boards from my show? Every dumb-ass from here to Seattle has posted an opinion. One girl's pissed be-cause she sees more in a Calvin Klein underwear ad. And the queers—they don't care about natural light and shadows. They just want a nice crotch shot."

Babe's eyes were stinging with tears. "What about you, Jake? How can you recommend the high road for me while you're pulling cheap stunts?"

"Because I'm a jerk. I saw those pictures in your apartment, and I knew it was a chance to put the screws to Dean Paul. That's all I could see. It's my blind spot. Rich guys like him always have been. But ever since college, he's come to represent the whole lot for me. Don't ask me why. I should probably be paying some therapist on the Upper East Side one-fifty an hour to help me figure it out. But instead, I tell myself that I work through all my problems in the ring when I bloody up my sparring partners."

Babe managed a faint smile. Jake had never been this candid before. Her urge to leave began to fade.

"I'll be honest. In the beginning, I only wanted you because of your history with Dean Paul. I knew that me being with you would drive him crazy. And I loved it. I wanted to hear you tell me that I was a better lover, that I made you come in ways he never could. But it's more than that now. You remind me of myself in a lot of ways. You're out there trying to prove something. Every day. No matter how far you go or how good people say you are, you never quite feel like you measure up. I know that feeling. It's like we're kindred spirits, Babe. But we spend all our time fighting each other. Why is that? It's so fucked up. Can you imagine how great we'd be if we supported each other? I think about that sometimes."

Babe put down her bags. The last thing she intended to do was walk out the door. That much she was certain of.

Jake stepped toward her. "Want to hear something funny?"

Babe nodded.

"It was Bizzie Gruzart who got me started on all this soul-searching."

"The PR girl who crashed her Vespa into Pastis?"

"Yeah," Jake confirmed. "My publisher tapped her to do the book party, and that bitch advised me to unload you. She thinks being with you will hurt my Q-rating with female fans. I told her to bag it. Like I'm here to please some cunt in the Midwest. Should I listen to Neil Diamond, too?"

Babe laughed.

Jake wrapped his arms around her and pulled her close, kissing the center of her forehead. "Do you know how many girls have told me 'we're over' the way you just did? Plenty. But you're the only one I've ever tried to stop. Every other time I didn't give a fuck. I knew I could hit a bar that night and find a piece of ass just as good or even better." He traced his index finger down the bridge of her nose, stopping at her lips. "I can't replace you so easily."

Babe kissed Jake James as if it were the first time. And in a way, she really thought it was. The aggression in his lovemaking disappeared. He handled her with great tenderness. He climaxed without the self-aggrandizing chant. At that moment, it was precisely what she needed.

But when he woke up with a start a few hours later, the original version of Jake was back. He roughly extricated himself from her embrace. "Shit! We fell asleep. Look at the time. Goddammit. This is why I only like to cuddle at night."

Babe watched him scramble into the bathroom and turn on the hot water.

Jake boomeranged back to rifle through his closet. "Hey, get dressed and go pick up my dry cleaning around the corner. My favorite shirt is there. I want to wear it to the book party tonight."

Babe sat up in bed. "Ask me nicely."

Jake cut a glance in her direction. "I just did."

Babe began searching for her clothes and thinking about what she might wear, too. "What time do you want me there? Another photographer from *212* is covering for me. I'll actually be able to enjoy the event."

He headed into the shower, calling out, "It doesn't matter.

Bizzie says these things are insane. Everybody will be pulling at me. I probably won't even realize that you're there."

Babe picked up his dry cleaning and shoved it into the first trash can within sight. Then she got in a cab and cried all the way to her apartment.

THE IT PARADE
BY JINX WIATT

Fill in the Blanks

There's a new monster "get" in town. You know the drill. Major scandal. Damsel in distress. Every bitchy interviewer with an eye toward ratings-sweeps victory elbowing her way to nab an exclusive sit-down. We've been here before. We'll be here again. But this time out the fight is fierce. It hasn't been this nasty since they were all wrestling over that intern with the pretty mess on her Gap dress courtesy of you-know-who. Yours truly just wonders which personality will show up for the chat. Will it be the ghetto-fabulous rapper or the Ivy League BAP?

14

Gabrielle

"Mrs. Foster, how did it make you feel when your daughter changed her name to Brown Sugar and denied ever being a part of this Grosse Pointe community?"

"You are trespassing on private property," Diahann Foster said, exiting her Mercedes E500 sedan with an imperial attitude.

Undaunted, the pushy *Hollywood Live* reporter trailed her prey all the way to the front door. "Mrs. Foster, what do you think about rap music? Are you proud to call Brown Sugar your daughter?"

"No comment!" Diahann screamed. "Now please get off our property and leave us alone!" And then she slammed the door.

"As you can see, Ainsley, in spite of our strongest efforts, there's still no official response from the Fosters in Grosse Pointe, Michigan. We know their daughter as the platinum-selling hip-hop diva Brown Sugar. They know her as the debutante Gabrielle. Where do the two intersect? No one knows for sure. Back to you in Hollywood."

Gabrielle zapped the remote control to obliterate the *latest development* from her life. It just wasn't fair. Her parents' lives were being turned upside down. Television crews were staking out her mother at the house and her father at his office. Ironically, Gabrielle was enjoying more of an escape in New York. Security at the Waldorf-Astoria had been militant about keeping prying media eyes at bay.

And then she had Baby Bear. He was fully recuperated, back on the job, and perfectly willing to body slam anyone who got too close. His loyalty was unyielding, even as her career limped closer and closer to death each day. In fact, Baby Bear had become her greatest cheerleader. "You'll come back, Sugar," he told her. "Stronger and harder."

It was an emboldening notion. But Gabrielle didn't believe him. The rap industry had closed ranks. Brown Sugar was out. Queen Bee was in. Other artists were speaking against her publicly. Big, powerful stars whom she admired. It was the most isolating feeling.

She had stopped listening to Shaniqua Jackson, if only to hold on to what remained of her sanity. The outcry from fans was just too brutal. They felt duped and manipulated. And Shaniqua put through only the angriest callers to vent on-air.

Anyone from her past looking for a quick ride on the scandal train had found their ticket. Theory stayed the busiest. That loser would show up anywhere to get a little attention at her expense. Even Morgan Atwood had joined in. Her first boyfriend. She had truly loved him. And it crushed her to see Morgan on television, looking smug, sounding mean. His print interviews were the worst. Nothing was sacred. Not even the night she had lost her virginity to him. In fact, that had merited a point-by-point account.

This was rock bottom defined. The world was completely against her. And that included her own record label, Riot Act. She saw the writing on the wall. "My Hot Box," the planned third single from *Queen of Bling*, had been scrapped. Even with 50 Cent guesting on the track, the suits didn't believe in it. Or her. Radio stations had stopped playing Brown Sugar music altogether. Sales plummeted. It was a total free fall.

AKA Bomb Threat had tried to comfort her with long-distance platitudes. "Just lay low, baby. All this will blow over. Everybody at the label is behind you."

Yeah, right. Those bastards were behind her. But only because that was the strategic place to be when they stabbed the final knife in her back. Maybe the label brass had actually started to believe the bullshit they put out there in her press biography. That she was some uneducated project ho with BMW dreams. Wrong, Mr. Executive. Brown Sugar was an Ivy League girl at heart. And she knew the deal.

Riot Act already had her replacement on the fast track. Diamonds and Pearls. Twin sisters with killer looks and bad-ass attitudes. Straight out of a rough neighborhood in Atlanta. They were the reason Bomb had yet to return from Los Angeles. He was working overtime in the studio prepping their debut. Identical Brown Sugar sound. Identical Brown Sugar image. Only these girls were authentic. There were no Queen Bees or Shaniqua Jacksons waiting in the wings to call them out.

Gabrielle needed to take action. Find out where she stood in terms of personal finances. Like most new artists, she had been so starry-eyed at the chance to work in the music industry that the good business side of her brain shut down. Bomb handled everything—the contracts, the money, the major purchases. He set her up in this penthouse and shoved a few credit cards with skyscraper limits into her hand, and she never asked questions. There seemed no reason to. Everything she wanted was a bedtime whisper or a signature away.

It was the oldest mistake in the book. Every Motown singer had learned it the hard way, and that was forty fucking years ago. So much for progress. Gabrielle had always told herself that she would investigate the finer points . . . later. Well, later was right now. And she had no leverage. Goddammit! A star had to be on the rise to put a bad contract in turnaround. There was incentive. The company wanted to keep you around. But a crisis case like Brown Sugar? Oh, God, Gabrielle didn't stand a chance.

How could she have been so naive? What good was the Ivy League degree if she failed to use it? To add insult to injury, she had started her career at MTV of all places. She had listened to the I-got-screwed stories firsthand. Yet here she was, starring in her own. Bomb had positioned her exactly where he wanted her to be—in the fucking dark, appeased by expensive clothes, flashy jewelry, a high-rise penthouse address, and slick promises that she would only get bigger, better, and richer. And Gabrielle had fallen for it. Hook, line, and Rolex.

As it dawned on her how ignorant she was, the realization triggered a cold, naked, helpless fear. Gabrielle had no idea how anything got done. Even the most simple responsibilities. For instance, when did Baby Bear get paid? And who paid him? Everything had been done for her. Like she was a child. Or some kept woman.

She stared down on the metropolitan matrix below, shame stabbing into her. To think she had created Brown Sugar as a means of empowering herself. From weakling to warrior. What bullshit that was. Nothing had changed. The players were new. The circumstances were different. But she was still a victim.

Come on, brown sugar. Give us some of that sweet chocolate.

The cruel voices from the past invaded her mind. After all these years, the memory remained so potent. If she just allowed herself to think about it, the nightmare felt as fresh as yesterday. Only the faces lived on in a constant blur. It had been dark, and it had happened so fast. She had just closed her eyes and submitted to the inevitable, merely waiting for the violation to end. But the voices. Oh, God, the voices. Even now she could hear them with such clarity. As if the monsters were whispering into her ear at this moment. When her brain played back the transcript from that horrible night, it was always the leader that she heard. The one who taunted her the most. The one who held her down . . .

The phone to the suite jangled, the rapid ring signaling an internal call.

Gabrielle let Baby Bear answer it. He knew the drill. No parents. No media. No so-called friends. The only people with clearance to get through were Lara and Bomb.

From his perch in the outer seating area, Baby Bear ventured quietly inside. "Sugar, there's a cat on the line named Dean Paul Lockhart. Swears up and down that you'll want to see him."

She just stood there, stunned.

"He's waiting downstairs in the lobby."

Instantly, Gabrielle's concern went to her looks. Was she presentable? Did she have time for a few quick improvements? It was an odd reaction, but Dean Paul conjured up those feelings in a way no other man ever had. Not Morgan. Not Theory. Not Bomb. She felt a flush of warmth. "Bring him up."

Baby Bear nodded dutifully and lumbered out, heading for the lobby.

Gabrielle stepped into the bathroom to check her reflection. For a moment, she didn't recognize herself. The woman in the mirror was stripped of Brown Sugar's dramatic hair extensions, war paint makeup, and glitzy, conspicuous, look-motherfucker-I-made-it trappings.

There was just her own close-cropped chestnut hair, loosely tousled, a sweep of mascara and a swipe of lip gloss, a chic Chanel J12 sports watch on her wrist, and a simple ensemble of white, fitted, ribbed cotton tank over pink low-waist Juicy Couture yoga pants.

Baby Bear had remarked that she resembled Halle Berry. Gabrielle disagreed. That beauty was a force all her own. She smoothed out an errant eyebrow and smiled. He deserved a raise just for saying it, though.

When Dean Paul walked into the suite, he just stared at her for one prolonged, glorious moment. Finally, he spoke. "Now there's the girl I remember."

She approached him, smiling demurely.

He kissed her lightly on the lips and embraced her, stroking the small of her back with his hand. "I'm sorry. About everything. How are you holding up?"

Gabrielle withdrew from him. It felt too damn good to continue. "Worse things have happened to me."

Dean Paul looked at her strangely. "What I've seen so far is brutal. Are you a veteran of some war I don't know about?"

Of course, he had no idea how loaded that question was. At first, Gabrielle said nothing. Then she sat down in her favorite chair and curled her bare feet underneath her legs. "I thought you were in Greece."

He planted himself on the sofa opposite her, knees akimbo, elbows on his thighs. There seemed to be a great deal on his mind. "We cut it short." One beat. "I've been worried about you, Gabby. Is there anything I can do?"

Gabby. Hearing him call her that always affected her. It did something to her central nervous system. She had always adored the sound of it tripping off his lips. Maybe because it was a nickname exclusive to him. "You could help me understand you."

His gaze was serious. "Understand *me*?"

"You've been silent for so many years. No contact at all. Not even a postcard. Now you're back." She glanced at the white-gold wedding band screaming from his ring finger. "And married."

Dean Paul stared down at his open hand. "It's not like I never thought about you, Gabby. Because I did. Often. But we didn't exactly leave things on a high note. There were no promises to exchange Christmas cards."

"As I remember it, you left me. Isn't that one of your relationship signatures? You always do the leaving, right?"

"I was just a college guy."

"And you're just a married guy now. One week in and already looking up ex-girlfriends. Impressive."

He looked uncomfortable. "I don't want to talk about that. I came here for you. I want to help. If you'll let me."

Gabrielle could tell that her calm intrigued him. What he didn't know was that she had tripled her Xanax dosage. A doctor had prescribed it years ago to curtail panic attacks after the incident at Brown. It had become a daily habit. Every morning she popped a Centrum and a Xanax. A long time ago she stopped thinking of it as a drug. That word made it sound sinister. She preferred the term "emotional vitamin."

"I don't know what you could do," she told him. "You're a very famous man, Dean Paul, but you don't have much pull in the black community."

He gesticulated in the wild, exaggerated manner of many hard-core rappers. "Hey, don't sell me short, boo. I can be down."

Gabrielle laughed at him. Really laughed. In a way that she had been unable to for days.

He grinned. "You have the sweetest laugh. It's good to hear it again."

Her amusement faded. There had been an intimacy between them at the wedding. There was an intimacy between them now. Confusion and fear swirled in her brain. If pressed, Gabrielle knew that she would give in to anything he wanted, no matter the consequences. The sanctity of his marriage. The safety of her heart. All of it was fair game. She felt that vulnerable.

"Why did you do it, Gabby?" His question caught her off guard. "I can see pursuing a career in music, but you completely reinvented yourself."

"You don't understand the world of hip-hop."

"And you do?"

She gave him a dumb look. "I am black."

"Congratulations. But if that's all it takes, why are you hiding up here?"

Gabrielle rose and stepped over to the window. Then she turned to face him. "I wanted to create another identity. To be someone else. The kind of person who doesn't let bad things happen to her."

Dean Paul regarded her intently. "I don't get it. You used to talk about home all the time. I think of you as being more spoiled than I was. To hear you tell it, Grosse Pointe was a plastic bubble."

"Maybe it was," she said quietly. "And that's the worst training for the real world."

He stood up, suddenly agitated. "What happened, Gabby? You were never the same after we broke up. Everybody used to say so. They put it all on me. Like I had just stomped on your heart and left you in ruins. I stayed away because I never wanted to own up to the fact that I could have such an effect on a girl. Just by leaving her? It was too intense. Scared the hell out of me. But that's not what changed you, is it?"

Gabrielle's lips were trembling. She was so close to telling him her secret. In fact, the first word was right there in her throat . . . but it died there, too. At the last moment, she spun to face the window.

"Gabby!" His plea was urgent.

She groped for the strength to not break down. "Did you come here to help or to perform some kind of mental exorcism?" Miraculously, there was a distinct wryness in her tone.

Dean Paul released a deep sigh. "Just tell me how I can make this easier for you."

"Tell Michael Jackson to get arrested again. Maybe then I'll catch a break from the reporters."

He laughed softly. "You've really gone and done it if it takes Wacko Jacko to knock you off the radar."

Gabrielle breathed a sigh of relief. The inquisition had ended. She was safe for the moment. Turning back to face him, she smiled. "Some PR flack in a cubicle wrote my press bio. Can you believe that? I know it's my own fault for going along with it, but I didn't dream up that nonsense."

"When you're dealing with the media, there's no such thing as context. My dad taught me that a long time ago." He grew quiet for several seconds. "Who's handling your requests?"

She stared back at him blankly.

"For interviews," he explained.

Gabrielle shrugged. "The record label, I guess. Baby Bear is taking whatever calls are routed here."

Dean Paul shook his head in severe disagreement. "That's no good. You need your own handler. Someone who's looking out just for you." He left her there and returned seconds later with a stack of pink messages in his hand. As he sifted through them, his eyes widened. "Shit, Gabby, everybody is courting you—Barbara Walters, Katie Couric, Diane Sawyer . . ."

"How long do you think it will take before they go away?"

He considered the question. "There's a snowball effect to scandals. Some begin to feed on themselves, and when that happens, you can only hold on tight for the ride. I think this one has that quality. At some point, you'll have to talk. You can't just stay locked up in this tower like Rapunzel."

Gabrielle knew that. But hearing confirmation of it still unnerved her.

"That guy outside is security. He's no publicist. You need to take control. The record label might own Brown Sugar. But you own Gabrielle Foster." He produced a Palm Pilot from his back pocket and began tapping the screen with a tiny stylus, his beautiful face rigid with determination. "Before I leave, you're going to have a publicist of your own." His tone was absolute.

A resistance rose up within her. "I don't understand why my record company can't act in that capacity. They have an entire PR department."

"Sure, that's looking out for their interests. Who's looking out for yours?"

"At the end of the day, I am their interest," she argued. "I still have two more albums on my contract."

He looked up from the little toy. "That doesn't mean they have to let you back in the studio. I have a friend who's an executive at RCA. When they want to burn out a contract, they release a hits compilation, maybe a collection of previously unreleased tracks that didn't make the grade for other CDs, anything to keep an artist on her way out the door from incurring new production costs."

Gabrielle was silent.

Dean Paul thundered on. "I don't think you realize how big this is. Everybody is interested in hearing your side of the story."

He waved the messages as evidence. "Katie Fucking Couric is ringing you up! You've crossed over, Gabby. There are people out there who have never heard a Brown Sugar song, but they know the name Gabrielle Foster. You have an opportunity here to turn this around."

His passion gave her a ray of hope. But the doubts still lingered. "You haven't heard the things people are saying on the radio. You haven't read the message boards on the Internet. So many people hate me."

"Rap fans," Dean Paul scoffed. "They're taking sides in a nasty street fight. Who cares? Wave the white flag. Let Queen Bee claim victory on the hip-hop front. It's the only win she'll ever get. Do you think Katie's calling Queen Bee for a *Dateline* exclusive? In her fucking dreams! A girl from the hood? There's no mystery there. I could drive out to Coney Island and find ten more Queen Bees on the same block. You're the one they want, Gabby. It's not Brown Sugar they're chasing after. It's you."

THE IT PARADE
BY *JINX WIATT*

Fill in the Blanks

The party wars are heating up. Event Planner #1 (Ms. Perfect Princess) is helming a major bash for those gorgeous Asian twins while Event Planner #2 (Ms. Vespa Road Rage) is giving a cable stud's book launch the full treatment. Why not just settle this feud with a slapping, scratching, hair-pulling slugfest in the middle of Times Square? Yours truly would gladly ring the bell and bellow, "Let's get ready to rumble!" This could get very ugly, darlings. Spies tell me there's more than professional VIP rivalry at stake. Let's see . . . two women plus mutual hatred equals . . . come on, this is easy math—a man. And not just any man. Girls on top don't slobber over the copy guy at Kinko's. They save the swooning for the rich and famous. And it doesn't hurt if he makes Brad Pitt look ordinary.

15

Dean Paul

"Why don't you take off your shirt?"

Dean Paul looked down at Finn Robards. "You've been waiting a long time for the chance to say that to me, haven't you?"

Finn's eyes were eclipsed by big, dark, and flamboyant Christian Dior sunglasses. He continued sunning on the lounger, betraying no reaction. "Maybe." His voice was singsong. "But you usually beat me to it. Let's face it. You don't exactly sit around waiting for people to ask."

Dean Paul took in the open view of the West Village and the Hudson River. They were poolside on the roof of SoHo House, a private members club and hotel on Ninth Avenue.

Finn wore one of those nothing-to-the-imagination Speedo numbers, the style favored by champion swimmers and fat European men. His body was bronzed, waxed, and sculpted to perfection. He sighed to announce his annoyance and tilted up his shades. "You're blocking the sun. Not to mention making me nervous." He tapped the lounger next to him. "Sit with me. Slip off your shirt. Have a drink. We'll visit. A little sun would do you good. Your Greek tan stopped just short of perfection. One more day and you would have had it."

There was a plush white towel neatly folded onto the empty chair. Dean Paul stretched it out, peeled off his Thomas Pink shirt, and kicked back. For September, it was uncomfortably hot. "Happy now?"

Finn smiled. "It's a mild improvement." He snapped the waist-band of his Speedo. "I can get you one of these . . ."

"I'll pass. But thanks."

A waiter approached.

Dean Paul ordered up a bottled water.

Finn shook his head, shooing the server away. "I'm sorry I couldn't meet you somewhere more convenient. But when I'm working, I have to protect those hours. It takes real discipline, you know. To be a writer."

Dean Paul cast an odd glance over to Finn. "Yeah, I can see that you really put yourself through the grinder."

"I'm thinking about my screenplay. I studied under David Helmore. He calls this Quality Reflection. It's as important as the actual writing itself. David's a Scientologist and knows John Travolta. He even went to his son's birthday party. Jett. He's twelve now, I believe. Anyway, David has serious Hollywood connec-tions."

"He's the guy who offers the two-day workshop for seven hundred bucks, right? I've seen his flyers around the city."

Finn blanched. "I've taken his seminar eight times. You always learn something new. When I finish my script, David's going to give me notes. That's why I'm so serious about Quality Reflection. I want the screenplay to be the best it can be before he looks at it."

Dean Paul felt an obligation to bat the conversational ball back and forth before cutting to the chase. "So what's the movie about?"

"My life," Finn said.

Dean Paul almost laughed. But he stopped with a big smile at the last moment. "Well, if *you* can't write it . . ."

The waiter returned with the water.

Dean Paul was thankful for the distraction.

"So how's married life?" Finn asked.

"It's great."

"Really? Not according to what I read from Jinx Wiatt."

"We didn't talk on the trip home because Aspen slept most of the way. She was zoned out on pills." He shook his head. "That woman gets one tip from a flight attendant and makes the leap that my marriage is in trouble."

"You did abort the honeymoon," Finn pointed out. "That's reason to wonder."

"You can thank my ex-girlfriend and her trailer-trash lover for that. My parents summoned me home."

Finn checked his Ritmo Mundo watch, then flipped over onto his stomach. "I take it you won't be at the book party tonight."

"Fuck no. Now, I would show up for a book burning."

Finn propped himself up on one elbow and regarded Dean Paul seriously. "I think you should go. If I were you, I'd cover it for *Hollywood Live*, too."

Dean Paul laughed. "Yeah, that's a great idea."

"It is," Finn insisted. "You showing up with your head held high and a production crew orbiting around you to promote *his* book would drive Jake James insane. Think about this for a minute. It reduces him to nothing. He bashes you in the book. He tries to humiliate you with the pictures. And you're still not pissed off enough to boycott his party. Even better, you're helping him out with the *Hollywood Live* bit." Finn giggled gleefully. "A medieval torture device couldn't cause that much pain. He'll be miserable on his big night. And you'll shine like a star. It's the perfect revenge."

Dean Paul grinned. He liked the sound of this. He liked it a lot. "I never pegged you as the Machiavellian type."

Finn straightened his arm and rolled back onto his stomach. "I've known that I was gay since I was six years old, and I've survived every species of bully. That's all Jake is. A big, loud bully. And the best way to fight bullies is to show them that nothing they do can rattle you."

Dean Paul looked at Finn in a whole new light. He had known

him since their days at Brown, but he had never taken him seriously, always reducing him to one-dimensional roles like Lara's gay friend or the rich homo who organized the elaborate parties.

There was a short stretch of silence between them.

Finn was the first to speak. "I was surprised when you called. I didn't figure you for the fag stag type. What's on your mind? I assume it must be Lara."

"I'm worried about her."

"Why? Because she's having the best sex of her life, and it's not with you?"

"She told you that?" There was genuine alarm in his voice.

"See that Chanel bronzing mist on the table?"

"Yes."

"Spray some on my back, would you please?"

Dean Paul picked up the bottle. With a reluctant awkwardness, he raised it over Finn's back and pumped out a few sprays. "Don't ask me to—"

"Just rub it in," Finn snapped impatiently. "If that fraternity in college didn't bring out your inner queer, then this certainly won't."

All of a sudden, Dean Paul felt silly. He shook his head and began to massage the oily mist evenly into Finn's skin.

"Oh, yes," the laziest writer in America moaned. "I always knew you had nice hands. A little lower . . ."

Dean Paul halted immediately. "That's it, Finn. I'm done." He used the towel to rub off the sun product from his hands.

Finn laughed. "God, you're so straight. It's ridiculous. At least tell me you've jacked off with a buddy before. That would make you hetero but human."

The thought repulsed him. "No, I haven't."

"Not even in high school?"

"No!"

"You know what's funny?" Finn asked. He raised up to carefully survey Dean Paul. "I can't even categorize you as a metrosexual. You don't try that hard." He glanced down at Dean Paul's hands. "When's the last time you had a manicure?"

"I've never had one. It's a waste of time and money."

"And yet your nails are perfect. It's sickening."

Dean Paul's expression was pleading. "Can we talk about Lara now?"

"I suppose."

"Did she honestly tell you that Joaquin was the best sex she's ever had?"

Finn sighed. "You know Lara. She would never say something like that out loud. I've just connected the dots." He paused thoughtfully. "Why do you care so much all of a sudden? You didn't have me on speed dial when Garrett the manic-depressive tennis player was making her miserable."

"Joaquin Cruz is sleazy," Dean Paul said firmly.

"Why? Because he's been with the Kometani twins at the same time, and you haven't?"

Dean Paul ignored Finn's question and pressed on. "I've heard stories about him from other guys on the charity polo circuit. He's got a friend in San Antonio—Eddie Azzar. Another high goaler. These two have a contest going on between them about who can sleep with the most upscale women. They call it the Top-Shelf Pussy Club."

Finn raised up. He removed his sunglasses and used his hand as a visor to look directly at Dean Paul. "Are you serious?"

He nodded severely. "They keep up the game everywhere they play—Buenos Aires, Sotogrande, Santa Barbara . . . the Hamptons. I've heard there's a Web site—a running tally of all the women, journal entries, some candid photos—but I can't find it on-line."

"Have you told her about this?"

"I tried, but she doesn't want to hear anything I have to say. I was hoping you would talk to her."

Finn looked worried. "I'll give it a shot. Lara's really got it bad for this guy, though. Do you know that she ditched me for lunch today? I think it was to meet him. I tried her cell phone for two hours, and she never picked up. In the middle of a business day? That's so unlike her. I wish we could find this Web site. I don't want to humiliate her, but she needs to see the truth."

Dean Paul stood up and slipped back into his shirt. "Work on that for me. Okay?"

Finn nodded, his face tight with concentration.

Dean Paul started to go. "This was fun, Finn. And I appreciate the advice on the book party tonight. I plan on following it to the letter." He winked and took off at a fast clip toward the elevator. Once there, he retrieved Jennifer Goldbum's cell number from his Palm Pilot and punched it in.

She answered right away.

"Guess who?"

He could sense her smiling over the line. "My new correspondent! I heard you were back early from Greece. Are you crazy? I would die to be there right now."

"Yeah, well, sometimes you don't have a choice."

Jennifer hesitated. "You know that we covered that story about your photos, right? We had to. It was major. But we kept things to a minimum."

"Hey, *Hollywood Live* has a job to do. I understand that. But I'm ready to be on the *reporting* end of the show for a change. What do you think about moving up my start date?"

"That sounds great!" Jennifer said brightly. "How soon?"

"Tonight. I want to cover Jake James's book party at Butter."

Jennifer fell silent. "You're kidding, right?"

"No, I'm dead serious. Why shouldn't I take the high road?"

"The story's already been assigned . . . to Brooke," Jennifer began, thinking out loud. "Bizzie Gruzart gave us an exclusive. We'll have the only broadcast team inside. Give me five minutes to work on this." She hung up and called back in two. "It's done. I'll meet you outside Butter at eight o'clock."

From the SoHo House, Dean Paul walked to his apartment, a massive loft in the Flatiron District off Fifth Avenue. He owned the entire top floor—over four thousand square feet. With views exposing north, south, east, and west, the natural light was amazing. There were two fireplaces, exposed brick walls, two and a half slate baths, and four bedrooms. The place was total Zen.

A note had been taped to the stainless steel fridge. Aspen was out to see Brian, her manager. Afterwards, she planned on meeting some other *Real World* vets for drinks. He shouldn't wait up.

Dean Paul didn't intend to. He knew that she would probably dance on a table like Tara Reid and come stumbling in sometime before dawn. The fact that she was in conference with Brian concerned him. After all, Brian wanted her to do that cheesy reality-star burlesque show in Las Vegas, and Aspen was just desperate enough to accept, if only to show her husband that she was indeed a sought-after commodity.

There was a message from his mother on the machine. He decided to put off calling her until tomorrow. The grande dame Sophia Mills could wait. She had laid out enough guilt this morning to last throughout the month. No way was he giving her another chance to light into him.

He had met his parents for breakfast at the Ritz-Carlton on Central Park South. They lived on a private tower floor in an opulent, ten-room condo that allowed them to take advantage of all premium hotel offerings, including room service.

It had been his mother's idea to grace publishing houses with her regal presence. That was her passive-aggressive way of telling them, "Don't make an offer on that slut's book about my son!" She had made quite a show about the physical and mental costs of her efforts—how tiring it was, how awful some of the editors were, how much she detested the younger agent who had taken over for her retired one.

Dean Paul had listened dutifully, and, when appropriate, he'd offered empty apologies for the whole sordid mess. But he knew better than to take his mother's bitching at face value. Sophia Mills wanted to get back out there and listen to people tell her how wonderful she was. His little scandal was just the push she needed to build excitement again for the memoirs she had been vaguely promising for the last two decades. Instead of sniping about it, she should be thanking him for showing his ass and peeping his cock to Babe's camera.

His father had been no easier to take. Robert Lockhart started in on the tired subject of law school, and dismissed the *Hollywood Live* gig as a job more suitable for former Miss Americas. Gee, thanks, Pop. Can sonny boy get that praise on a plaque for his home office? Parents. Sometimes they could drive you up the fucking wall.

He didn't allow the lack of enthusiasm to get him down. Would it be nice to have their support? Yes. But could he live without it? In a heartbeat. Deep down, Dean Paul knew that he stood the greatest chance of making his mark in entertainment. It coursed through his veins. Hell, growing up, he had figured out his best angles before he learned the letters of the alphabet.

He slid a Coldplay CD into the stereo, twisted up the volume, and hit the shower. As the song "Clocks" played, he lathered up in preparation for a shave, and thought about Gabrielle. There had been that moment today . . . she was so close to confiding in him. What kind of demons was she fighting? At least he had helped out on the publicist front.

Dean Paul felt certain that Bizzie Gruzart would serve Gabrielle well. Though disliked by many, Bizzie's name carried clout, and she had instant access to connections that mattered. Anything was an improvement over Baby Bear scratching down messages from Diane Sawyer.

The phone rang.

He finished rinsing and stepped out, picking up the extension in the water closet.

It was Finn. "I found the Web site."

"Shit. That was fast." Dean Paul wrapped a towel around his waist.

"I just started playing around on-line. You know, it's not just gay porn on the Internet. There's a lot of straight porn, too."

"I'm shocked."

"I tried Google and got swamped with hard-core sites. I hope I don't lose my membership at this club. Their computer froze under the avalanche of pop-ups. I had to reboot."

"What did you find?"

"They don't seem to be registered with any of the search engines. Not yet, at least. Anyway, I played around with the URL. You just had to add a "the" to 'topshelfpussyclubdotcom.' I'm staring at Joaquin's mug right now. He and his friend Eddie are grinning like two boarding-school brats who just finished a panty raid at the sister school."

"How bad is it?"

"She'll never speak to him again. That's what you want, right?"

"Believe me, I'm not happy about this. If she were head over heels for a nice banker, I never would have bothered you."

"Lara never got over you. Are you aware of that?"

Dean Paul mulled the question. But he chose to ignore it. "She seems to have moved on quite nicely. I'm not in her thoughts right now. I know that."

"Joaquin is just sex. Once the smoke clears, she'll be pining over you again. I don't understand how you can pass up a woman like Lara to marry an Aspen Bauer."

"It's complicated, Finn."

"She would kill me for telling you this, but I think you need to know. Lara spent over five thousand dollars on a signed first edition of *The Great Gatsby.* That's your favorite book, isn't it?"

"Yes."

"Does Aspen know that?"

He didn't answer.

"Lara keeps it on her bookshelf. She has this fantasy of getting back together and you finding it on a rainy Sunday afternoon."

Dean Paul gripped the receiver tightly and looked up at the ceiling. There was true ache in his heart. "I have to go, Finn. Thanks for the detective work. You'll break this ugly news to Lara?"

"I usually love gossip like this." Finn's voice was heavy. "But not when she's the victim. Why can't this be happening to someone who actually deserves it?"

"Things are rarely that balanced." Dean Paul hung up and dressed quickly, choosing a lapis blue shirt that brought out his eyes. He dismissed the idea of a tie and left the top three buttons undone.

Butter was located on Lafeyette Street in Greenwich Village. From its launch, the bar/lounge had become a favorite celebrity haunt. Matt Damon lived in the neighborhood and popped in regularly. It was so VIP-friendly that Britney Spears could burn through endless cigarettes in defiance of Manhattan's smoking ban for mere mortals.

Dean Paul saw the *Hollywood Live* van and went straight to it.

Jennifer embraced him warmly and offered platitudes about how much she looked forward to working with him. Then she introduced Thumper Thomas, an athletic black cameraman and a dead ringer for Jesse L. Martin from *Law & Order*.

She got down to business and discussed the plan of attack. Jake James might be a name on the rise, but he was no Matt Lauer. Originally, the coverage had been budgeted for a thirty-second tease. But the fact that it was now Dean Paul's debut boosted the story to feature status and two minutes. Jennifer wanted crowd shots of beautiful New Yorkers, an interview with the guest of honor, and maybe a sound bite from an A-list name in attendance. When she finished, Jennifer parted Dean Paul's shirt so that more of his chest was revealed. "And I want to show lots of you."

He just smiled at her. It didn't make him feel uncomfortable, because the gesture carried no sexual import. It was simply a good television maneuver. A jolt of inspiration hit him. "Can we try something outside? Right here in front of the door. I've got an idea for an intro."

Jennifer looked intrigued. "Sure. Why not?"

Thumper positioned himself on the sidewalk.

Dean Paul took possession of the microphone outfitted with

the *Hollywood Live* logo. It felt good in his hand. Then he grabbed a copy of Jake's book.

The area bustled with activity. Party invitees were still streaming through the entrance, and a gaggle of spectators had gathered to watch the TV crew in action.

Dean Paul didn't have a script. The words were floating somewhere in his head. He just hoped they found their way out of his mouth.

Thumper gave him a signal.

And then he jumped off the proverbial cliff. "This is Dean Paul Lockhart reporting for *Hollywood Live*." He could feel the energy infused in each syllable. The realization was instant. This was his destiny. "I'm here outside the Manhattan nightspot Butter for a party celebrating Jake James's new book, *Put Up Your Dukes*." Dean Paul raised a fist in mocking tribute to the title. "He's the host of MSNBC's *In the Ring with Jake James*. Just between you and me, I don't have my TiVo programmed to record that on a season pass. I went to college with the guy. Let's just say that we ran in different circles. Maybe you've heard about those seminude pictures of me taken by my ex-girlfriend and his current one that he plastered all over his show? I'll admit it—at first, I was embarrassed. But then I remembered something that J.R. Ewing once said on *Dallas*. It goes, 'Never get caught with a dead woman or a live boy.' I was alone in those pics, so the way I figure it, I'm safe." He winked. "Now let's move past the velvet rope and find out who's here and what they're saying." He held up the book. "By the way, chapter seven really beats up on me. Jake James knows how to throw a punch, I'll give him that. But you won't catch me in a rumble." He pointed to his perfect nose. "Does this look like it's ever been broken? I'm a lover, not a fighter." He flashed his killer smile, the one that could get any woman he ever wanted into bed. "Follow me." And then he opened the door and disappeared inside. A few seconds later, he doubled back.

Jennifer was holding her head between her hands. "That was amazing. You did it in one shot. And off the cuff! It was brilliant."

Dean Paul grinned.

"I think I'm going to come," Jennifer said.

Thumper howled with laughter.

Dean Paul cracked up, too. "It's that easy? You must save your boyfriend a great deal of anxiety." He opened the door and motioned them through. "Come on. After we wrap this fucker, dinner's on me."

Butter resembled an indoor tree house with its wood-paneled walls, chairs carved out of timber chunks, and the gigantic birch forest photograph that commanded an entire upstairs wall.

Bizzie Gruzart rushed them upon entry. "Dean Paul! I never expected to see you here tonight." She gave him a faux scolding with her index finger. "This is my party. You better be good."

Dean Paul raised the peace sign. "Scout's honor." He put an arm around the homely Bizzie and led her away for a confidential conference. "Thanks for taking Gabrielle Foster on. She really needs someone in her corner right now."

Bizzie beamed up at him.

"I'd consider it a personal favor if you gave her situation your very best effort. She's being shot at from all sides." He paused. "That's a poor choice of words considering the incident on Park Avenue. But you know what I mean."

Bizzie grinned. "Don't worry. I'll come up with a plan."

A thought struck him. "When are you meeting with her?"

"Tomorrow morning."

"If you don't mind, I'd like to be in on it."

Bizzie narrowed her gaze curiously.

"Gabrielle's in a very vulnerable place," he explained. "I don't think she's aware of how much she has to offer. And I really believe that if handled shrewdly, she could emerge more successful as herself than she ever was as Brown Sugar."

"How does the new Mrs. Lockhart feel about you getting this involved in the welfare of an ex-girlfriend?" Bizzie asked silkily.

Dean Paul released his arm from her shoulder. "I have no idea. But I'm sure I'll read about it in Jinx Wiatt's column."

She gave him an empathetic look. Not long ago, Bizzie had been the subject of every obvious blind item. "Ten o'clock at her hotel," she said.

"I'll be there." He rejoined the group. They began pushing through the thick crowd of cable news players, assorted models, publishing types, and the usual social suspects who would show up for the opening of a ketchup bottle if it meant free booze and hors d'oeuvres.

Dean Paul spotted Miles Weatherly, the lawyer who years ago had parlayed the O.J. Simpson trial into a steady career as a television legal analyst. Lara had been involved with him once. He wondered what had happened between them. When he witnessed Miles pretending to give one woman his attention while he checked out the ass on another, the answer for the unraveling became clear.

But his eyes were zeroed in on no ordinary ass. It belonged to Babe Mancini.

Dean Paul clocked her with his gaze. She looked beautiful and miserable at the same time. There was a drink in her hand. It didn't appear to be her first one. It didn't appear to be her last.

Babe made eye contact and took in the *Hollywood Live* entourage trailing him. She raised her glass in a mock toast and clearly mouthed the words "Fuck you."

A strong hand grabbed his arm violently. "What the hell are you doing here?"

Dean Paul stared into the angry face of Jake James. He jerked his arm free. "I tell you what, between you and your girlfriend— this is a tough room." With a tilt of his head, he gestured to Jennifer and Thumper, who were coming up from behind. Then he raised the *Hollywood Live* mike as evidence. "It's your big night, Jake. You should smile for the camera."

The realization seemed to rise up on Jake as certain as a brand-new morning. "I should've expected a cocksucker like you to pull something like this."

Obnoxiously, Dean Paul shoved the mike in front of Jake's

mouth. "Don't worry. We're not taping yet. I assume that was just for me. Or do you want to repeat that for our viewers at home?"

Jake stood there, fuming in silence.

Jennifer and Thumper caught up.

"Let's roll," Dean Paul said.

Once more, Thumper gave him the signal.

"I'm here with the most important man at a Jake James book party. And that would be Jake James. How does it feel to be a published author?"

Jake was so pissed off that when he smiled for the camera, it had that rigid, cringe-inducing quality of an unnatural politician on the campaign trail. "It feels good. I think America's ready for a man who's not afraid to tell the truth about what's wrong with our country. I say what's on my mind, and I say it loud. That's why I called it *Put Up Your Dukes*. Because I'll stand behind every word in this book with my fists if I have to."

Dean Paul saw the opening and went for it. "You stand behind every word, but do you stand behind every image?"

Jake looked at him strangely.

"A lot of attention is being paid to this revealing cover photo of you stripped down in the boxing ring," Dean Paul began, holding up the book for the benefit of Thumper's lens. "We live in a high-tech digital age where photographs can lie. So here's your chance to address a rumor out there firsthand. Is this one hundred percent Jake James? Or is this your face superimposed on another man's body?"

It wasn't anger blasting from Jake's gaze. It was poison. He knew exactly where this was going. And there wasn't a goddamn thing he could do to stop it. "Of course, it's me. Like I always say, never trust a man who doesn't power-train his mind *and* his body."

"So you're telling me there's no airbrushing at work here. This is Jake James from head to toe."

"You're damn right it is."

"Now's your chance to prove it." Dean Paul addressed the

crowd already several drinks into a good time. "Who wants to see this man take off his shirt?"

There were whoops and cheers of approval.

Jake glared at Dean Paul as he tore off the tie. He didn't bother with the buttons on his oxford. One ferocious rip and it was raining plastic onto the floor of Butter. The realization that he had walked straight into this trap was all over his face as he paused for the final act—pulling the undershirt over his head. And then he stood there, nostrils flaring, massive chest heaving, powerful arms rippling, six-pack abs proving once and for all that the photograph hardly did him justice.

Catcalls and whistles erupted from the crowd.

Dean Paul flashed that smile again for the camera. "Ladies and gentlemen, this man will do *anything* to sell books. I'm Dean Paul Lockhart for *Hollywood Live*. Back to you, Ainsley."

Jennifer gave him a double thumbs-up.

His eyes blazed a look of triumph. "Okay, Jake, you can put your shirt back on. It's getting a little obvious. Some of the closeted boys are starting to sweat."

Dean Paul left him there and searched for Babe. He found her near the bar.

She was half drunk and regarded him coldly. "Congratulations. You made him look like an idiot."

"I'd like to think I had very little to do with that. Let's give Jake some credit."

"I don't know where this rivalry is going. But with two ego-driven males, it usually comes down to one thing. So take it from a girl who knows. His cock is bigger than yours. Sorry, Dean Paul. You lose."

"This isn't news to me, Babe. Jake's always been the bigger dick."

She grinned in spite of herself.

He smiled back. "What are you doing, Babe? Let's get out of here."

"Why? So you can make him look like a buffoon *and* walk out with his girl? That would be a real knockout punch." She looked at her empty glass, then stared helplessly at the busy bartenders.

"I don't give a shit about Jake. I care about you."

Babe laughed in his face. "Oh, my God, you're hilarious. Fuck *Hollywood Live*. You should do stand-up."

Dean Paul held out his hand. "I'm serious, Babe. Let's go somewhere and talk. This guy is toxic. He's no good for you."

"And I suppose you're my white knight?"

It was as if no years had gone by at all. Babe was still that girl from college. Hurt was what she knew best. And she never let you forget it.

"Let's see . . . I could stay with him . . . or I could leave with you. I should just flip a coin. Either way I lose."

Dean Paul opened his palm. "Not this time." His fingers were almost touching hers.

Babe looked across the room at Jake James. Then she looked at Dean Paul. Tears filled her eyes. But she took his hand.

Dean Paul led her out, moving fast through the crowd. They passed Jennifer and Thumper, and he promised a rain check on dinner. Now his hand touched the door. Freedom was one push away. He turned back.

Jake James was watching them.

Babe stared at Jake for a long, heavily calculated moment. Then she raised her hand, the one that was joined with Dean Paul's. And she followed him into the night. They walked in silence for several blocks, but Babe never let go of his hand.

"Where are we going?" she asked, finally.

"My place. We can talk there. I'll make some coffee."

"What about Aspen?"

"Why is everyone so concerned about my wife?" His tone was snappish. But then he softened. "I'm sorry. It's just . . . She's out for the night."

They continued walking, lost in their own thoughts, until Babe stopped suddenly on Union Square and released his hand.

"You don't have to do this. You don't have to be nice to me. After what I did . . ."

"Babe—"

"But I didn't give those pictures to Jake," she blurted. "I want you to know that. He stole them from my apartment."

Dean Paul didn't doubt her word for a second. "I believe that." He paused. "But there is the matter of the book proposal. Jake isn't responsible for that."

"You hate me, don't you?"

"No, I could never hate you. I—"

"Even if I had sold that book?" she demanded. "Because I would have. At one point my agent was talking a million dollars. Can you believe that? And you and your lawyers and your god-damn family fucked it all up! *A million dollars!*"

"That's the price tag on what we had together?"

Even in the darkness, he could sense Babe's face reddening. She was furious. "What did we have? You just gave me a tour be-cause you wanted some real sex and thought too much of Lara to ask her for it. Did she gag deep-throating you? Did she let you give it to her in the ass? Did she submit to your public-sex fantasy at that bar in Providence? Yeah, I bet! You respected her too much to pull that shit. But I was the latchkey kid from the other side of the tracks. I was barely hanging on at Brown with my student loans and my part-time jobs. So I must have been the perfect choice to be your bedroom whore. You were smooth about it, though. For a time, I actually believed that I was your girlfriend."

Her words lashed out at him like a whip. They hurt so much that he turned away from her. The emotion rose up suddenly. It lodged painfully in his throat. And then the tears came to his eyes. God, he was crying! A woman had never made him cry before. He spun to face her.

Babe took one look at the water in his eyes and simply froze.

"Jesus Christ, Babe. How could you ever think that about me?"

She didn't answer him.

"I respected you. God, there was a time when I worshiped you. Babe, you made me feel like a man. I didn't know what sex was until I met you. After our wild nights, I wanted to send letters of apology to all the girls from high school. Even Lara, too." He laughed and wiped away his tears.

Babe laughed, too.

"Every relationship is different, you know? Lara and I . . . I don't know. It was strange. Right away we were as placid as a comfortable married couple. Does that make any sense?"

She nodded intently.

"I don't mean for that to sound negative. What we had was beautiful. But then I started developing feelings for you . . . and . . . it was altogether different. From the start we had intense sexual fireworks. You brought out that part of me. And I've always been grateful to you for that. We had our own kind of magic." He opened his arms to embrace her.

Babe fell into him and held on as if for life. Now she was crying and laughing at the same time. "And all this time I thought I was just an easy lay."

Dean Paul held her face in his hands and gazed into her eyes with real affection. "You're so beautiful, Babe. You're so special, too. Jake isn't worthy." The urge to kiss her proved overwhelming. When his mouth met hers, their lips parted in unison. It was soft and wet, tongues engaging in a brief dance. And then he withdrew.

"That was nice," Babe said. She took his hand again. "Do you still want to go back to your apartment?"

"Yes." He squeezed her hand and led her down the block, wondering all the way home if the whole lot—Lara, Babe, and Gabrielle—would have been better off never having known him.

They took the private freight elevator that opened to the floor of his loft. As it journeyed up, he could hear booming music. The turgid rock and roll of the Strokes, in fact. He knew the song. "Between Love and Hate." At first, he thought a neighbor was having a major blowout. But when the elevator creaked to a stop and he lifted the door, the real story became clear.

The party was happening in his apartment.

He stepped into his living room and searched the drunken throng for a familiar face. Oddly, they were all vaguely recognizable. Aspen had submitted him to endless hours of *The Real World*—highlights from every year, though she always declared her own season the best and most dramatic.

Dean Paul spotted her dancing with an alumnus from Hawaii whose name escaped him. He marched over and broke up the suggestive gyrations. "What the fuck is this?"

It took Aspen a few seconds to focus. She was drunk out of her mind. But sober enough to understand that he had brought Babe home. "What? I can't have a party, but you can walk in here with your ex-girlfriend? You didn't think I'd be here! Well, I've got a better question. What the fuck is *that*?"

An equally drunk castmate from the Boston season got in his face. "Man, this place is awesome! How much is your rent?"

Dean Paul stepped around him. "Aspen, I'm going to take Babe home, and when I get back, I want these people out of here and everything in its proper place." He glanced around at the wasted losers milling about. They were all living on yesterday's fifteen minutes of fame. "You didn't say anything about a party."

Aspen's red eyes blazed the worst kind of inebriated defiance. "And you didn't say anything about bringing one of your ex-sluts up for a quickie. I guess we're even."

He stormed back to the elevator where Babe stood waiting.

"Maybe you should stay," she said. "I'll catch a cab."

"No. I need some air. Let's go."

They were silent until reaching the sidewalk.

"I don't think it's a good idea to go back to my apartment," Babe said. "I fought with Jake. You fought with Aspen. It's too easy. And it's not right."

"You shouldn't be alone tonight."

"I'm fine."

He shook his head. "You shouldn't be alone. I know someone else who shouldn't be, either. Come with me." Raising his right arm, he stepped into the middle of the street and aggressively hailed a taxi.

"Where are you taking me?" Babe asked.

"Just get in." He tumbled inside after her and told the driver to take them to the Waldorf-Astoria.

Traffic was light. They went through the Park Avenue tunnel and were there in less than ten minutes.

Dean Paul took Babe's hand and piloted her into the lobby and straight to a bank of guest phones. He asked the operator to connect him to Gabrielle Foster's suite.

Baby Bear answered.

"Hey, man, it's Dean Paul. How's our favorite girl?"

"What's up? She's doing okay. Got a friend here tonight. Things are cool."

"Yeah? Well, I'm downstairs with a friend, too. We want to come up."

"Sounds like a party. I'll be right down."

Dean Paul looked at Babe.

She was on to him now. "What is this? Gabrielle and I are supposed to have some kind of pity party?"

"I have a feeling there won't be much pity to it."

They waited outside the elevator for Baby Bear. He alone had the special key that provided access to the penthouse floor.

"I'll push you over the balcony if you even think about suggesting a three-way."

Dean Paul smiled flirtatiously. "Come on. I've gone to all this trouble."

The doors opened. There stood Baby Bear. He took one look at Babe and broke out into a wide grin. "Uh, oh. It's sho'nuff gonna be a party."

Babe leaped into the elevator and hugged his massive neck.

Dean Paul was puzzled. "You two know each other?"

"We partied in the Hamptons together," Babe explained.

"Correction—*they* partied," Baby Bear said. "I just tried to keep them girls out of jail."

When they got to the suite, Babe rushed to embrace Gabrielle . . . and Lara.

Dean Paul was shocked to find her there. As they regarded each other, a palpable tension filled the room. Lara seemed downright angry. He couldn't imagine that she was still mad about his phone call.

Lara stepped out onto the balcony.

He followed her.

The view was spectacular. The sounds of the city sang from below. But all of that seemed lost on her as she stared at him as if he were a mess on the side of the road.

"Have you talked to Finn?"

"Yes." Her tone was clipped.

"I think you should save that look on your face for Joaquin. He's the one who deserves it."

"This isn't about Joaquin." She glanced back into the suite and lowered her voice to a hiss. "This is about you hiring *Bizzie Gruzart* to represent Gabrielle!"

The attack caught him completely off guard. "Am I missing something here?"

"Gabrielle's situation is serious. She needs quality representation, and the best you can come up with is Bizzie Gruzart?"

"The record label has frozen her out. Before I got involved, her representation was a three-hundred-pound bodyguard with a message pad."

Lara opened her mouth to argue.

But a memory clicked in Dean Paul's head that triggered a quickly lit anger. "I was in Greece when this happened. But you were right here, Lara. And as I understand it, you were the first to see her after the shooting and the breaking of the 'Smoking Gun' story. If *quality representation* is so fucking important, why didn't you suggest it then? Maybe you weren't thinking straight. Maybe your mind was all wrapped up in hitting the sheets with your polo stud."

Lara's face was a masterpiece of humiliation and guilt.

Instantly, he felt a stinging sense of regret for coming down so hard. "Lara, I'm sorry. I didn't—"

"No," she whispered, looking shell-shocked. "As much as I hate to admit it, you're absolutely right."

Lara never ceased to amaze him. She was a class act. The kind of lady that parents didn't raise anymore. Any other woman would still be fighting right now, if only to get a few digs in, but Lara had recognized her own weakness and stopped the argument cold. He would never get that from Aspen. Dean Paul thought about what Finn had told him regarding Lara's purchase of *The Great Gatsby*. Suddenly, he just wanted to take her into his arms.

She turned to grip the balcony rail with both hands and glanced down. "I have a friend at PMK. I should've called her. I just wasn't thinking." Lara's voice sounded far away.

"Bizzie will do fine. It's not a long-term pairing. She's just someone to help Gabby through this rough patch."

Lara sighed and twirled around to face him, her long hair blowing in the breeze. "I don't hate many people in this world. But I do hate Bizzie Gruzart. Forgive me if I'm high-strung where she's concerned."

Dean Paul pulled her in for a quick embrace and kissed her cheek. As always, she smelled magnificent. Hints of gardenia and ylang ylang clung to his nostrils. "Why do you even bother yourself with someone like Bizzie? You're light-years ahead of her. You put on fantastic events that take people to another place. You've helped raise millions for charities. What you do is an art form. Bizzie hires a caterer and books a band. It's no contest. I thought she could help Gabby because the major networks are involved. With Bizzie in the mix, all of this will get sorted out fast. Her last name alone will make sure of that."

For the moment, Lara appeared satisfied with his explanation. "Okay. I won't poison the well tonight. If the subject of Bizzie comes up, I might even put in a decent word."

"That's my girl." He took in a deep breath and glanced at his watch. "I'd better go. I have quite a mess waiting for me at home.

Besides, the sooner I get out of your way, the sooner you girls can start your slumber party. Is it still all about junk food, pillow fights in your pajamas, and prank calls to boys?"

Lara smiled and hooked her arm through his as she walked him out. "Better take your phone off the hook."

And then Dean Paul left them to their female bonding—the two women that he used to love . . . and the one that he still did.

THE IT PARADE
BY JINX WIATT

Fill in the Blanks

Heartfelt apologies to Tara Reid! She's not the only girl who stumbles around with a lampshade on her head. Yours truly has it on very good authority that the three exes of a certain recently married American prince are at it again. East Hampton is still reeling from that wild, post-reception private party at Mr. Thuggish Roguish Mogul's pad. Now spies report that the Waldorf-Astoria is the scene for their latest sorority meeting. But you know what they say about sisters who share sweaters. They do so often—and with much argument.

16

Lara

"Privi, please. I'll be your best friend."

Finn was whining.

Lara was dying. Again.

Privi sighed the sigh of the defeated. "Okay. But then you have to go. Lara needs her rest." She pursed her lips in disapproval. "Why can't you sit on the chaise in the corner? It's not proper for you to be in the same bed."

Finn crossed his ankles and sank a little deeper into the pillows. "I'm gay, Privi. There's nothing improper about it. Just try to think of me as her sister."

Privi shook her head. "What would you like to eat, Finn?"

He clapped his hands in delight. "A grilled cheese sandwich. Make it exactly like you did that time I came over to watch the *Felicity* marathon."

"And how was that?" Privi asked.

"I think you used Gruyère cheese. The bread was brown but not too brown. It had the most perfect crunch. And you cut off the crust."

Privi beamed a disappointed look at Lara. "I used the last of the whole milk making my banana bread for Yari. I'll have to step out to the market."

"Since you'll be out," Finn began, "bring back today's *Examiner*. I'm dying to see what Jinx Wiatt has to say."

Finally, Lara attempted to speak. "No, Privi," she croaked. "It's raining. You're not going anywhere."

Finn scowled at Lara. "It's not raining *inside* the building. There's a market on the first floor."

Privi's expression was iron-fisted stubbornness. "I can't make Yari's hangover cure without the milk."

Lara steadied herself with both hands. The nausea grew so intense that she ended up closing her eyes. "Please, I beg you . . . don't mention food . . . of any kind."

Beside her, Queenie scratched at the covers to nestle the perfect napping spot.

Lara gave her a loving stroke.

Privi looked on sternly. Her sympathy had its limits. "I thought you learned your lesson from that last night of debauchery. Yari's husband had cirrhosis of the liver. Is that what you want?"

Lara smiled weakly. "That's from long-term alcohol abuse, Privi. I'm guilty of two isolated incidents. Incredibly stupid. But isolated just the same."

"Actually, it's three," Finn put in. "Remember our junior year at Brown? The Naked Party?"

Privi gasped in horror.

"Yes, thank you, Finn," Lara grumbled. She held up three fingers. "Okay, three times. And I'm almost thirty."

Finn looked at Privi. "She's a saint. Kids today have three incidents before they turn thirteen."

Lara touched his leg to silence him. "You're not helping."

"I'm going out for the milk."

"Privi, please don't. This time is worse than the last. I know I'll never get the cure down. I just need to sleep it off."

But Privi would hear none of it. She stepped around to fluff Lara's pillow into shape and patted Queenie on the head. "Young lady, you will take every drop, and if this happens again, I'll be on the phone to your parents. And Queenie is overdue for a grooming."

"Call Hernando," Lara said softly. "He'll come here to do it. Queenie doesn't like that other place. It's too loud. Besides, the carrier makes her nervous. We only have one tranquilizer left, and that's for her next vet visit."

"That dog sounds like Neely O'Hara," Finn cracked.

Privi felt Lara's forehead with the back of her hand.

"Am I warm?" Lara wondered. "I feel warm."

Privi bent over to open the mini ice box near the bed. She produced a cold gel mask and carefully placed it over Lara's eyes.

The cool sensation instantly soothed her. "Oh, that feels marvelous. Privi, why didn't I think of this?"

"Maybe because alcohol destroys brain cells," Privi said.

"Actually, it doesn't," Finn argued. "Alcohol damages dendrites. Those are the branched ends of nerve cells. And it's not permanent. They repair themselves."

Lara and Privi regarded him curiously.

"I saw a special on the Learning Channel. Ironically, I was in bed with a hangover at the time."

Privi adjusted Lara's comforter. "I'm going out for the milk." She started for the door.

"I'm so jealous right now I can't stand it," Finn called out. "Can I stay over whenever I have a hangover?"

Lara peeked out from her mask.

Privi was looking at Finn warily. "I'm almost afraid to ask. How often is that?"

"Pretty much Thursday through Monday." Finn paused. "And the occasional Wednesday. Tuesday is trash-disco night at Wet Heaven."

Privi shook her head and disappeared without a word.

Lara put the mask back in place and grinned. "You drive her crazy."

"I want a Privi," Finn announced in his baby voice.

Lara was appalled. "She's not an object, Finn. She's a person. Privi's been with my family since the day I came home from the hospital."

Finn sighed restlessly.

Lara could tell that his mind had already raced on to another subject.

"I can't wait for Mio and Mako's party. You've seen them up close. Do you think they've had work done?"

The mere mention of the Kometanis produced a surge of anxiety. "Oh, God, Finn, please don't mention anything about work. Between Joaquin and this debilitating condition right now, I'm so far behind it's unthinkable."

Finn rambled on. "I heard one of those gossipy Japanese TV shows reported that they were actually in their late twenties, and that they got the idea from the Jennifer North character in *Valley of the Dolls*."

"Oh, that's ridiculous," Lara said. "That's a thick book. I honestly don't think they would have the attention span to get through it."

Finn sighed again. "What would you do if Dean Paul got divorced?"

Lara removed her mask and stared at her friend. "Where did that come from?"

"His marriage won't make it," Finn said. "And it will go down as one of the most inexplicable unions in history. Like Julia Roberts and Lyle Lovett." One beat. "Robert Evans and Catherine Oxenberg." Another beat. "Carmen Electra and Dennis Rodman."

"Okay, Finn. I get the point."

"Wait. I've got one more. Drew Barrymore and Tom Green."

Lara decided to play. What else could she do? "Michael Jackson and Lisa Marie Presley."

"Doesn't count," Finn said. "Anything associated with Michael Jackson is inexplicable."

"I give up then. Anyway, it hurts too much to think."

"So you never said. What would you do?" Finn asked.

They were back to the subject of Dean Paul. Wearily, Lara reapplied the gel mask. "I don't know, Finn. I suppose I would just hope that Aspen didn't get my wedding gift in the settlement. I spent two hundred dollars on that vase. It's a gorgeous Raku piece."

"That's no kind of answer."

"It's the only one I can come up with right now." But the question was stuck in her brain.

"Could you handle the idea of being his second wife?"

"I don't care if Dean Paul gets divorced tomorrow. I'm not going to marry him. Ever."

"Why not? You still love him. And he still loves you. That fling with Joaquin drove him insane."

"And now that it's over, he'll probably lose interest again."

"I just think—"

"Finn, if I had the strength, I would push you off the bed."

There was a long silence.

Lara broke it with a confession that surprised even her. "I'll always love Dean Paul. But it's a painful kind of love, because I know it will never be realized. Not because of me but because of him. I can't trust him with it. He means well . . . but at the end of the day . . . I think he's incapable of loving one woman. Last night when he and Babe walked into Gabrielle's hotel room . . . oh, God . . . all of that history flashed before my eyes. For a moment, I was back at Brown. Seeing them on campus together for the first time after their liaison at the Biltmore. I can't ever go back there, Finn. I just can't. It's too risky. I could never truly relax being with Dean Paul. His devotion to me wouldn't last. Not in the purest sense. I'm not enough for him. Maybe no woman is. He would probably always come back to me, but I'm not willing to settle for that. Why should I? I'd just end up hating him in the end. I feel sorry for any girl who decides that he's the one. There will always be a Babe on the horizon. Two nights at the Biltmore that change everything. I won't live that way. But I'll still measure every man I meet against him. Isn't that pathetic?"

In answer, Finn silently reached for her hand.

They were quiet for a long time. Eventually, he drifted off to sleep, but Lara lay there, wide awake now, fully cognizant of every throbbing pain in her head and every rumbling wave in her stomach. She had not been exaggerating to Privi. This was indeed worse than the last time. But it had been worth all the discomfort . . .

The trouble started just minutes after Dean Paul left. Room service brought up three bottles of Cristal.

Lara shouted at the attendant when he rolled the cart inside, "Sir, there's been a mistake. Get that out of here!"

Gabrielle rushed to intercede. "Don't pay any attention to her," she told the young man. "She has these episodes from time to time. It's very sad." With that, she pressed a crisp twenty-dollar bill into his hand.

The attendant left happy.

The cart stayed.

Babe popped the first bottle. She screamed as the cork exploded, fizz shooting out like a geyser, drenching the floor.

Gabrielle stood waiting with her glass, practically jumping up and down in anticipation. "Me, me, me!"

Babe, the de facto bartender, took care of Lara next.

But Lara refused. "No way. I swore to myself after the last time. I almost died. I'm serious."

"You have to take one sip!" Gabrielle demanded. "I have a toast!"

Babe nodded encouragingly and held out the glass.

Reluctantly, Lara took possession of it. "Okay. *One toast*. But that's all."

They formed a circle, a troika of Dean Paul Lockhart survivors—the tall, patrician blonde, the edgy, striking brunette, and the beautiful Black American Princess. Together they raised their glasses.

"In the words of Willa Ford," Gabrielle began.

The name didn't ring a bell. "Is she a poet?" Lara asked.

Gabrielle smiled. "Um . . . sort of."

Babe laughed.

Lara could tell she that was on the outskirts of an inside joke. "What?"

"She's a pop . . . *tart*," Gabrielle said, giggling. "A Britney Spears type."

"A poor man's Britney Spears," Babe added.

Lara was still confused. "Well, this should be interesting."

Gabrielle cleared her throat. "I'm paraphrasing, so bear with me. Okay. Here's to the men we love to love . . . here's to the men who passed on us . . . fuck the men, let's drink to us!"

From that first sip, Lara was a goner. It was a sentiment that she could really drink to. And she did.

With the opening of the second bottle, Babe stepped up to recite the brilliant toast, and she put her own spin on it. "Here's to the men we love . . . here's to the men we can't trust . . . fuck the men, let's drink to us!"

"Yes!" Lara squealed, thinking of Joaquin Cruz and downing her glass. She was the first to demand a refill.

And then came the ritualization of bottle number three. Lara's turn at the invisible podium. By now, she was buzzing like a chainsaw, silly and loopy and thrilled to be with her friends of yesteryear. She raised her glass, but every time she started to speak, an attack of the giggles sidelined her.

Gabrielle was laughing so hard that her body shook. "Baby girl, you've got to get through it. Now stop. Be serious."

Babe looked at Lara, then back at Gabrielle. "I don't think this girl can do it."

"Yes, I can!" Lara insisted. "Just don't look at me. If I make eye contact, I'll lose it again."

Babe turned to the exit.

Gabrielle focused on the balcony.

And then Lara took in a deep breath. "Here's to the men who . . . wait a minute . . . let me start over . . . here's to the . . . you know what . . . forget all of that." Her words were slurring a bit, but she knew what needed to be said. "There's only one part of this toast that really matters. Do you know what I mean?" She stood up on the coffee table, wobbling a little. "Fuck the men, let's drink to us!"

Babe and Gabrielle screamed in unison.

Even as tipsy as she was, Lara could sense her eyes widen in disbelief. "Oh, my God! I said *fuck*! I've never said that word before in my life!" And her champagne glass went bottoms up in celebration of the act.

Babe and Gabrielle moved fast to negotiate her down from the coffee table.

"You are one drunk bitch," Gabrielle told her, making the horrible word sound like a term of endearment. "Keep both feet on the ground. Okay, baby girl?"

Lara's head began that awful spinning sensation. "Am I your bitch?" she asked. "Isn't that what they say?"

"Yes, girl," Gabrielle answered, putting an arm around her shoulder. "You're my bitch."

Lara reached out for Babe. "And you're *my* bitch."

Babe tossed over a look of amusement. "And you're the whitest girl I've ever heard try to talk black."

Everybody howled with laughter, and the slumber party rocked on.

Remembering the endurance trick from that night at AKA Bomb Threat's house in East Hampton, Lara raided the minibar and chased down a can of Red Bull.

Babe commandeered the stereo, choosing a satellite station that specialized in hits from the early nineties. It was a nonstop mix that brought back a flood of college memories. "Shoop" by Salt-N-Pepa. The reggae-tinged "Can't Help Falling in Love with You" by UB40. The female anthem "I Don't Wanna Fight" by Tina Turner.

Gabrielle ordered a feast from room service, one of almost every single item on the menu. They sampled each dish greedily, and the sustenance went a long way toward soaking up some of the alcohol in their empty stomachs.

Baby Bear kept a discreet eye on the activities but mainly tried to avoid them altogether.

The room service carts were wheeled into Gabrielle's bedroom. Then everybody stripped down to undies and big T-shirts (courtesy of AKA Bomb Threat's drawer) and piled onto the king-size mattress to finish pigging out.

Babe dunked a luscious lump of lobster into melted butter and chunked it into her mouth. She stretched out to grab one of the empty Cristal bottles. "I've got a question for Lara."

Gabrielle's perfectly waxed eyebrows perked up with interest.

Lara experienced a subtle sense of dread as she wondered what could be coming down the pike.

"We got you to say *fuck*, so I'm hoping you'll just continue this evolutionary shift into the trashy girl we always knew was dying to break out of that prep school shell." Babe grinned. She held the champagne bottle by the neck. "I've heard that Joaquin Cruz's dick is this big. You're the only one in this room who knows for sure."

Lara just sat there. She may have been drunk, but she was still mortified. A blushing heat rose to her cheeks. "I can't talk about this! No matter how much I've had to drink!"

"We're your bitches," Gabrielle pressed. "Just give us a hint. Come on, this is a pajama party. We're supposed to talk about men and sex. It's a rule. I think it's officially in the girl code."

Lara covered her face with her hands, then played peek-a-boo just long enough to say, "It's *huge*," before diving headfirst into the pillows.

There were squeals of laughter.

"Jake is big, too," Babe said. "But that dick is just a memory now. I'll never let it near me again."

Lara rose up, her giddy mood deflated. "The same goes for me. Not with Jake, I mean. That other louse. What's-his-name."

Babe and Gabrielle searched Lara's face.

She told them about Joaquin's friendly rivalry with Eddie Azzar and their sick game's accompanying Web site.

"The Top-Shelf Pussy Club?" Babe repeated incredulously. "How about the Sleazy Dick Society? What a misogynistic pig. Christ, his mother must have done some kind of number on him growing up. Why else would he have such contempt for women? And the scary thing is that he hides behind all that charm and those slick seduction moves."

Lara shook her head. "It makes me feel like some kind of desperate woman who got bilked by a grifter."

"You shouldn't feel that way," Babe said firmly. "This isn't the kind of man that you look at after the fact and go, 'What the fuck was I thinking?' Joaquin pushes all the right buttons. I've seen him do his thing at parties around town. You'd have to be inhuman or a total dyke not to respond. How was the sex?"

"The earth moved," Lara said matter-of-factly.

Babe shrugged easily. "Well, at least it wasn't a total loss. I've slept with more than a few creeps who were terrible in bed. Now that's when true regret sets in. Realizing that you put yourself through hell and couldn't even get a decent orgasm out of the deal."

"Are you nervous about ending up on that Web site?" Gabrielle asked.

Lara said nothing. But the fact was, fear of that gnawed away at her.

"Don't worry. I'll take care of that fucking Web site," Babe announced.

Lara was moved by the protective tone in her voice. "What do you mean?"

"I know a computer geek. He helped me set up a file transfer program for special projects. This kid can do anything. I'll have him crack into that site, destroy it, and leave a special little message for that son of a bitch."

Lara couldn't stop the smile from curling onto her lips. "But isn't that illegal?"

"Technically, yes," Babe admitted. "So is cheating on my taxes. I still write off every trip to the spa as a work-related expense. Relax. This is a no-sweat gig. My guy can get through any firewall or intrusion-detection software. But I bet this site is a homemade job. Consider it blasted out of cyberspace."

Lara smiled gratefully at Babe. There was something she wanted to know, though. It could possibly cast a pall on the camaraderie, but she decided to take the chance. "Dean Paul seems to have accepted the idea of your book project."

"What book project? His family put an end to it."

Lara and Gabrielle traded meaningful glances.

"That movie star mother was the real trump card. But we hashed out our problems tonight, and things are fine between us. It was a cheap, moneygrubbing move on my part. I'll admit that. Still, I felt entitled. And I think he understands where I was coming from."

"It's all for the best," Lara said. "Your first book should be a celebration of your style and talent. When all was said and done, I think you would have regretted that book. Especially the way it got played up in the columns. You're an artist, Babe. A good artist. I've always thought of you that way."

Babe grinned wryly. "Jesus, I've been a hack for so long that I don't know what it means to be an artist anymore." She turned to Gabrielle. "You're awfully quiet."

There was a beatific smile on Gabrielle's face. "I'm just listening. I love this. Us, I mean. All defenses down . . . and we're . . . here for each other. I can't explain the feeling. It's just really nice."

Babe yawned, stretched, and fell back onto the bed.

Lara dropped next.

Then came Gabrielle.

Shoulder to shoulder they lay there, gazing up at the ceiling, giggling like schoolgirls at a sleepover.

It was Babe who started the call-and-response game. "Okay. Secret celebrity crushes. Everybody fess up. Mine's Colin Farrell."

"George Clooney," Lara said.

"Brad Pitt," Gabrielle chirped.

"Long hair or short?" Babe asked.

Gabrielle thought about it. "Long."

"Okay," Babe began. "Let's see . . . uh . . . the first time you had sex. Who was it and where did it happen?"

"You first," Lara said. She nudged Babe playfully.

"Chad Lafferty. I was fifteen. He was the ticket taker at the multiplex. We did it in his brother's Dodge Charger." Babe bumped Lara.

She hesitated a moment. "Believe it or not, my first time was with Dean Paul. At his apartment."

"Wow," Babe said. "That explains a lot. Gabrielle, what about you?"

"Morgan Atwood." Her voice had an edge. "We were sixteen. It happened in his bedroom on a Saturday night when his parents were out of town. And if you watch *Inside Edition* and read *Star* magazine, you can learn every thrilling detail. Straight from the source."

There was a pregnant pause.

Babe broke it. "One more—scariest experience of your life. I guess mine would be the time I got mugged at gunpoint. I was running on the Williamsburg Bridge. Three years ago. The guy was high. I really thought it was over for me."

"Oh, God!" Lara exclaimed. "I can't imagine that kind of violation." She mulled the question for her own answer. "I suppose my scariest experience would be getting lost at the beach when I was four. My parents couldn't find me for two hours. I'll never forget that. I had nightmares for years."

"Gabrielle, you're up," Babe said.

But not a single word was spoken. The silence ticked away.

Babe yawned again. "She must have fallen asleep."

Lara sensed otherwise and turned to see for herself.

Gabrielle's eyes were wide open. She looked terrified. . . .

Lara was shaken from her reverie by the distinct aroma of the cure as Privi came shuffling into the bedroom with the magic recipe—a steaming cup of beef bouillon and a glass of cold whole milk.

Privi glanced at the sleeping Finn. "You're the one who's supposed to be resting."

"It's just a catnap," Lara whispered. "He'll wake up any minute and start asking about his grilled cheese sandwich."

Privi muttered something under her breath and walked out.

Lara adjusted Queenie's blanket.

The telephone blasted to life.

She reached for the cordless, which forced her to face the bouillon and the milk. Not an easy confrontation. "Hello?"

"I left messages on your mobile phone and with your house-keeper." It was Joaquin. "Why haven't you called?"

"I've been under the weather," Lara said.

"I could come over and give you a sponge bath."

She had hoped that the sound of his voice would do nothing for her, that all of her desire for Joaquin Cruz would have simply evaporated. But none of that was true. In spite of everything she knew, Lara still wanted him.

"Are you there?"

"Yes, I'm here."

"So tell me what can I do to make you feel better. I'll do anything, baby. Just say it."

Go to hell. Three little words. So easy to say. So appropriate to deliver. Oh, God, she wanted to tell him exactly that! Yet what came out of her mouth was entirely different. "Tomorrow."

And then Lara hung up and began to sip on the bouillon. She planned on taking in every drop. The milk, too. *Come on, cure. Work your magic. I need to get better. Fast.*

Finn began to stir next to her. His eyes fluttered. "Who was that?"

"Wrong number."

THE IT PARADE
BY JINX WIATT

Fill in the Blanks

Don't you just adore a sweet reunion story about star-crossed lovers finding romance again? Maestro, please play Vanessa Williams's "Save the Best for Last." It could be happening with Princess Smile-For-My-Camera and her Former Big Man on Campus ex. That tacky tell-all book business is already ancient history, and this twosome could be looking at an empty pair of datebooks. Her hot fling with the feisty cable guy is ice-cold, and rumors are in the wind that his new marriage to Missy Reality Star is on the endangered list.

17

Babe

This was a stealth mission, and she had brought out her heavy artillery—the Nikon D1 with the 400mm 2.8 telephoto lens. You couldn't see her. But she could see you. So clearly that if you were due for a pore-extraction facial, then her picture would tell the story.

Come on out and play, you piece of shit.

Babe waited. Across the street in the vestibule of another building. What had once been a giant coffee lay littered at her feet. She was wired. Jesus Christ, this stakeout was for justice, not for cash. When would she see a little action?

A Toyota Tacoma with a double cab cruised down Second Street at a suspiciously slow speed. The windows were tinted.

Instantly, Babe knew.

The truck stopped directly in front of her. The driver's window eased down. The man behind the wheel gave her a creepy smile. He looked like he was on crystal meth. "Heyyou'rethatbitchwhogotmyshotofGwynethparkingonthesidewalk."

Shit. She was made.

Glancing around, she started for the truck. Just her luck. Any second now, her prey would probably surface, and she would be otherwise engaged trying to convince this asshole that her story wasn't worth jumping on.

"YeahyoufuckedmeupthattimemaybeI'llwaitaroundhereand-fuckyouup." It took her a moment to get used to his impatiently fused word strings. He was a skinny little bastard. Tons of hair—long and stringy. Under a baseball cap worn backwards. They called him NPP. Short for No Piss Petie. Why? Because he could knock down Cokes like ninepins and never leave his post to take a leak.

Babe noticed the black felt curtain he had rigged to darken the shooting area in the cabin. This dipshit was a true pic hunter. Notorious for trailing A-listers without mercy.

He even considered their kids fair game. Babe had heard a story once about his relentless pursuit of the daughter of an action star and a top model. The little girl fell off her bike trying to get away from him. He got several shots of her crying on the street with badly skinned knees and walked away. The pictures earned him a bundle.

"Mightaswelltellmewhoyou'reaftercuzI'llbeonyoulikefliesonshit."

Once more, Babe struggled with the language. But she got the gist. "This is personal. The mark's semi-famous at best. Not worth your time."

No Piss Petie smiled bigger this time. His teeth needed brush-ing. His eyes were bloodshot. He had probably been up all night long chasing some starlet from bar to bar.

The CB radio crackled.

"Gwen Stefani is on the move! I repeat: Gwen Stefani is on the move!" The voice reported this news as if it were a matter of in-ternational significance.

No Piss Petie eyeballed the area. The debate was raging on his face. To follow orders and go after a sure thing or to get revenge and stick around for a mystery shot? "JustwaitI'llfuckyouupone-day." And then he slammed his foot on the accelerator.

Babe breathed a sigh of relief as the truck screeched away. She raced back to her spot and settled in for the wait. Where was her quarry?

About a half hour later, she got some activity.

Joaquin Cruz emerged from his apartment building. He was shirtless and barefoot, wearing a pair of faded, five-button-fly jeans, the first three undone to advertise the fact that he hadn't bothered with underwear.

Babe captured him in the viewfinder. She zoomed in. God, what a hot son of a bitch. He oozed sex. This stud was fucking nuclear. Her index finger pressed down on the blessed button.

Click. Click. Click.

He took a final drag of the cigarette hanging from his lips and tossed it into the street. For a split second, his dark eyes flashed in her direction.

Babe's heart lurched. *Shit.* Had he noticed her?

The answer became clear when he casually turned around to face his own building.

A sigh of relief passed her lips.

What happened next shocked the hell out of her. She had hoped to find something here. She had never dreamed of finding this.

A woman stepped out of the building. She gave Joaquin an intimate lover's smile and kissed him on the sidewalk.

A tingle of illicit discovery ran up and down Babe's back. Her stomach tightened. As the viewfinder jammed harshly against her cheek, the ball of her forefinger adjusted the focus. It had to be perfect. This must be what it feels like to shoot with a gun. The couple was in the crosshairs. Babe Mancini had the kill shot.

Joaquin Cruz . . . and Aspen Bauer-Lockhart.

Her finger froze on the point of fire. And then she unloaded her ammo.

Click. Click. Click.

Babe found herself stuck at the edge of the picture. She couldn't move. The enormity of the moment lanced into her brain. Seeing Dean Paul and Aspen fight over *The Real World* revelers was one thing. But seeing this was quite another. Where the former hummed with possibility, the latter sang with conclusion. Dean Paul would soon be free.

In the lens she still had them. Body to body. Face to face. They were amplified. The polo-playing cocksman and the new wife of America's golden son. The image stayed sharp as the molecules rearranged themselves in Babe's mind. They were no longer man and woman. They were now letters of the alphabet.

D I V O R C E

Babe's internal jukebox began to play the old Tammy Wynette song.

Aspen's face suddenly took on a weird intensity.

Just as quickly, Joaquin craned his neck toward Babe, his eyes sizing up the scene and her place in it. Right away, an insolent self-righteousness seemed to consume him.

Babe went numb. For a fleeting moment, she felt the guilt of voyeurism, of impoliteness. The accusation in their eyes affected her more deeply than she ever realized it could. So this was how it felt. To be caught in the act of privacy invasion. Nobody had ever spotted her before. She always managed to slink away unnoticed.

At first, Joaquin and Aspen stared right through her. Then they formed a united front of aggression and stepped into the street.

"You fucking bitch!" Aspen screamed.

Joaquin glanced around. He walked more gingerly now.

Babe could see the soles of his bare feet turning black from the concrete.

"I want that film." His hand reached out, palm facing upward as if to pantomime the ridiculous request.

Babe lowered the camera. "I want Madonna to quit while she's ahead. Doesn't mean it'll happen."

Joaquin stopped for a car, keeping a firm hand on Aspen, who seemed more than willing to take her chances with the glistening BMW X5 moving past.

"I'll break that fucking camera on your face!"

Joaquin gently restrained his venom-spewing lover. He smiled at Babe disarmingly.

She calculated the distance between them. A good twelve to fourteen steps. If things got ugly, the advantage would be hers.

Joaquin couldn't run too far without shoes. And Aspen was in heels.

"Come on, Babe," Joaquin said. "If that picture gets out, people could get hurt."

Babe laughed in his face. "Since when do you care about other people's feelings? The Top-Shelf Pussy Club hardly reads like a Hallmark card."

Joaquin's luscious mouth tightened.

Aspen continued to glare at Babe. But there was a question in her eyes. "What the fuck is she talking about?"

The polo player didn't answer.

"Ask Joaquin about his friend Eddie," Babe shouted.

Aspen turned to him, curiosity morphing into suspicion.

"Your lover there has a running contest with a buddy," Babe went on. "You can read all about it on thetopshelfpussyclubdotcom. They like to bed down classy ladies and brag about it on the Internet. I'm sure you'll make the grade, Aspen. After all, you're Mrs. Dean Paul Lockhart. That's real Top-Shelf quality." She paused a beat. "At least on paper."

"Is this true?" Aspen demanded.

"It's just a prank, baby. She's making it out to be something it's not." Joaquin reached for his latest conquest.

But Aspen pushed his hand away.

Two taxis and a Volkswagen Beetle zipped past.

Aspen ventured farther into the street, closer to the holder of the candid proof that would be her marital waterloo.

Babe watched a Lincoln Town Car coast onto the scene. To avoid mowing down Aspen, it stopped just ahead of Joaquin's building. The rear door opened on the opposite side.

Lara stepped out. She didn't see Babe. She didn't see Aspen. Her concentration on Joaquin was absolute.

Babe knew the affliction well. She had felt it for Jake James once. And the disease didn't disappear overnight, no matter what you were aware of or how badly you were treated. Proof of that was all over Lara's face. The desire for Joaquin had gone to her head like a shot of tequila to a teenage brain. Babe watched her shut the car door and seek him out with a fuck-me need in her eyes.

But then Lara saw Aspen. She froze. As she took in a shocked breath, her face was wiped clean of expression. A second later, Lara registered Babe's presence, too.

Babe knew that this would go down in Lara's personal history as one of her most humiliating moments. That contract was all drawn up. It only needed to be signed.

Lara looked across the street.

Babe beamed back a telepathic message of support and understanding. And then she moved her head up and down in a severe nod that translated: *Yes, that bitch is fucking him, too.*

Joaquin couldn't seduce his way out of this situation. He looked uncomfortable as hell. All that liquid charisma seemed to be freezing up as he stood there, speechless on Second Street.

Aspen took a step forward, scowling at Lara. "What are *you* doing here?"

Lara stiffened haughtily. "I have no idea." She looked at Joaquin. "But it won't happen again. You can bet on that." Then she slid back into the Town Car, and the driver whisked her away.

Joaquin shook his head and retreated to his building. At the door, he turned to Aspen. "Are you coming?"

"Fuck you!" Aspen screamed.

Joaquin shrugged and disappeared inside.

Babe hiked her camera bag over her shoulder.

"I want that film! I mean it, bitch! I want it!" But Aspen made no move to make good on her threats. She just stood in the middle of the road and screamed like a mental patient.

Babe started down the sidewalk. She slipped on her iPod headphones to tune out Aspen. The sleek little music device was cradled in her left hand. She scrolled down until the playlist titled DP lit up. Phil Collins's "Groovy Kind of Love" began to serenade her. It had been playing in the bar that night at the Biltmore. God, she loved this song. She loved Dean Paul, too. Back then . . . and right now.

Several blocks later, Babe called his mobile.

He answered on the second ring but sounded distracted.

Right away she heard voices in the background. "Hi, it's Babe. Is this a bad time?"

"Kind of. I'm in a meeting with Gabrielle and Bizzie Gruzart. What's up?"

"We need to talk. It's important. Can you meet me somewhere?"

There was a hesitation. "Not now. We're in the trenches here. And if I don't work off some stress at the gym later, I just might kill somebody. How about tonight?"

As she tried to mask her disappointment, the mercurial history of Dean Paul's attentions stalked her mind. From the center of his universe to a casual acquaintance. "It would have to be early," she managed to say with an easiness she didn't feel. "I'll have to start the photography gauntlet by eight."

"How about six? Where do you want to meet?"

She thought about it. Sixes and Eights came to mind. But so did Hue, the multilevel Vietnamese restaurant and lounge. She liked the seating in the two-room bar. Very sexy. A strong hooking-up vibe. There were intimate couches, too, even a few beds. "Hue," Babe decided. "It's on Charles Street."

"Yeah, I know," Dean Paul said. "I'll see you there." He hung up.

Babe stared at the phone and told herself not to read anything into his curt manner. Just then, a tiny fear registered. Could he know about her involvement in the tabloid photo spread from his wedding? She stopped herself, realizing that *involvement* was too innocuous a word when she had been the goddamn mastermind.

Yesterday Babe had come so close to confessing. She had been so angry that she wanted to rub it in his face. At the very last moment, though, she'd backed off. A gut thing told her to. She had earned big money off those pictures and made the Lockharts a laughingstock in the process. She smiled as the image of his mother popped into mind. Babe had luckily captured Sophia Mills during a priceless millisecond when she had lipstick on her teeth. The rag published it under the snarky caption READY FOR YOUR CLOSE-UP, MISS MILLS? No, it would never do to come clean on that scheme.

Her ill-fated book deal was altogether different. The Lockharts had squashed her like a bug on that one. It was easy to forgive a failed attempt at betrayal. That's why Dean Paul had been comforting and had given her the you're-so-beautiful pep talk. So the girl from the broken family had thrown a punch and swung into the air. No harm done.

Babe went back to her apartment and proceeded to go about the dreary task of collecting faxes, e-mails, and voice messages for the night's events. She was reading the guest list for a Faith Hill CD listening party when Linda Konner called.

"I've been thinking about you," Linda said without preamble. "We should do a project together."

Babe experienced an overwhelming sense of relief. For a moment, she thought her old book proposal was about to come back from the dead and fuck up her life.

"So I'm reading the new issue of *212*," Linda went on, "and I see your name and think, 'What about a coffee-table book on the New York nightlife scene?'"

"That sounds fantastic." Babe felt excitement bubble up to the rim. It didn't quite boil over. This wasn't a sale, after all. Just an idea. She told Linda about her photographic style on the social scene during her days at Brown—the violently cropped images, the edgy lighting techniques, the disoriented, drunken point of view.

Linda was encouraging.

"I still shoot that way," Babe said. "I sneak in several images at every event. You know, to keep those muscles flexed. Of course, *212* would never use them. The editors there want the *Town and Country* vibe. Everybody looking rich and beautiful. In my storage files, I must have thousands of images to choose from."

"I think we should pursue this," Linda said. "Give it some

thought, and we'll talk in a couple of days." She paused. "Does *212* have you covering the birthday party for the Kometani twins?"

"Probably."

"I thought so. I'll see you there. Maybe we can steal a few minutes over a drink."

Babe laughed a little. "I have to work the event. What's your excuse?"

"I represent Mio and Mako. In fact, I just sold a beauty book they're writing to St. Martin's Press. Well, I should say they're posing for the pictures. One of my ghostwriters is doing the actual writing. Anyway, I have to turn in an appearance and wish them well. It's the least I could do. I earned a nice commission on that book. But I still plan to be home in time for *Law & Order*, so let's try to visit early into the evening."

Babe said her good-byes and hung up as if on a cloud of wonderful, cotton-candy air. This was no deal with the devil for a moment of notoriety. This was a real chance to display her talent. The possibility was incredible. She tried to imagine what her name might look like on a book cover. BABE MANCINI. And what would she call it? Let's see . . . the title had to be provocative and sexy . . . something that smacked of eroticism and decadence. Suddenly, inspiration struck. The hair stood up on her arms. *Night Sweat*. That would be the name of her first book, and she knew that it was fucking gold.

The rest of the afternoon flew by. She plotted out her wardrobe to meet Dean Paul, deciding on a Zac Posen denim jacket, a ribbed cotton tank, and a lace-overlay chiffon miniskirt by Valentino R.E.D. Then she slipped into a pair of Marc Jacobs python sandals, tossed her essentials into a Badgley Mischka beaded satin bag, and hit the door.

Babe walked into Hue at six on the dot and went straight for the flawless mahogany bar to order a Rolling Blackout—a potent mix of Stoli, Kahlua, and espresso.

She slapped down a twenty for the drink and told the could-be-a-model bartender to keep the change. He had that gorgeous frat-boy look that ruled Hilfiger campaigns.

Babe stalked the two-room lounge, sizing everything up, sorting everything out. There was an interesting mix of hard chargers and hot players. Model (of course—they swarmed the city spots like locusts), musician, magazine editor, artist, designer, HBO writer.

A familiar actor approached. "Hey."

She knew the face but not the name. Tragedy of the semi-famous.

He shook his index finger at her. "I think I know you."

Babe gave him a look. "Is that a line, or do you have a bad memory?"

His forehead crinkled. Apparently, anything more than half a sentence was heavy-duty social intercourse. "Hold on a minute . . . what?"

Babe avoided eye contact and watched the entrance for Dean Paul. "I'm waiting for someone."

He opened up his arms. "I'm here. And I'm on TV. Every week."

"So is Maury Povich. It's nothing to brag about."

"You're a smart-ass. I like that. Haven't you ever seen my show?"

Babe shook her head.

He called out the name of a bad sitcom on the WB.

She nodded politely, having seen half an episode once. The name came to her now. Tate Barbour.

"Today's my birthday," Tate said.

Babe stifled a groan. What were the odds? Every time she met a jackass in a bar, it happened to be his birthday. One asshole had lucked out with a blow job this way, and the rest of the female population had to suffer.

"What kind of present do you want to give me?"

"Something you really need—acting lessons." And she walked away to enjoy her drink elsewhere.

A quarter past six came. Then six-thirty. Still no sign of Dean Paul.

It occurred to her that he could be in some kind of heated row with Aspen.

Just as she began to really worry that the night would be aborted, he showed up, effortlessly stylish in a Brown University T-shirt, lived-in jeans, and a six-hundred-dollar pair of Prada boots. He reduced every other man in the bar to troll status.

"Shit, Babe, I'm sorry." Dean Paul's breathing was labored as he kissed her cheek. "I ran most of the way. Can't you tell?" He smiled at her, and his high concept could be summed up in three little words: God among men. "Drink first." He glanced at the one in her hand. "Can I get you another?"

She held it up. "This is serious enough. I have to work later tonight."

Dean Paul dashed to the bar and came back with a Surfer on Acid—a kick-ass blend of Jagermeister, Malibu coconut rum, and pineapple juice.

Babe gestured to his concoction. "Are you embracing your inner college boy?"

He grinned, checking out the crowd, vibing to the trance disco beat of a remix of Sting's "Send Your Love."

Bodies filed in. Alcohol flowed. And the background noise went up a notch.

"I'm a fucking idiot," Dean Paul said in a louder voice. "I completely forgot about us meeting here." He shook his head. "You'd never believe the day I had."

Babe smiled vaguely, playing it cool, even as the fire of embarrassment burned inside of her. He had forgotten about the date. She had lived for it all day. The incongruity was off the charts. "You know what? I think I will have another," she said, pushing her almost empty glass into his hand. "Rolling Blackout."

If only she could—black out, that is.

His retreat to the bar gave her a few moments to collect herself.

But Dean Paul was back too soon, and she still felt . . . uncol-
lected. The drink helped. She sipped the poison greedily until
slight buzz became solid buzz. Now she could deal. Enough of the
edge was off.

"Do you want to sit?" He gestured to a cozy, unoccupied
couch in the corner. It had everything but a neon sign that read
MAKE OUT IN PUBLIC RIGHT HERE.

Babe slid onto the soft leather seat. She glanced down at her
dangling purse. Inside it was the end of his marriage. The reality of
that resonated. To have expectations for tonight would be foolish.
It's not like Dean Paul was going to review Exhibit A and say, "Oh,
that sucks. Guess I'll divorce the bitch. Let's start things up again.
Are you free later tonight?"

He leaned back on the couch. "So what's on your mind. You
said it was important."

She reached for her Mischka bag. "Important but not pleasant."

Dean Paul tensed. A wary look swept across his face. "If this has
anything to do with Jake James . . ."

"This isn't about that asshole. It's about another one. Joaquin
Cruz."

He seemed to relax a little. "I know all about that."

Babe unsnapped the purse closure and pulled out two digital
prints. "I don't think you know about this." She passed them over.

Dean Paul studied the evidence. A strange sort of determination tightened his jaw, as if he were a kamikaze psyching himself
up for the inevitable and honorable end. He looked at Babe. "Are
you doing surveillance work now?"

It was an odd response. As she opened her mouth to explain,
Babe braced herself for the shoot-the-messenger routine. "I
promised Lara that I would take care of Joaquin."

"*Take care* of him?" There was a hint of hostility in his tone.
"Okay, Babe Soprano, go on."

"At first I just intended to destroy the Web site. I work with a kid who can do anything with computers—hack 'em, crack 'em, build 'em. You know the type. He's twenty-one, and I don't think he's ever so much as held a girl's hand. Social retardation in the Internet age."

Dean Paul continued to absorb the pictures.

"I just had a feeling that I could find something on Joaquin if I put in the effort. I don't know. Call it a sixth sense. When it comes to scams, his stripe of worm typically operates on the edge. So I found out where he lives and decided to . . . observe."

Dean Paul's face went through a repertoire of disappointed expressions. "Jesus, Babe, I never knew you were one of them. And I've had eyes on the back of my ass to spot 'razzis since I was a toddler."

Babe stared back at him. This was the last thing she expected. To play patient teacher to a dense pupil who didn't get the lesson. "Then maybe you need to stand up to look at these. That's your wife."

He looked at Babe. Really looked at her. As if the idea of her being a paparazzo was creeping inside his brain and slowly rotting it. He gave the pictures one more glance and handed them back. "Soon to be ex-wife." He announced this with little emotion.

"I'm sorry."

"Your little peep show comes as a surprise, but it's not a two-by-four over my head. Aspen accepted a job in Vegas this afternoon. Some kind of strip show with other women from reality television."

There was a long silence.

Awkwardly, she slipped the photos back into her bag.

Dean Paul worked on his drink. "So what do you plan to do with those? A big paycheck is sitting in that purse."

"I would never do that."

"Oh, really?"

The fear of what was coming next consumed her.

Dean Paul's brilliant blues told her that he knew the things she didn't want him to know—about her . . . about everything—that her Chanel cuff bracelet had smuggled in an uninvited guest to his wedding, that the media megabucks were drawing interest in a secret account, that no matter how much pain and embarrassment her mercenary act of subterfuge had caused his family, she would always feel a smug sense of victory over him, over everything and everyone that he represented.

"How did you find out?" Babe asked, her voice barely a whisper as the sad reality began to take shape.

Those Lockhart eyes bored into her soul. "You just told me."

Babe felt the heat rising on her cheeks. Twin spots of glowing redness. When she finally spoke, her voice was urging, yearning, begging for some less than neutral response. "Please don't hate me."

"I don't hate you." But even as he said it, there was a change in the way that he looked at her. Things were different now.

Babe felt less certain that the sun would rise tomorrow. There were no words to offer him. She could apologize until her voice gave out, and it would still sound hollow. "No hard feelings?"

Dean Paul stood up. "No feelings at all, Babe." And then he walked out into the New York night.

She sat there for a long time, finishing her drink, thinking about the mess that was her life, wondering how she would go on.

"You shouldn't have spent your time waiting around for that guy."

Babe glanced up to see Tate Barbour.

"Maybe you're not such an idiot after all."

He laughed. "Well, I was hoping for a little more encouragement than that. But it's a start."

Babe realized that she must look like an easy mark for hunters of the hooking-up set. She was alone, all dressed up in her *Sex and the City* best, and reeling from a public rebuke.

The old Babe would have given this C-list actor the time of day, flirted some more, benefited from a free drink or two, and before the night ended, gone over the business of who lived closer. But a new Babe was emerging in the final act of the Great American Drama that was her history with Dean Paul Lockhart. And this Babe wanted a new beginning.

She stood up.

"Can I buy you another round?" Tate asked.

"No, thanks. I just got a better offer."

He looked around as if he had missed something. "From who?"

"Myself."

Babe walked back to her apartment, changed into her cashmere Juicy sweats, and dug out every New York party picture she had ever taken. Work could wait. She sat there at her worktable, under the soft light of the task lamp and above the harsh brightness of the negative viewer, and pored over the images, singling out the best ones.

It was a fresh challenge. Her own book. *Night Sweat.*

The new mood flowing through her left her strangely exhilarated. On this—one of the saddest nights of her life—she had never expected to feel . . . happy . . . positively happy . . . for perhaps the first time in her life. That realization merged with the high energy of her creativity. She got a whiff of the future. And it smelled good.

Smiling, Babe peered through her magnifier at a great shot of Dean Paul at a glitzy benefit for amfAR. She stared deep into those impossibly devastating eyes, took in the aquiline nose, the sensuous mouth. All of a sudden, a train of thought began to chug along.

He had taken all the punches a little too easily tonight. A wife's infidelity. An ex-girlfriend's cruel deception. Yet none of it seemed to really penetrate. Upon reflection, she now sensed a bulletproof quality to his reactions. As if he knew that there was a safe place for retreat, that emotional succor was waiting.

Something clicked in her mind. Cynics had that defense mechanism. It was their own harsh view of the world. But people deeply in love had it, too. And it was the object of their affection.

Dean Paul was a romantic at heart. There was the answer to one question. Now Babe wondered about the other. She might be down for the count, but Lara and Gabrielle were still in the running.

Who would get him?

THE IT PARADE
BY JINX WIATT

Fill in the Blanks

Those poor, pitiful Japanese twins. The beautiful sisters are all dressed up, and they definitely have a special place to go ... but nobody cares. Only the truth here, darlings. Sure, their spare-no-cost birthday bash is generating priority buzz. That doesn't have anything to do with them, though. It's the RSVP list that's wagging tongues like crazy. A former rap diva is set to make her first public appearance since that self-imposed exile following a shooting, a scandalous PR hoax, and the loss of a career that went poof overnight. Hmm. Any coincidence that it's happening on the eve of her highly anticipated TV interview with *Hollywood Live*'s delicious new correspondent? Yes, darlings. Mr. Wonderful beat out Barbara, Katie, and Diane for the biggest monster get of the year. Sorry, girls. If only you had slept with the gorgeous liar back in college, too. Maybe then you would be asking the questions. So much to look forward to at the birthday party. And there will be cake! What more could a nosy scribbler want?

18

Gabrielle

"Hello? *Hello?* Would you please stop calling this number!"

Gabrielle shut her eyes as the connection went dead. She was dialing home just to hear their voices now. She knew what times her mother would answer. She knew what times her father would, too.

But she could never find the strength to speak. There was always that tentative intake of breath, the intention to say the words, to say anything at all, and then in the end . . . nothing. They always hung up before she found the final courage.

Her world had turned upside down. Again. Only now she wanted to run to Matthew and Diahann Foster, not away from them. Gabrielle's mind rolled over all the accusations and resentments she had silently heaped upon her parents. The walls she had put up. The emotional banishment she'd subjected them to. And the years. Oh, God, the years! Of estrangement. Of loneliness. Of secret yearning. It all seemed so pointless now. And the regret weighed her down.

They had given all that they were capable of giving. They had done their very best to protect her. She understood that today. But back then, on that horrible night at Brown, and almost every day after that until recently, Gabrielle had blamed them. For surrendering every shred of their blackness to guarantee their place among the elite. For conceding their culture so completely as to raise a little girl who had no concept of the things people could say or do based on the color of her skin.

Gabrielle had studied the Civil Rights Movement. She had seen movies like *Mississippi Burning*. But one was a history that her parents rarely spoke of. And the other was just a Hollywood film that seemed so far removed from her own experience. As far as she was concerned, those issues had nothing to do with her. Inevitably, though, there was always a price to pay for denial.

Come on, brown sugar. Give us some of that sweet chocolate.

And that night she had paid hers. Or so she thought . . .

The telephone jangled.

A sharp fear registered that it could be her mother calling back. But then Gabrielle assured herself that she had effectively blocked the number to prevent that from happening.

She let Baby Bear do the honors.

The phone rang less and less these days. People trying to reach her knew to contact Bizzie Gruzart, and now that the interview details had been disclosed, those hoping to break her story accepted the obvious and stopped trying.

It made perfect sense to grant *Hollywood Live* and Dean Paul the exclusive. Telling the world what happened might be one of the hardest things she would ever do. Because she planned on setting the record straight. For herself. For her parents. And that would mean revealing everything. No more secrets. No more lies. No more shame.

She wanted someone who really knew her to ask the tough questions, not a newsmagazine harpy who would play chemistry for the camera. By *her* she meant Gabrielle. Not Brown Sugar. That woman had ceased to exist. She had been a creation, an image to flaunt, ethnic armor to wear, a product of a deal that attempted to cheat the devil.

Tomorrow. The time and place was all set. Here in this suite. At two o'clock. It still seemed so far away. The panic came in waves. Occasional fits and starts, the dull fear of not being able to go through with it. Gabrielle tried to shield herself from the media buildup, only it was impossible to escape. The interview had been programmed for the full promotional blitzkrieg. Typically, Paramount's *Entertainment Tonight* steamrolled over its rivals. But *Hollywood Live* was rising. And the accompanying excitement for the coup of pairing Dean Paul with his tabloid-scarred ex-girlfriend had narrowed the viewer margin to a single ratings point.

Baby Bear stepped into the room. "Sugar." He used his hand to put an imaginary receiver to his ear. "It's your number one ace boon coon—Lara."

She smiled at the sweet giant who had taken a bullet for her. "I know this is going to take some time, Baby Bear, but I told you that I don't want you calling me Sugar anymore."

"I'm trying, Su . . ."

She saw him wince at his second mistake, and picked up her extension.

"Gabrielle!"

It sounded like she was calling from a construction site. "Lara? I hope you're wearing a hard hat!"

"I'm at the warehouse. There's so much to do. I'll never get out of here. Privi's bringing my clothes for the party and checking into the Hotel Gansevoort. It's right nearby. Poor Queenie. She's out cold from a tranquilizer. But it's for the best. She's never traveled well. Listen, I won't keep you. Just want to let you know that my car service will be there by seven."

"That's not necessary. I can get myself—"

"It's final," Lara cut in. "I'm not giving you an opportunity to change your mind. You haven't ventured out of that suite even once since the uproar."

Gabrielle laughed. "Dean Paul calls me Rapunzel."

"Well, I'm not going to tell you what Finn calls you. You'll slap him silly."

"No, tell me. I'll see him tonight. Maybe I'll push him headfirst into a gondola."

Lara hesitated.

"Tell me," Gabrielle insisted.

"Okay. But don't hold it against me. I'm just the wire service."

"Deal."

"He says you're an agoraphobic with twenty cats, only minus the twenty cats plus one Ruben Studdard lookalike who can't sing."

"That shit!" Gabrielle squealed with good humor. "Ugh! I'm going to get him!"

"Isn't he awful?"

"He's beyond awful. Have you heard from Babe?"

"Not really. She's obsessed with that book proposal for her agent. But she'll be here tonight." Lara paused for a moment. "Oh, fuck. One of my sculptures just fell into the lagoon."

"You're sober. I can't believe you just said fuck."

"You and Babe are a horrible influence. I'd be wise to cut my losses and befriend a couple of born-again Christians."

"Yeah, maybe the three of you could sit in a circle and pray about Joaquin Cruz's d—"

"Gabrielle!" Lara exclaimed. "I expect that kind of vulgarity from Babe, not—"

"See? You haven't been corrupted *too* badly. That dignified lady is still lurking."

"I'm not sure if someone who once called herself 'Super Bitch' is authorized to make such pronouncements," Lara teased. "Anyway, I thought we agreed to never mention that name again."

"Sorry. I forgot."

"Gabrielle, I'm concerned," Lara said, her voice dripping with faux distress. "Memory problems and agoraphobia? Perhaps you should just skip Mio and Mako's party and go straight to Lenox Hill."

"Hey, anything to get me out of tomorrow's interview."

"Nervous?"

"Terrified."

Lara's tone changed on a dime. "You're in good hands. He'll take care of you."

"I know."

"Okay, Rapunzel. I better run. I feel like the architect of disaster right now. This place will never be ready in time."

"Don't be ridiculous. Everything's going to be perfect," Gabrielle assured her.

"It better be. There's no dress rehearsal for events like this. I'll see you tonight." As Lara was hanging up, she began to scream at one of the subcontractors, "Get those red linens out of here! They're supposed to be black-and-white checkered!"

Gabrielle smiled. It was all in the details. . . .

And that's when an unfinished one crashed back into her life. She froze. Just hearing his voice in the outer seating area filled her with repulsion.

" 'Sup, Baby B? Heard you ran into some trouble! You handled that shit, though. One bullet don't stop no Bear. I told Queen to get rid of that punk-ass nigga cousin. Fucking crackhead."

Gabrielle seethed in a cauldron of used-to-be memories, realizing how much she hated the industrial-strength ghetto bullshit, wondering how she'd endured it for as long as she had.

AKA Bomb Threat loped into her suite as if he owned every square foot of the hotel. It was Halloween, and he was going as the Fairy Tale Thug Prince, his costume tricked out to the max— Armani on the body, Gucci on the feet, Oliver Peoples over the eyes, full-length ranch mink over it all, and fuck-you-I-got-bank jewelry flashing from ears, neck, wrists, and fingers. Gold shouted little-boy money. Serious motherfuckers busted out the diamonds.

Following a few reverential steps behind this hip-hop cartoon was the servant Gabrielle knew as Ice Man. Always in his Sunday best, always discreet, always silent. His only job—to carry a velvet-lined box containing more of his master's diamonds.

Movie stars pranced around film locations with personal umbrella handlers trailing them like tails on a comet. AKA Bomb Threat did them one better. He shadowed his every step with a personal *diamond* handler.

"Hello, Bomb," Gabrielle said with all the coldness she could muster.

He eyeballed her. Slowly. Up and down. Noting the total absence of the product he owned. Brown Sugar had been in-your-face style. The woman front and center was subtle grace. His chin jutted up like an exclamation mark. "What's this? You look just like that bitch I rescued from Vibeology." He laughed a little. "Remember? You were nothing back then."

Gabrielle straightened her spine. Her eyes blazed defiance. "You're wrong, Bomb. I became nothing when I signed on the dotted line with you."

For a moment he paused. Then a peal of mocking laughter exploded from the depths of his bull neck. He waved Ice Man out of the room as if swatting a fly. Suddenly, the laughing eyes were narrow. "Bitch, I fucking *made* you. Don't stand up in this penthouse crib I'm paying for and try to tell me different. Who the fuck do you think you are?"

"The name is Gabrielle Foster." The present tense strangled her voice with emotion. "And trust me. She's no one you need to know."

He smoothed down the nonexistent creases in the jacket of his two-thousand-dollar suit. Eventually, his hand grazed over his crotch, watching her as he crudely adjusted himself. There was a dismissive shrug. "Different name. Same pussy."

Gabrielle hated that word. But she hated the speaker more.

Bomb walked quickly to the bar and fixed himself a Courvoisier. "The label's pissed about this interview. They sent me here to deal with your out-of-control ass."

"You mean they dragged you away from the making of Brown Sugar part two? This must be serious."

He banged back the liquor in a single gulp. "Should be. To you. Think any other company will sign you? You're still under contract. Don't fuck around with that."

Gabrielle thought about what Dean Paul had told her and decided to test the water. "Does that mean I can go back into the studio?" She gave him her best provocative smile. "I want to do some new tracks. Don't you think I should answer Queen Bee?"

Bomb gestured to her haltingly. "We don't need to do that right now. Let's just chill for a minute. Give this shit a chance to ride out." His tongue flicked out to moisten his upper lip.

It was the answer Gabrielle expected. She switched the weather on her smile, going from hot to cold faster than Beyonce could shake her ass. "That's a pretty lame pitch." The expression on her face said she knew the deal.

Curiosity shone in his eyes.

"Let me guess," Gabrielle said. She eased down onto the plush sofa and crossed her legs. "You plan to burn me off with a greatest hits set and whatever else you can package quickly and at little expense."

Bomb looked at her savagely. He preferred women listening to his business lectures. Not the other way around.

Gabrielle seized the moment. She had become a thundercloud full of hidden lightning. Time to strike again. "It would be better for me to stay underground, right? That way the Brown Sugar mask stays on, and there's only one product to focus on. The one you control. And with all the controversy, you might be able to squeeze out a few more sales before shipping me off to Vanilla Ice Island." She changed her tone to singsong. "But if Gabrielle Foster starts getting all the attention . . ."

Bomb slung the fur over a chair. His face telegraphed the title of Nelly's biggest hit, "Hot in Herre." But he wasn't shooting steam or spitting game. Just staring, his mind putting together her intentions like a child's jigsaw. Suddenly, he erupted. "Bitch! I made you!"

Gabrielle kept her voice even. "I think groomed is a better word for it. You approached me, remember? You responded to my poetry. I wrote every lyric on those CDs." She paused, thinking of the way he had pushed her to compromise her material. He had all but forced her into writing about the genre's default subjects for female artists—men, money, their own vaginas. "My voice was diluted, but a part of me was there."

His smile was cruel. "You think people were jamming to your

poetry? It was my beats, girl. I could've gotten any bitch off the street to rap the Yellow Pages over those tracks and still had fucking hits!"

She tried to stay calm. Part of what he said was true. But so what? His attack only served to end the argument. "If it's so easy, then you shouldn't care what I do. Find another bitch. This one's out of here." Gabrielle stood up.

Bomb lurched forward to get right in her face. "Where are you going? You don't have shit. I own you." His hand dug into her arm.

"Let go of me."

Bomb twisted harder.

"Baby Bear!" Gabrielle called out.

One blink. And he was there. "Step off, Bomb. That shit's not right."

Bomb's temper ticked up even higher. "Who the fuck do you think you're talking to? You work for me. My company pays your fat ass. If I tell you to suck my dick, then you get down on both knees. No questions asked."

"I work for Su . . . I work for *Gabrielle*. Check your fax machine for my letter of res. Now. Like I said. Step the fuck off."

It was *High Noon*. Baby Bear, sumo body lurching, was ready to pounce. The threat was crystal clear. If Bomb didn't release Gabrielle's arm, then he would be a diamond-studded pancake.

The thug-mogul's face talked major-league disbelief. He gave orders. He didn't take them. But finally, he removed his hand. Then he looked around the room, as if he half expected Ashton Kutcher to run out and scream, "Dude, you've just been punk'd!"

She stared for a long time because this was how she wanted to remember him. With a chink in the macho armor. "I had an independent lawyer review my contract. You screwed me, Bomb. You screwed me good. And you screwed me better with that deal than you ever did in bed. That's for goddamn sure."

The humiliating words whacked into their target. An accusation to a black man that he couldn't fuck. The ultimate abuse. And right there in his eyes was the force of the hit.

"I could never have recouped those expenses." She laughed at the crime that was her slave agreement. "Well, maybe if I sold ten million. Anyway, that wasn't a contract. It was a sucker's loan. So good luck paying it off to the label. Like you said, Bomb, you own me. Brown Sugar is Riot Act's problem now, not mine."

He bounced a look to Baby Bear. "You like working for free, man? This bitch ain't got no money."

Gabrielle tackled the end of his words. "I sold the jewelry." She flashed her bare extremities as evidence. "Those were gifts. Mine to keep. Mine to sell. And don't try to evict me from this suite. It's paid up through the weekend. Your accountant was late with the bill, but I settled the matter with management. I'm the registered guest now. I could have you thrown out. But watching you walk away with your balls in your hand will be satisfaction enough. Of course, you probably won't do the heavy lifting. Chances are you'll make Ice Man carry them."

"You greedy little—"

"Oh," Gabrielle cut him off. She just couldn't resist. "FYI— Baby Bear is getting a raise. Plus better benefits. I can't believe you didn't offer a dental plan."

"Yeah, man," Baby Bear chimed in. "What's up with that?"

She smiled at AKA Bomb Threat to show him that she still could, to prove to him that the career apocalypse had only made her stronger. He never saw the distinctions between Brown Sugar and Gabrielle. Until this moment. And that's when she picked up Bomb's fur and shoved it into his arms. Her final words were the sweetest she had ever uttered to him. "Now who's the bitch?"

A few hours later she was twirling in front of the mirror, checking out her simple Narciso Rodriguez spaghetti-strap cocktail number. God, she was practically naked. No jewelry. Minimal makeup. Just a black dress. But this is what *Gabrielle* would wear. A soaring feeling of liberation sluiced through her veins. Officially, the occasion might be Mio and Mako Kometani's birthday celebration. *Unofficially*, though, it was a coming-out party for Gabrielle Diahann Foster.

As promised, Lara's Town Car idled outside the Waldorf-Astoria.

The anxiety of leaving the hotel settled in Gabrielle's stomach and stayed there, even after the driver zoomed away from the curb and into the dark forest of the Manhattan night.

Slow, deep breaths.

That got her through the first difficult minutes. Ultimately, her agitation receded, and she began to enjoy the fact that for the first time since the woman formerly known as Brown Sugar hit it big, the woman known once again as Gabrielle was out in the city . . . completely alone. No puppet-master producer. No entourage. No bodyguard. Free at last.

In no time, they were coasting through the Meatpacking District. The driver stopped somewhere on Ninth Avenue. Gabrielle's Manolo Blahnik heel stepped out onto the cobblestoned street. She loved this area. The mix of old meat warehouses and retrofit storefronts against style-heavy restaurants and flagship fashion posts from the likes of Stella McCartney and Alexander McQueen was the kind of urban, eclectic success that only New York could claim.

Outside, the building was a massive, easily ignored zinc-colored metal structure. But the buzz of activity surrounding its perimeter hinted at something exciting inside. As a torrent of anticipation surged through her, Gabrielle breezed past a gaggle of smokers and into . . . another world. Oh, God! Yes, it was another world. She was in Italy. This was Venice!

Somehow, Lara had managed to fit into the space a replica of the Grand Canal with actual water and authentic-looking gondolas. Massive, hyper-realistic murals of the Basilica di San Marco and Palazzo Ducale rose up like mirages from a blue lagoon. The exhaustive attention to detail created a transporting effect.

Byzantine. Gothic. Renaissance. The exotic melange of styles ruled in its own way. The party had just started and already had a life all its own. Full of secrets. Teeming with romance. Open to pleasure.

She surveyed the crowd so far. The pretend city in the pretend country was overflowing with famous-energy New York.

The rich. The hot. And the sexy.

Gabrielle hit the least crowded drink trough. There was still chemical-seeker gridlock. But she killed the time with a second-tier model, going back and forth on a love-your-dress routine. Then she was up. "Raging Bull!"

It packed an eight-ball wallop—the adrenalizing caffeine sugar drink and the shot of seventy-proof Smirnoff. She downed it. She felt it. And then left in search of the kick-ass social equivalent.

Gabrielle saw Lara just beyond a Eurotrash clique, and screamed out her name.

The long blond hair was slicked back. The way-above-ten body was parading in a black catsuit. She turned, beamed at Gabrielle, mouthed something into her headset microphone, and dashed over to embrace her. "You made it!"

"What you've done is incredible!"

Lara's smiling reply was modest.

Gabrielle fiddled with the headset. "I like this. Very Janet Jackson."

Lara laughed. "Thanks." She pointed to the stage and catwalk. "You might be interested to know that I'll be performing 'Rhythm Nation' later."

Babe appeared out of nowhere, forefinger already easing down on the shutter release of her Contax G2. "Okay, my bitches, smile for *212*."

Click.

"I want one with the three of us together!" Gabrielle insisted.

As if on cue, Finn showed up, his eyes falling on the camera clutched in Babe's hands. "I'll take it."

Babe hesitated. A nanosecond later, she was giving him a quick lesson in good party photography.

Finn listened. Barely. "Enough, Professor Leibowitz. Get in the picture already. This looks just like my Polaroid Joycam."

The expression on Babe's face told the rest of them that he would have been better off calling her mother a truck-stop whore. A tight tension descended.

Finn sliced through it. "I'm kidding. Touchy. I know women who aren't that sensitive about their own babies."

There was a burst of laughter, and then they formed a chain of impossibly photogenic female solidarity. The embraces were warm, the smiles real, and the feelings for each other as comforting as cashmere.

Click.

As easily as if someone had yelled, "Courtney Love!" they suddenly scattered, Lara to deal with an emergency, Babe to chronicle the VIP night, and Finn to finagle an introduction to *CSI* stud George Eads.

And that's when Gabrielle saw him making his way down the narrow, faux-Venice street. For a moment, he took her breath away. His smile is what got her. It started slowly on the outside of his lips, lit up those baby blues, and opened up his gorgeous face like a delicate flower in sunlight.

Gabrielle tensed. There was something about the way that he looked at her. A strange, emotional entreaty. As she struggled to make sense of it, the butterflies flew loose in her stomach.

"I've never seen you so beautiful."

She laid her fingers on his arm as he leaned in for a kiss, his lips touching hers one second longer than casual social manners allowed. A whiff of work sweat hit her nostrils. You could bottle it and earn a fortune. No-Nonsense Masculine by Dean Paul Lockhart.

"Are you here to work or play?"

"Both. We just wrapped our piece." He smiled. "I did a Q&A with the guests of honor." One beat. "Longest five minutes of my life. They're pretty, though. Did you know that people actually pay them to show up at parties and be boring?"

Gabrielle laughed. "Lara has told me stories."

He gave her that look again. A brave honesty sparkled from his eyes. "Jesus, Gabby, I feel like I'm about to explode. We have to talk. I've got to tell you something."

Gabrielle took a deep breath as he piloted her away from the crowded bar and toward a less populated area close to the catwalk. She bit down on her lip, chewing on it gently.

Around them, the crowd partied on.

And there was that look again. It arrowed through to the part of her that she had shut down long ago. Steeling herself, Gabrielle groped for air.

Dean Paul's hands took her bare arms gently. "I love you, Gabby."

She said nothing. The silence stretched on and on.

A shadow of confusion darkened his face. "Did you hear me? I said I love you."

Gabrielle stared back, touched by the adoration in his eyes. It spoke of true commitment, a lifetime together, even grand-children . . . at least for right now.

Suddenly, in the face of the reverse heartbreak in the making, she discovered true amusement. *Did you hear me? I said I love you.* If a collection of Dean Paul quotations were ever published, that one would have to make the final cut.

Gabrielle found herself smiling at the sweet narcissism of his expectations. In his mind, he had just said three very important words. *I love you.* Of course, she loved him and would say them right back. He was, after all, Dean Paul Fucking Lockhart.

"Gabby, say *something.*"

"You just got married."

"That was a mistake. It's over."

"Has Aspen's plane even touched down in Las Vegas yet?"

He shook his head. "Aspen doesn't have anything to do with this, Gabby. I felt this way at the wedding. I thought about it on my wedding night with her sleeping right there. Everything makes sense to me now. You're the one that I want. Don't you under-stand? I love you."

Gabrielle's hand was still gripping his firm forearm. She squeezed tighter and smiled calmly. "Right now I believe you mean that."

Dean Paul reacted against her placid demeanor. There was a wild look in his famous eyes. "What do you mean *right now?* I love you. Period."

"My God, think of everything that's happened. Just between the two of us. Your marriage. Your new job. The end of your marriage. And me—I was shot at. I became a tabloid fixation. My career went from platinum to ashes. How can you be sure of *anything* in the cyclone of such craziness? And I didn't even include Lara and Babe's public dramas. Don't think they don't play a part in this, too."

His face was stubborn. "This has nothing—"

"This has *everything* to do with them. It always has. It always will. You've had a lot of girlfriends in your life, Dean Paul, but we're like some sacred fucking harem to you. It always comes down to one of us. Who you want to fight with. Who you want to save. Who you want to love."

"Jesus, Gabby, what's wrong with you?"

She knew her eyes were blazing now. "Why does something have to be wrong with me? So you tell me that you love me. Am I supposed to fall to my knees and say, 'Yes, he loves me! Now I can live!' " She pounded her chest dramatically. "Because that era has passed. Your chance for that kind of worship was back in college."

He glanced around temporary Venice, fuming. "This is what you want to do? You want to withhold your feelings from me because I ran out on a college romance?"

"You haven't even asked me what my feelings are. You just assume that I'm in love with you. Well, alert the media. Go get your *Hollywood Live* crew. Because I'm not. I *love* you. But I'm not *in* love with you. Do you want to know what I'm in love with? Do you really want to know?"

Dean Paul's lungs grew still. His heart—if it was still beating—was slowly breaking.

Gabrielle swallowed hard. It pained her to hurt him, but she had to get this out into the air. "I'm in love with the friendship I've rediscovered with Lara and Babe. Don't get me wrong. You've been wonderful to me throughout this ordeal. You really have. But those two *anchored* me. Especially Lara. It's like, I look at them . . . and . . . I see a clearer reflection of myself. And I know that if I got back together with you . . . I would lose that. I've already lost it once. Back in college. Over you. I'm not going to lose it again."

For a long, simmering moment, Dean Paul just stared at her, as if he were angry at getting bumped to second string for some girls' club. "Honesty seems to be your theme for the night. You're being honest when you say you don't love me. How about being honest about what happened to change you. Why did you write off your parents? Why did you fall into that Brown Sugar masquerade in the first place?"

The instant horror began to tumble over in her mind. She pushed it away. "I won't go into that. Not tonight. Not here."

Dean Paul didn't budge. "Then when? Goddammit, Gabby! When?"

"Ask me tomorrow. You've got the exclusive, remember?"

She left him to seek out the bar. God, she needed a drink. Maybe two. Shit, just give her three. People were laughing, dancing, and talking animatedly around her. But all she could do was wonder if she had just made the biggest mistake of her life.

Gabrielle stood alone, chasing down Raging Bull number two, gearing up for a third. Her body language spelled out ALOOF— KEEP MOVING in big neon letters. And to think that she had secretly thought about this event as *her* party. Some party. It sucked. Were Mio and Mako having a good time? They should be. It was their fucking birthday.

From behind, she felt two male hands on her bare arms.

At first, she thought it was Dean Paul. But then her body suddenly recoiled from the touch. Bourbon breath rained down on her neck. The voice whispered in her ear . . .

"You're the one who calls herself Brown Sugar, right? Tell me, baby. Where'd you get a name like that?"

Gabrielle froze. A chilling fear called up the memory.

Come on, brown sugar. Give us some of that sweet chocolate.

Her brain ran the frightening test, comparing the haunting voice in her head with the live voice in her ear. It was a match.

With a counterfeit calm, she slowly turned to face him. She had to look him in the eyes. She had to hear him say it again. She had to be sure. "What did you just say?"

"You're Brown Sugar, right? Where'd you get a name like that?"

If a black girl could go pale, then Gabrielle Foster would have been as white as a ghost. Her heart stopped beating. It was him.

She fled imitation Venice. Minutes into her search for the Town Car, she gave up and took a cab back to the hotel. Baby Bear's presence gave her a renewed sense of safety. But there would be no sleep for her tonight. She lay in bed wide awake, living out the horrible memory over and over again in her mind . . .

"Come on, brown sugar. Give us some of that sweet chocolate."

Gabrielle continued walking, ignoring the obnoxious drunk and his two equally drunk buddies.

It was after midnight.

There was a great deal on her mind, and none of it had anything to do with the beer-fueled taunts from three horny and dateless college losers. Dean Paul had moved on. She was stuck in a forlorn rut. Something had to give.

"Come on, brown sugar. Give us some of that sweet chocolate."

The voice was closer now. An awareness rolled over her that this could be more than a boys-will-be-boys catcall.

"Hey, guys, I've never dipped my stick in black pudding before. How about you?"

Gabrielle stopped and turned angrily to face them.

In the darkness, it was difficult to make them out, their faces partially shielded by baseball caps, their clothing nondescript.

"Leave me alone." Her voice was loud, firm, and clear.

"What was that? I can't hear you, tar baby. Speak up." It was the same voice—the leader, the straw stirring this increasingly sickening drink. His two companions were obvious underlings.

She surveyed the scene and experienced a mounting panic. Tuesday was not a typical party night, and as her watch ticked past one in the morning, this area of the campus appeared to be deserted. The sense of invasion infuriated her. All she wanted to do was take a fucking walk, get some air, and clear her head.

Spinning back around, she extended her walking strides and hoped they would lose interest. When she heard them approach, it was too late.

"Don't play so hard to get, brown sugar." He grabbed her and pulled her in the direction of a wooded area.

Gabrielle got in one scream before the hand clamped over her mouth, silencing her. She tried to fight back. But his strength overpowered her at no contest.

They forced her deeper into the woods and shared jokes, as if the inevitable were a spirited group-sex adventure and not rape. "I can't wait to get a taste of this brown sugar. I bet that boyfriend liked it. Now I'm going to try it."

The reference paralyzed her. Was this just trash talk? Or did he actually know Dean Paul? Gabrielle tried to adjust her eyes. But the mixture of her fear with the darkness left her almost blind.

They pushed her down into the dirt. The leader went first. He tore into her roughly as the others chanted him on. In a minute or two it was over. The next man took his turn. But his penis was soft.

"Maybe you'd get hard if we'd run into a black boy."

He gave up under the harsh ridicule as the third man forced himself into her mouth.

"Look—this black bitch is sucking him good."

By then her mind had shut down. He was only half erect at first, but grew firmer. Finally, it was over. All Gabrielle could think about was how out of the realm it was. Beyond any ken of her understanding. Her parents had raised her in their white Utopia, a place where she thought nothing bad could ever happen. And right now she hated them for it. Would she ever be able to forgive?

When they stumbled away, Gabrielle mechanically put herself back together and returned to her on-campus apartment. She went to bed and woke up the next morning in the same clothes. If there had not been dirt in her underwear, she never would have believed that it had happened. . . .

She prepared herself for the full day ahead. Bizzie Gruzart was meeting her at the hotel for breakfast. There were hairstyle, manicure, and makeup artist appointments. After that, she would rendezvous with Lara at Bergdorf Goodman to select a wardrobe for the interview. Dean Paul had told her to expect the *Hollywood Live* crew at about one-thirty.

Gabrielle took in a deep breath as she slowly conjured up the courage to speak of that horrible night for the first time. She had never uttered a word of it to anyone. But today she would break her silence about what had happened to change her. And, more importantly, who had been responsible.

Come on, brown sugar. Give us some of that sweet chocolate.

Now Gabrielle had a face to go with that voice.

It was Jake James.

THE IT PARADE
BY JINX WIATT

Fill in the Blanks

It's called gravity, darlings. What goes up, must come down. And did that quick-talking, hard-punching cable creep ever fall fast. Certainly you tuned in months ago when the hip-hop queen for a day told that harrowing tale of college rape. Riveting television. Mr. Motor Mouth can deny, deny, deny, but is anybody on his side? Not a certain news network. The suits booted his show off the air. Another book? Don't hold your breath. The first one had a successful launch, but tanked once the bombshell detonated. Another job on TV? Not in this lifetime. Analysts say the man is walking anthrax to female viewers. Spies report that a criminal case never got off the ground because the accuser would not submit to the he said/she said ugliness of a trial. Is she scared of a

defamation suit? Not this tigress.
Rumors insist that she's ready to
countersue in civil court if he so
much as looks in her direction. One
of those high-powered agents told
moi that this former up-and-comer
has sunk so low that he's considering a local talk-radio job in Nebraska.
How delightful to hear that they have
radios in the state. Yours truly thought
they just grew corn there.

19

Dean Paul

"We could be in bed." Emma Ronson placed her hand on the inside of Dean Paul's thigh as she said this.

"That's false advertising. If we were, you'd be sleeping right now."

Emma gave a defeated little sigh. "You try getting up at three in the morning five days a week."

"Hey, I kiss you good-bye."

"You lay there like a crash test dummy. Occasionally, you pucker your lips."

"Like this?" Dean Paul did the honors.

Emma leaned in to meet her luscious, glossy lips with his. "Mmmm . . . are you sure we have to do this?"

He skated his tongue softly along the ridge of her lower lip. "I'm positive."

"I don't know which is worse," Emma said.

"What's that?"

"A man who's still on good terms with his ex-girlfriends or a man who's not."

Dean Paul hooked an arm around her, his fingers grazing the fine silk of her Hermes blouse. She could protest from here to Sixty-First Street. But Emma Ronson was ready to see the women who had come before her. And she was ready for them to see her, too.

Along with the insanely expensive blouse, she wore a Gaultier tweed skirt, black Wolford tights, and smart Prada flats in a country brown. She looked very adorable. And very cool. With her knife-blade-straight blond hair and rose-cheeked complexion, it was stylish English schoolgirl all the way. The kind of beauty that women envied supportively and men coveted respectfully.

For a girl under thirty, Emma Ronson had accomplished a lot. There was the double degree from the University of Miami in broadcast journalism and political science. The quick ascension at NBC-owned NewsChannel Four to weekday coanchor of the top-rated *Today in New York*, which aired from five to seven each morning.

That meant rising out of bed at the ungodly hour of three. It also meant no sex after eight o'clock. She was Manhattan's girl. The city had an intimate relationship with her. Everybody woke up with Emma Ronson. But Dean Paul went to bed with her. Game, set, match. Her universal appeal only seemed to tick upward each day. Emma could do something as quotidian as admit her personal finance frailties in one segment, and then hold her own against Donald Rumsfeld in the next.

As the cab slowed to a stop in front of Feinstein's at the Regency, he laced a hand through hers and squeezed tightly. They swung out of the taxi at eight twenty-nine. The show started at eight-thirty. On the street a ripple of awareness began to percolate. Inside the elegant cabaret it reached full potential. She was New York's favorite girl. He was America's favorite son. They were together. And the sighting was an event.

The house lights went down.

Dean Paul guided Emma to the reserved cafe-style table near the front. Gallantly, he ushered his fiancée into her chair. Then he slid into his own seat like a little boy late for assembly.

A few tables away he saw Lara and Babe. Two parts of an unbeatable trinity here to support the third. They looked amazing.

Life agreed with Lara. It always had.

And Babe carried herself with a new confidence, the kind that radiated true internal worth, not external arrogance subbing for insecurity.

The offstage announcer made the simple introduction. "Ladies and gentlemen . . . please welcome Varese Sarabande recording artist . . . Gabrielle Foster."

The soft, theatrical gel lights went up.

She walked out onto the small stage in an Atelier Versace mermaid gown. The Swarovski crystals sparkled. The hand-painted silk tulle gleamed. Her deep copper skin glowed.

Applause erupted.

The loudest appreciation came from her parents, Matthew and Diahann Foster. They were standing up, whistling like mad, and beaming with pride in tribute to the daughter who had come back to them.

After the bombshell interview that had destroyed Jake James, Gabrielle returned home to Grosse Pointe, Michigan. The sojourn lasted a few months. It was a time to heal and reconnect with the world and the people she had rejected. The reunion proved enriching, both emotionally and creatively.

Dean Paul learned this for himself when he conducted the follow-up story for *Hollywood Live*. Gabrielle, back in the postcard-perfect place of her youth, enjoyed long, lazy days. She spent countless hours with her mother and father's old record collection, immersing herself again in the soft, easy listening sounds of Barbra Streisand, Neil Diamond, Rita Coolidge, and Roberta Flack.

The rediscovery of the soundtrack from her childhood elicited a new discovery of the voice within. Her voice. Gabrielle could sing. It was a subtle, sultry instrument, a pure talent never hinted at during the staccato rapping sessions from her work as Brown Sugar.

Varese Sarabande, a boutique recording label based in California, signed her with great alacrity. Soon after, she began the process of recording her first traditional vocal CD, a collection of contemporary standards that her parents had taught her to appreciate. It was their culture. It was hers, too.

Months later, her new project enjoyed a quiet release. By then, the bombastic tabloid attention was gone. There were new scandals to pound mercilessly into the public consciousness. Like the one involving Aspen Bauer in Los Angeles. His ex-wife and Joaquin Cruz had fled the scene of an accident that left a young pedestrian in a coma. Criminal charges were pending.

Dean Paul shut his eyes for a moment as the piano player's fingers danced across the keys in the opening bars of Gabrielle's first number. He thought about what she had told him, about this second chance in the music business being so much sweeter. She preferred the intimacy of a small label. It left her free to connect with the music. And here tonight, in this venue that seated no more than a hundred and forty, it left her free to connect with the audience.

The piano player found the melody.

Gabrielle closed her eyes, parted her lips, and swept him away. Her vocals were as close as a whisper in the ear, her delivery as heartfelt as a woman thinking while writing a letter to a lover.

Dean Paul Lockhart eased back and sipped his Skyy on the rocks. He watched the gorgeous singer. He listened to her beautiful song. And it dawned on him that the lyrics were the story of his life.

"I'd rather leave while I'm in love . . . while I still believe the meaning of the word . . ."

THE IT PARADE
BY JINX WIATT

Fill in the Blanks

"The more things change, the more things stay the same." If this scribbler had a dollar for every time dear sweet Granny said that, you could pick any finger and be sure to find a nice-sized pink diamond on it. The woman was brilliant! Don't believe *moi*? Read on, darlings. It's been a year since the wedding of the century (which became the quickie divorce of the century), and the groom's sassy exes have moved up and on. Missy Party Planner is sporting a rock from that scrumptious young plastic surgeon. A cutie, a doctor, and free Botox! All together now . . . *we hate her.* Missy Shutterbug is all the rage with her coffee-table book on New York nightlife and a series of exhibitions in snooty art galleries. Don't worry. She's not crying herself to sleep. Spies say she's keeping company with a hunky Broadway star. And Missy Rapper-Turned-Chanteuse is packing them in at that intimate cabaret spot. Plus, rumors are swirling that she's singing love songs to her own musical director. Ooh—very Michelle Pfeiffer in *Fabulous Baker Boys*. Are you wondering about Mr. Wonderful, that miracle man who once had all of them in a tizzy? Well, you can't teach an old dog new tricks (another one of Granny's favorites). His exclusive relationship with Missy Morning News Anchor is kaput. How does yours truly know this? The poor thing was sobbing about it to her girlfriends just one table away at Sixty-Six. It's a paradox for the ages. How a woman can go from Supergirl to Basket Case based on one man's attentions. Quick! Somebody stamp a warning label to this guy's forehead: DANGER—HEARTBREAK AHEAD.

ABOUT THE AUTHOR

Kylie Adams is the author of four previous novels, *Fly Me to the Moon*, *Baby, Baby*, and the *USA Today* best-sellers *The Only Thing Better Than Chocolate* (with Janet Dailey and Sandra Steffen) and *Santa Baby* (with Lisa Jackson, Elaine Coffman, and Lisa Plumley). She is a contributing editor to *The South*, a regional bimonthly magazine that features her pop culture/humor column, "Kylie Says." She lives with her Shih Tzu, Bichon Frise, and bitchy Persian in Brandon, Mississippi, where she is currently at work on *Ex-Boyfriends*, the follow-up to *Ex-Girlfriends*.

To contact Kylie, visit her on-line at www.readkylie.com. Or write: Kylie Adams, P.O. Box 320702, Flowood, MS 39232.